Fixing Delilah

by

SARAH OCKLER

LITTLE, BROWN AND COMPANY
New York   Boston

Copyright © 2010 by Sarah Ockler
Excerpt of *Twenty Boy Summer* copyright © 2009 by Sarah Ockler

Little, Brown and Company

Hachette Book Group
1290 Avenue of the Americas, New York, NY 10104
Visit us at lb-teens.com

Little, Brown and Company is a division of Hachette Book Group, Inc.
The Little, Brown name and logo are trademarks of Hachette Book Group, Inc.

The publisher is not responsible for websites (or their content) that are not owned by the publisher.

First Paperback Edition: December 2011
First published in hardcover in December 2010 by Little, Brown and Company

"Sigh" lyrics written by R. Alex Morabito.

Library of Congress Cataloging-in-Publication Data

Ockler, Sarah.
Fixing Delilah / by Sarah Ockler. — 1st ed.
p. cm.
Summary: When Delilah, her mother, and her aunt spend the summer in Vermont settling Delilah's estranged grandmother's estate, long-held family secrets are painfully brought to light and Delilah finally learns some difficult truths about her family's past.
ISBN 978-0-316-05209-2 (hc) / ISBN 978-0-316-05208-5 (pb)
[1. Secrets—Fiction. 2. Family problems—Fiction. 3. Single-parent families—Fiction. 4. Depression, Mental—Fiction. 5. Grief—Fiction. 6. Families—Fiction. 7. Vermont—Fiction.] I. Title.
PZ7.O168Fi 2010
[Fic]—dc22

2010008631

10 9 8 7 6 5 4 3

RRD-H

Printed in the United States of America

Book design by Saho Fujii

The text was set in Electra.

For my mother, Sharon Ockler,
who keeps the family stories,
photographs, and treasures,
and for my father, Steven Ockler,
whose love of maple sugar candy found
its way to Red Falls.

fix *n*

1: a position from which it is difficult to escape; a predicament

fix *v*

1: to repair something broken, damaged, or spoiled; to mend
2: to make amends for something wrong
3: to restore a relationship by resolving a disagreement or rift

chapter one

"Claire? It's Rachel. I'm afraid I have some bad news."

Chapter two

Mom and I didn't sleep last night. She spent the predawn hours packing and mail-forwarding and making lists with colored Sharpies while I hung out on the couch, drinking cold coffee and trying not to ask too many questions. I was in enough trouble already — and that was *before* Aunt Rachel's phone call sent her into overdrive and hijacked my summer plans.

"Here we go," Mom says now, clicking the power locks and backing us down the driveway in the dark blue Lexus sedan. Actually, it's a *black sapphire pearl* Lexus sedan, not dark blue. The bill for the custom paint job is tacked to the bulletin board over my desk — a constant reminder that I still owe her for the dent-and-scratch combo I added when she was out of town last month.

Including the backpack between my feet and a long black dress for the funeral, I brought three bags of stuff for the whole tragic summer. The rest of the *black sapphire pearl* trunk and the *cashmere* leather interior is full of Mom's matching luggage and carefully labeled boxes of file folders, gel pens, computer cables, a printer-scanner–fax machine, and — should she be required during our dysfunctional family trip to showcase her management prowess — a collection of smartly tailored pantsuits in taupe, navy, and classic black.

"Left turn in four. Hundred. Feet."

An invisible electronic woman navigates us toward the highway from the distant planet Monotone, where everyone is tranquil and directionally adept, but Mom isn't listening. As vice president of marketing for DKI Group — "the most prestigious branding firm on the east coast" — Mom *gets* multitasking. She could eat a bagel, scan the morning headlines, *and* get to I-78 with her eyes closed. Even deprived of sleep she drives effortlessly, one hand on the wheel, the other tapping manicured fingers on the dash-mounted touch-screen phone. It takes her eight separate calls to her assistant's voice mail to convey what I did in one text message to my non-boyfriend, Finn:

major family shit going down. off 2 vermont
4 the summer. L8trs.

"Merge on right. In one. Point five. Miles."

Mom checks her rearview and eases the Lexus into the right lane. "Eyes on the road, mind on the goal, and everything will be okay," she says, patting the steering wheel. It's her corporate road-warrior mantra, and she's already said it three times this morning. Usually, Mom's mantras are pretty poster-worthy. Mom on doing homework without her help: *The more you put into it, the more you get out of it.* Mom on working weekends: *You've got to plant the seeds of hard work to reap the harvest of a satisfied client.* Mom on home cooking: *I'm stuck at the office tonight, Del. There's money in the coffee canister for pizza or Indian.*

I want to believe her today, but the view isn't looking too hot from the passenger seat.

Despite all evidence to the contrary, I'm really *not* the car-denting kind of girl. I'm also not the lipstick-stealing, school-skipping, off-in-the-woods-with-someone-I-barely-know kind of girl, or the kind who loses all of her dignity over a scandalous cell phone picture on a trashy blog. But that *is* the evidence, exhibits A through E, all stacked up against me, and now I'm like the bad guy on one of those cop shows, handcuffed to an airplane seat. Only instead of getting the handsome, tough-but-emotionally-wounded police escort, I'm stuck on a seven-hour road trip with Commander Mom and her arsenal of mobile communications devices.

I turn away from her and put on my sunglasses so she can't see the tears stinging my eyes, but it's too late.

4

"Delilah, we've been over this already. You can't stay here in Key. Period." She says it like it's some big edict passed down by the Supreme Court. It's all I can do not to play the "I wish my father was around, because he'd [insert better parenting strategy here]" card.

Mom continues, tapping my leg for emphasis. "It's not just the sneaking out or the shoplifting." *Tap, tap, tap.*

"How many times do I have to tell you?" I ask. "It was an *accident!*" It *was.* I didn't even realize the lipstick was still in my hand when I walked out of Blush Cosmetics yesterday, bored and tired from wandering the mall alone.

"An accident," Mom says. "Like the car? Like your grades?" She shakes her head. "It doesn't matter, Delilah. There's a lot of work to do up there." *Tap, tap, tap.* "Other issues aside, you'd still be going with me."

Right. I'm letting her think she's won an important strategic battle in our ongoing war, but if things were different between us, more like they used to be, I'd *want* to go — not just because I need a break from Finn and pretty much everyone I know in Pennsylvania, but because nothing would be as important as helping my mother and aunt through this tragedy and tying up its many loose ends — the three remaining Hannaford women united and strong as an unsinkable ship.

But things *aren't* different. She's her and I'm me and surrounding us is an ocean of mess and misunderstanding, full of pirates and sharks just waiting to see who slips in first.

"Stay on interstate. Seventy-eight for. Fifty. Miles."

After the directive, Mom cranks the air and switches off the freakishly calm GPS woman. Back here on planet Stress, it's just the two of us, all the unsaid stuff made more unbearable by the artificial cold.

"Now that I have a captive audience," she says, setting us on cruise control as the road opens up, "who did you sneak out with last night?"

Last night.

You'd think someone who's seen you half-naked would be a little more enthusiastic about picking you up on time. Not Finn "forty-five minutes late" Gallo. From the driver's seat of his old silver 4Runner, Finn crushed a spent butt into the ashtray and turned down the radio, blowing out a plume of blue smoke from between his lips. He didn't say anything, like, "Thanks for waiting in the dark for me," or "I'm sorry I put your life in danger with my lateness," or "Allow me to apologize with this exquisite lavender rose bouquet." He just pulled me to his mouth with one hand cool and firm on the back of my neck and somehow made up for everything bad he'd ever done in his whole entire life.

At our spot in the woods by Seven Mile Creek, Finn parked between two big pine trees and killed the engine. He asked me what was up, and I shrugged. I'd spent the whole night arguing with Mom about Blush Cosmetics and didn't feel like talking. Finn and I aren't that good at talking, anyway.

So we didn't.

Aunt Rachel says that the universe is always trying to speak to us, and that the universe doesn't waste time speaking about things that aren't within our direct power to influence or change. But if that's true, the universe needs a better signal. Because when Finn kisses me, hot and fast like each time might be the last, everything else in my life goes like the New England evergreens in a morning fog: gray, hazy, and just about gone.

Last night, I felt the familiar solidity of Finn's body against mine, midnight air cool on my cheeks, rocks and sticks and living things pinned beneath me, bits of moon falling through the branches in the tall pines bent over us. At the end of it all, Finn sucked a crackle from another cigarette and stood, reaching down to help me to my feet. I shook out the blankets and rolled them up and he pulled the leaves from my hair. One by one they floated and swirled and fell to my feet, and when he flashed his up-to-no-good smile with the moonlight soft and blue on his skin, I wanted to stay there forever. To hide. To forget. To numb the dull ache of something missing. To erase my mother and her expensive car and late nights at the office. To fill the empty spaces left by my father, killed before I was even born, with something other than endless unanswerable questions.

But it was time. Finn dropped me off on the corner. He called me *Lilah* with that devious smile and shook his head in that "you're nothing but trouble" sort of way that gives me chills, but he didn't say good-bye. Or wave. Or wait in the shadows until I was safely back in my house. He just drove away, and I walked on in the other direction, the distance between two points growing long and cold.

When I got back inside, Mom was there on the edge of my bed, a new eyebrow crease invented especially for the occasion of my tumbling through the open window at two in the morning with leaves in my hair.

"Get in here, Delilah," she said, tugging me the rest of the way inside. *I'm not playing games.* Only she didn't actually say the games part. She didn't have to. I climbed in and sat on the bed and chewed on my thumbnail as she recounted the last fifteen minutes in alternating bursts of finger-wagging and foot-stomping. She'd been waiting for me (wag) in the bedroom (stomp) the entire time (wag) with news from Aunt Rachel.

I spit out a piece of my thumbnail and met her eyes, matching the curious exasperation behind them as she passed along her sister's announcement, direct from the staff at Maple Valley Hospital up in Vermont.

Elizabeth Rose Hannaford, the grandmother whose name I hadn't been allowed to speak in over eight years, was dead.

"I told you last night," I say to Mom, inching down the window to thaw the freeze in the car. "I needed some air."

Mom's voice is about to jump an octave. I see it coming and make a silent little wish on the dash lights that somewhere among all those tailored pantsuits she's packed her

8

Xanax. For now, I imagine how much better life would be for all of us if her lectures were delivered through the GPS device.

"Delilah. I had. To. Leave work yesterday. To. Pick. You up from Blush." *In six point. Four. Miles.*

"So?"

"You were supposed to be grounded! You almost got *arrested* yesterday!" she says, as if I could forget the detective's dramatic lecture on the downfall of our nation's youth. "*One more dollar in merchandise,*" he'd warned, knuckle jabbing my shoulder, "*and we'd have to press charges.*"

"Prisoners don't deserve *air*?" I ask. "Why don't you just pull off my fingernails next time."

"Unbelievable, Delilah. I really thought I could count —"
Bzzzz.

"Hang on. I have to get this." Mom touches a button on the dash and activates her public persona. "Claire Hannaford speaking."

She has a plaque on her desk at work by the phone:

☺ **SMILE before you dial! SMILING helps you sound more relaxed on the phone!** ☺

She does it, too. Even in the car. No wonder she's so great at rebranding entire corporations for DKI. She rebrands *herself* every fifteen minutes.

I lower my window all the way down and stick out my arm.

The breeze whooshes through my fingers and carries my hand over the highway, zooming past lines of orange cones and construction signs until Mom nudges my ribs. "I'm on the phone," she mouths, still smiling but eyes mad and wide as she circles her finger in the international gesture for "roll up the windows." I pretend to turn the nonexistent crank on the door. She raises my window from the button on her side and locks the controls.

"Sorry for the background noise," she continues into the earpiece. "Yes, the final invoice was sent on Thursday with a thirty-day grace."

The sun is fully up now, bleaching the sky from orangey-pink to a pale, sad white. Corpse-white. It's horrendously early and the daylight hurts the stuff behind my eyes. It rained earlier this morning, though — right after I heard about our disastrous summer plans, which I thought was fitting. Now the road is all patent-leathery and sets our wheels to a whisper, raspy and hypnotic like the ocean. The sound reminds me of this Memorial Day road trip Mom and I took to the Connecticut coast when I was six — just the two of us. New London — only time I've ever seen the ocean. We couldn't swim the first day because it rained, so we just walked along the shore with bright yellow raincoats buttoned up over our bathing suits, looking for shells and sea glass and dizzy little hermit crabs. The rain kept coming the next day, so we stayed inside the motel eating Doritos from the vending machine and watching movies on cable — a luxury for us back in Mom's pre-DKI days. Even when I accidentally pulled the pin out of the motel fire extinguisher and shot a blast of white across the floor, she laughed, chasing after my little white footprints as I ran into the bathroom to hide. On the last day, the sun came out and we swam in the ocean, no lifeguards, just Mom's hand firm in mine as the waves crashed around us.

On the way back to Pennsylvania, late at night on the road, she smoothed her hand on my cheek and sang classic rock songs with the radio on low, and I pretended to be asleep so she wouldn't stop.

After her call, Mom clicks on the radio and I turn away, my breath fogging the glass of the passenger window. As the all-news-all-the-time station drones on about the latest economic trends, I trace a bead of leftover rain along the bottom edge of the window and watch it pass over my shoulder. Sometimes I think about telling Mom how much I hate being home alone every afternoon, turning on the television just to pretend there's company. All those takeout dinners at the big dining room table, chairs empty, invisible guests eating invisible soup and drinking made-up wine in my head. I want to shake her and scream and tell her that for all her hard work to secure our future, the snake plants in the foyer know more about my life than she does. That I'd strike a single match and raze the whole damn place to the ground if it meant we could start over with nothing but the ocean, potato chip vending machines, and free cable.

Then again, I don't need an arson charge on my record.

"At this rate, we'll never get there," Mom says, turning toward me to check the right lane as she merges back in. In the stifling beige-ness of the car interior, she looks weak and defeated and ten years older than she did yesterday, before she knew her mother was dead. She wears it like makeup—a paper-thin layer of unwavering resolve flaking away to reveal all the broken parts underneath.

"Mom, I'm . . . I'm really sorry about —"

Bzzzz.

"Hold on, Delilah." Mom keeps one hand on the wheel, the other searching for the right button, fingers poking around the dash like a bird for worms as the unsaid end of my sympathy stumbles and slips back down my throat. On the phone, Claire Hannaford Speaking betrays none of our troubles, but as she engages her award-winning, smile-as-you-dial communication skills for the caller, a thing that's been sitting like a rock at the bottom of my stomach grows an ounce heavier.

Dread.

Cold and unmoving, it drips with the murky memories of that place we're going to. That place where she and Aunt Rachel shared their childhoods and, though my recollections are hazy, where I spent part of mine. That place I was ordered to forget right after my grandfather's funeral more than eight years ago. That place yanked suddenly from the dark of the cellar, all those black-tarred Hannaford secrets still stuck to it like giant, undustable cobwebs.

The tension is crawling across my skin and making me itch.

I dig a Snickers bar from my backpack and offer Mom the first bite, but she refuses, waving her hand in front of me as if shooing a fly. After her call, she lets out a long sigh, tugging the phone device from her ear and flipping the GPS back on.

"Recalculating route for. Red Falls. Vermont."

"Mom?"

"Not now, Delilah. I'm driving."

"Location triangulated," Lady GPS announces. "In two hundred. Four. Miles. You will reach your destination."

Chapter three

Mom is missing.

The car windows are open, and a soft breeze blows over my skin, jostling the branches of a giant weeping willow next to the unfamiliar driveway where we've stopped. I peel my cheek from the *cashmere* leather seat and shake off the road-sleep, scooping up my backpack and climbing out of the car.

At the top of the driveway, there's a house, big and solid, mustard yellow with white trim. It's framed on both sides by rows of giant sugar maples that seem to reach all the way up to the sky.

I know those trees.

This is the house at Red Falls Lake where I spent every summer for eight years. My grandparents' house. We're here.

The old place seems only to have changed in relation to me. I'm bigger. It's smaller. I'm older. It's *ancient*. It's still the same color that I remember, but now the paint along the bottom peels down in golden curls like lazy spring daffodils. The shutters are loose and crooked, some open on both sides while others are shut or half-shut, sneaking looks as if after all these years, the house no longer recognizes me.

I pull my backpack tight over my shoulders and walk alongside a row of maples that leads me around to the back. Warm and honeyed in the sun, the yard yawns and stretches its way down the hill to Red Falls Lake. The water, which is neither red nor falling, looks like a giant blue whale, shimmering peacefully behind the bleachers on the western shore. They used to hold boat races down there, loud and growling and filling the air with smoke. I remember hiding under the bleachers with Little Ricky from next door, creeping through the dirt in search of discarded soda cans that could be converted to nickels for candy at Crasner's in town.

Little Ricky. I look across the yard at the neighboring blue-and-white Victorian and wonder if his family still lives there. We were so close back then — best summer friends. I remember the feeling even now; an inescapable stickiness to each other like magnets on the fridge. It's funny how someone can be such an integral part of your life, like you laugh at the same jokes and eat your ice cream cones the same way and share your toys and dreams and everything but your heartbeats, and then one day — *nothing*. You share *nothing*. It's like none of it ever happened.

Only it *totally* happened, I know it did, the memories of it forced suddenly from their hiding places by the reality of this house. My chest tightens, a lump rising up inside me with everything I want to scream at my mother. It's *her* fault my grandmother died alone here, forgotten. It's *her* fault our days back home melt into one another in their dreary sameness, a thick gray soup of *don't wait up*. *Not tonight. Not now.* I look at the trees and the grass and the lake and wonder — is this my destiny, too? In twenty years, will I drive across the states with my own daughter, back to my mother's house in Key, back to bury the things I tried for so long to forget?

When I find my mother at the top of the slope, I wipe my eyes on the back of my hand and stomp across the yard, ready to let loose all that I'd bottled up on our long drive from Pennsylvania. But as soon as I see her up close, sitting there in the grass and looking out over the town's namesake lake beyond, all the fight in me scatters, clearing the way for something worse.

Fear.

In these quiet moments, Claire Hannaford doesn't belong; her face is vulnerable and far away. She watches me awhile with a tilted head, strands of brown-and-gray hair blowing gently over her eyes as I approach. I wonder if she's thinking about her departed mother, or Aunt Rachel, or the sister that died when they were younger, or the call from the Blush Cosmetics security guard, or maybe the cattails at the edge of the lake — how she used to cut them with a pocketknife and chase me with them, all the while my grandfather laughing from his wheelchair parked in the grass, pointing out circus animals in the clouds overhead.

"Mom?" I rub my arms as I get close to her, though the air doesn't seem chilly enough to make my skin prickle.

"I couldn't go in," she says, yanking up fingerfuls of grass. "I got all the way up the driveway, but once I smelled that honeysuckle, I couldn't go near the front door."

I sit down next to her on the ground, not touching or talking, wedged into the familiar space between the rock part of me that mostly hates her and the hard-place part that dies to see her so uncertain.

"I just can't believe my mother is dead, Honeybee."

Like the fragile side of my mother, her old nickname for me no longer fits. Awareness of its long absence creeps between us like a serpent in the grass of her childhood home, and Mom shakes her head as if to erase the word, looking back out over the water.

We sit for a while, watching the lake breeze carry seagulls in search of castaway popcorn along the shore. The birds sing to each other in a mournful way, the echo of their calls floating up from the beach, and I try to imagine what it's like for her — eight years dodging that one phone call, that one ringing in the middle of the night, the death knell for someone she once loved. I think about the Hannaford women and can't help wondering if we're all alike — me and my mother, she and hers, all of our problems starting this way. A tiny crack in the previously solid understanding of one another. A crack to a fissure. A fissure to a break. And then a gulf, big and empty and impossible to cross.

"Aunt Rachel will be here soon." Mom stands to brush the grass from her pants and holds out a cool hand. I take it without hesitation because I don't want to hurt her feelings. Because I don't want to know the lost side of her, and I need to feel her hand in mine, familiar and strong and absolutely certain again. Because I need to know that eyes on the road, mind on the goal, everything really *will* be okay.

But I can't know that, and neither can she. The old house on Red Falls Lake is like a cemetery now — hallowed. Haunted. Not the place for questions.

I squeeze her fingers anyway.

Mom takes a deep breath and marches us toward the driveway, shedding her frailty like a jacket too warm for summer.

"Let's move this stuff into the house," she says, dropping my hand. "I'd like to get my workspace set up before Rachel arrives and the arguing starts."

"What time is she coming?"

"She said two o'clock," Mom says. "That means four."

Ignoring the front door, we head for the porch that starts on the side of the house near the maples and wraps around back in a giant L. The third stair creaks loudly as we land on it, one foot after the other, marching up to the unlocked side door and through it, into the kitchen.

"Wow," Mom whispers, setting her purse on the counter. "It's the same. Exactly the same. Even the curtains." I follow her gaze to the white fabric panels hanging limp over the sink, tiny red-and-gold roosters trotting across the bottom in pairs. The cupboards are the old kind — wood painted white with windowlike panes so you can see the dishes inside. On the spots where the sun hits sideways, the blocky, black-and-white-tiled floor reflects in the glass. The skin on my arms prickles again as the breeze moves through the screen door, the red-and-gold roosters marching back and forth, back and forth as the curtains sway.

I leave Mom with her memories and start unloading the car, never venturing beyond the kitchen entryway, never raising my eyes more than the transfer of our belongings from the *black sapphire pearl* car to the black-and-white-tiled floor necessitates. As I travel from the car to the driveway to the third creaky stair to the kitchen and back, the series of accidental screwups that earned me a summer of estate sale duty fades from my mind, clearing the way for the scattered memories of our last trip to Red Falls — the yelling. Tears.

Flashes of the fight between my mother, Aunt Rachel, and my grandmother that sent us packing. It was at Papa's funeral, after the church service but before the burial. They'd said I was too young for that part — the burial — but after all the screaming, Mom and Aunt Rachel didn't go to the cemetery, either. As we backed out of the driveway — gravel back then, I remember it crunching under the tires — I watched the house and the willow tree in front of it get smaller and smaller until they both disappeared.

It was the last time any of us saw my grandmother alive.

I want to ask a hundred questions now — all the ones I held back in the car and in the yard, still pinned beneath my tongue by a waning sympathy for my mother's pain. But we lose our words easily here. I don't ask, she doesn't offer, and through our mutual silence we set about our work efficiently, all the kitchen windows opened, me bringing in boxes and Mom sorting their contents into stacks and rows.

On my last trip to the car, Aunt Rachel's rickety black pickup bleats and bumps its way up the driveway, late as Mom predicted. As my aunt approaches, the sadness of the house reflects in her face, just as it did in her sister's.

"Aunt Rachel!" I wrap myself around her and my heart unsticks, just a little. She rubs my back and kisses the top of my head, squeezing me tight as a line of jingle-jangle silver bracelets slides down her arm, a small hiccup catching in the back of her throat.

We all look alike, the three remaining Hannaford women. Same hazel eyes with various brown flecks. Same small ears. Same unruly eyebrows. Same long, wavy, chocolate-brown hair. And we all have those parentheses around our mouths — the ones that betray everything we feel and say all the things we don't. I haven't seen her since my solo trip to D.C. last Christmas, but feeling her warm against me with her cinnamon ginger breath and homemade lavender soap–scented skin erases all the time and distance between us. Her light blue vintage T-shirt (*Annapurna — a woman's place is on top*) is soon covered in our mixed-up tears.

"I have no idea how to handle this," I say, kicking the driveway with my flip-flop as we break our hug. "Mom's in total denial, as usual."

Aunt Rachel blots her eyes with her shirtsleeve. "I think we all are, hon." She tries to laugh, but it's as sad and faraway as the seagull songs, and I know she doesn't mean it. She and Mom haven't seen each other in two years — not since my aunt's last Thanksgiving visit. She only stayed two of the planned five days. And Mom — well, the closest she gets to Rachel's apartment is dropping me off at Philadelphia International Airport for the Philly to D.C. nonstop.

When we reach the porch, Mom opens the side door and leans forward like she's going to envelop her sister in a hug but stops just short, her shoulders tightening from the effort of holding back. "Rachel?" she whispers.

The maples near the porch shake their rustling green heads in the breeze, but Mom and Aunt Rachel don't notice. They just stare at each other, standing here in the middle of things with their arms dangling and the screen door half-open, the same blood flowing through their veins and a thousand pounds of unspoken words keeping them apart.

Chapter four

"Come on in," Mom says, holding the door. "I haven't looked at the rest of the place, but the kitchen's dreadfully the same." Her laugh is forced and uncomfortable—an olive sucked through a straw.

Inside, my aunt glides along the perimeter of the kitchen, one hand running over the countertops and curtains and one in her pocket. Behind her, two ants march out from under the stove to investigate a sticky-looking stain, completely unaffected by us and my grandmother's death and everything that happened before.

"Oh, sis," Rachel says. "How did we get —"

Bzzzz.

"That's mine," Mom says, digging through her purse.

"But I —"

"Hang on, Rach."

"Claire?"

Mom nods but holds up an index finger to put her sister on pause. She wraps up quickly, but that doesn't earn her any points with Aunt Rachel, who's steaming against the counter with her arms folded over her chest.

"Rachel, I told you last night," Mom says, pulling out her earpiece and sashaying back into the conversation like we're milling around the hors d'oeuvres table at a cocktail party. "If anything important comes up at the office, I have to make myself available."

"Burying your dead mother isn't important?"

"That's not what I said."

"I can ask someone else to help if it's too difficult to manage your schedule," Rachel says.

"Manage my schedule? Look, I realize that you can come and go wherever the wind blows, but my work is a little more —"

"Important, right? Because catering for movie crews isn't important? People need to eat, Claire."

"I was going to say structured."

"Structured? You don't know anything *about* my work. You've never even been on a set, so how —"

"Let's not do this right now." Mom grabs her purse,

digging into the front pocket and producing the small tin where she keeps her Xanax. "We have a lot to sort through tonight. I have to finish unpacking and do a preliminary walk-through…call the funeral director…her friends…" She grabs a glass from the cupboard, fills it with tap water, and chases down a little white pill. "I haven't even picked up groceries."

"I'll go," Rachel says. "Need anything specific? Milk? Toilet paper? Compassion, maybe? I'll get a bunch. I probably have a coupon. You know how we *unstructured* people are about our coupons."

"I'm going with her," I say. Both of them look at me like they forgot I was in the room, and before Mom can object, Aunt Rachel takes my hand and leads us out through the kitchen door.

"I'm sorry," Rachel says as we reverse down the long driveway and onto Maple Terrace. "I promised myself I wouldn't let my sister upset me today, and I blew it in five minutes. The tarot cards told me to prepare for conflict. Why didn't I see it coming?"

"That's just Mom's way. I think it's the assertiveness training she gets at work. 'Close the deal' and all that stuff." I make air quotes around the deal phrase with my fingers.

"That bad, huh?" Rachel asks.

I shrug. "Pretty much."

"Here." She fishes a miniature spray bottle from the

glove box and gives it a few rigorous pumps. "Frankincense and orange oil," she says. "To increase happiness and peace."

"Perfect. When we get back, could you, like, spray that directly *on* her?"

"If you think it'll help, Del. If you think it'll help."

As Rachel navigates Red Falls' "bustling" commercial hub, a few kids on bikes slow to check us out, waving as if we're a parade float throwing candy. A woman in a purple apron chats with coffee-drinkers as she sweeps the sidewalk in front of a funky-looking café called Luna's. The view of the sky over Main Street, sapphire blue, is interrupted only by a single banner suspended from Sweet Thing Chocolatier on the left side of the road to Bender's Hardware on the right, announcing with many exclamation points (!!!) and Random Capitalizations:

Red Falls' 50ᵗʰ Annual Fourth of July Parade
And Sugarbush Festival!!!
July 4th!!
Featuring Log rolling, Pony rides,
Maple Sugar candy, Maple Cream, Maple fudge, and
our WORLD famous Maple Drizzlers!!!!

We turn into the lot at Crasner's, which has since my last visit expanded from a humble general store into a bona fide Food Dynasty, minus the burned-out *d* and *Dy* on the neon sign. As Rachel settles on a parking spot, I ask the question that's weighed me down since we arrived in Vermont, made heavier now by my recollection of Sugarbush Festivals past.

"Rachel, what happened that day at Papa's funeral?"

Rachel turns off the truck and unbuckles her seat belt, staring at the CRASNER'S FOO NASTY sign until her eyes go blank, her hands curled in her lap like dried leaves.

"Every day you wake up and think, we'll fix things tomorrow," she says, still staring at the sign. "Or the next day. Or maybe the next. But now...there won't *be* a next day. Mom's...she's just...*gone*. Like *that*." She snaps her fingers.

"I'm sorry. I thought —"

"I have this memory of shopping here for school supplies," she says, turning the silver bangles around her wrist. "Your mom and I always swapped bags on the way out to the car to see who got more loot."

I try to picture Mom and Rachel as kids, digging through bags of pencil cases and folders and erasers and Elmer's glue, but there's someone missing from the story. We don't talk about her often, my other aunt. I've never even called her *Aunt* Stephanie. Dead at nineteen from cardiac arrest, she didn't live long enough to come into the title. And though Mom gave me her youngest sister's middle name as my first, by the time I was old enough to ask questions, she'd buried the entire history of it with *I'm sorry, Del...I really don't want to talk about it.*

I want to ask Rachel about Stephanie now, but I don't get much further than the S.

"Sss...hard to imagine Mom as a little girl," I say instead.

"Claire *lived* for back-to-school time. She was very methodical about it. She'd spread everything out on the bed and organize it into categories. Then she had this whole special way to load up her backpack."

"You should've seen her this morning," I say. "Notice all the boxes and matching luggage?"

"Yep."

"She brought pantsuits, Rachel."

"Pantsuits? Are you serious?"

"I wouldn't kid about something like pantsuits."

Rachel shakes her head. "It's a wonder you've survived this long, Del."

"Just barely," I say, remembering Mom's face when she picked me up at Blush yesterday. "Things at home aren't exactly splendid."

Rachel shifts in her seat to face me. "Okay, I'm totally ambushing you here. What's going on with you? Your mom told me last night you've been getting into some trouble."

I laugh, shaking my head. "You and Mom talk like once a year. *Now* she decides to be chatty?"

"She's worried about you, Delilah."

I put my sunglasses on top of my head and look out the passenger window at two men in cutoff flannel shirts having a spitting contest on the curb.

"She worries about all the wrong things," I say, more to the guys outside than to Rachel. "I'm fine."

"Right. I was on the phone with her last night when she discovered you'd snuck out, presumably with some dude."

"Finn," I say, "is not some dude."

"Boyfriend?"

"Not exactly. We just kind of…it's nothing, really."

"I get it." Rachel's hand turns my face away from the window. "Boyfriend. Dude. Nothing really. Please tell me that you're at least being…*safe*?"

I think about waiting in the black space of the street corner for Finn, who's always late, and the way he drops me off for the walk back to my house alone. I recall the spin of the tires on the pavement last night as he swerved to stay on the road after sliding his hand up my shirt before we got to the woods. I feel the bark of the tree outside my bedroom window scraping my fingers as I pulled myself back up to the second floor. *Safe?*

"God, Rachel. Yes, we're safe. I'm not stupid, despite what my mother thinks."

"She knows you're not stupid, Del. Which is why she says your behavior lately doesn't make any sense."

"Great. Now you sound like *her*." I put my sunglasses back on and turn away again. The spit champs are gone. "I thought you were on my side."

"There aren't *any* sides," she says. "I just want you to be okay. I'm worried about you, too."

"Then be straight with me. What happened back then? I was young, but I remember you guys arguing with Nana, and then Mom packed us up and we left. I wasn't even allowed to *talk* about Red Falls after that. It's like Mom wanted everything...erased. And now we're back here eight years later and no one is saying anything."

Rachel taps her fingers on the steering wheel, but she doesn't offer any answers. "The three of us need to sit down and talk about things, hon. And we will. I promise. I'm not trying to put you off. But for now, let's just get the groceries so we can get back to the house and settle in. It's our first day together in years, and it's not going to be easy on anyone — especially your mom."

"I guess."

"Can you do me a favor?" she asks. "Promise me you'll hang in there a little longer?"

I take her outstretched hand. "All right, Rach. I promise."

"Good. Now let's go find the bakery case and see if they still make those delicious maple walnut muffins."

Rachel hits a bell on the counter and smiles as a woman in a white paper hat emerges from behind a row of giant ovens.

"Good afternoon, ladies. What can I get for you today?" she asks as she carries out a tray of golden buns. "Just took out a fresh batch of... of... Rachel *Hannaford*? And... oh my *God!*"

She drops the fresh batch of Rachel-Hannaford-and-oh-my-God.

Her hands cover her mouth.

And she shakes her head, staring at me with wide, watery eyes as if I'm a ghost.

"For a second it's like I was looking right at her," she tells my aunt.

"Claire?" Rachel asks.

"No. Stephie."

"I can't believe you're almost seventeen," Megan the Baker says, taking her break with us in the bakery department's small eating area. "I used to change your diapers."

"Really?" I manage a weak smile, wondering what's in those fresh-baked buns to make a total stranger think such an announcement is okay.

"Del," Rachel says, "why don't you go find some snacks for the house? I want to catch up with Megan a little." She pushes the cart toward me. I wheel over to the junk food aisle without her, trying not to look offended.

As I check out the cookies and potato chips and snack cakes, I can't shake the feeling that everyone in this town is watching me. Like if there was a record playing, it would've scratched and skipped the second I walked through the door, and everyone would just wait for me to make some big dramatic announcement, hands on their guns just in case.

This town ain't big enough for the both of us.

When Stephanie died, she was just a few years older than I am now. I probably *do* look a lot like her, but I've never seen any pictures — not even at my grandparents' house. Just the one Mom keeps tucked away in her nightstand drawer — the three sisters holding hands and jumping off a dock into the lake. You can't even see their faces.

As I reach the end of the aisle, I peek at the bakery department to check on Megan and Rachel. Their hands move quickly as they talk, landing on each other's shoulders like small, pink birds. Their faces are sad and serious and when Megan puts her arms around my aunt, I see her face again and I finally remember it.

When we reunite a few minutes later, Megan ambushes me with a bear hug, smothering me against her bread-and-flour bosom.

I hug her back.

"Mom and I will stop by the house tomorrow," she says, handing Rachel a box of pastries. "Most of us heard the news yesterday, and now that you're in town, I'm sure you'll get visitors. Actually, here — better take a few more pastries. On the house." She loads up another bakery box with an assortment

32

from beneath the glass case and hands it over, kissing us each on the cheek one more time.

"I remember her," I tell my aunt as she takes over the cart and leads us to the produce. "She was always at the lake with us."

"She loved hanging out with you."

"How do we know her?"

Rachel looks back toward the bakery. Behind the pastry case, Megan blots her eyes with the edge of her apron, the white paper hat drooping on one side over her forehead. "Megan was Stephanie's best friend."

"Whoa."

Rachel nods, pushing the cart toward the fresh vegetables and steering us into the section with the eggplants.

"Aunt Rachel? I don't mean to be...I mean, I know it's really hard to talk about because she died so young, but... how come we don't...there aren't any..." I don't know how to ask, so I just leave it there, half-said.

"You know, hon, after Stephie died, we *never* really talked about her," she says, her hands tight around the cart handle. "There's a lot of pain there. Still. I guess we feel like we failed her. Like maybe if we were home instead of away at college, we could've done something to fix her. Something my parents and the doctors and her boyfriend missed. Sometimes I think I don't have the *right* to talk about her. Like at the end, I didn't know her well enough to say anything. So much of her life became secret. She spent all of her time with her boyfriend, and when she was home, her nose was buried in her diary. I swear that diary was her best friend, even more than Megan."

"Did you ever read it?" I ask.

"No."

"Not even after she died?"

Aunt Rachel shakes her head, removing an eggplant from the middle row and pressing her fingers against its flesh. "To this day, I don't know if I would've, either. We never found it, Delilah. It's like she just...took it with her."

An involuntary shiver crawls across my skin as Rachel bags the eggplant and sets it in the cart, moving us on to the lettuce. I want to ask more about Stephanie, about the diary and her boyfriend, about what her life was like and what made her heart stop working. But Rachel's shoulders seem heavy under the burden of remembering this much, so I close my mouth, focusing instead on helping her find fresh watercress and the romaine with the crispest, greenest leaves.

We keep the conversation deceptively light when we discuss the imported cheese selection, when we pick out cereals, and when we stock up on cleaning supplies. At the end of our shopping mission, we cruise through the bakery to say good-bye again to Megan, and I help Rachel unload the groceries from our cart onto the checkout conveyor belt. As we watch the cashier scan and drop our items one at a time into brown paper sacks, we don't say anything else about Stephanie or the family fight or the past. We just smile and pay and wheel everything out to the parking lot, the cloudless blue sky making everything seem better than it is.

Chapter five

"What's that smell?" I set the last bag of groceries on the kitchen counter, waving a hand in front of my face to clear the smoke.

"Sage." Rachel points to a stick of incense burning on the windowsill. "You burn it for an 'out with the bad, in with the good' kinda thing. Negative energy attaches to the smoke and flows out — see?" A long wisp of smoke rises like a ghost and wraps around her finger, trailing through the open window over the sink. It reminds me of Finn, blowing out the smoke of his cigarette in the truck last night.

So much has happened in twenty-four hours that it hardly

seems real, the smoke just another part of a long, uninterpretable dream. As soon as I open my eyes, I'll wake up in my own bed, half-asleep with the television on, sunlight sneaking in through the windows to remind me that it's time for school.

"Great. FedEx them tomorrow for priority delivery," Mom says from her newly established office — a folding table in the back corner of the kitchen, flanked by a dry erase board and a giant wall calendar. I'm surprised the sage isn't interfering with her corporate chi.

"Also," she continues, "I got a call about the invoices." Her back is to us as she chatters away at an efficient clip, confirming details and setting goals and exceeding expectations, one hand smoothing her hair, the other pressing her ear to her assistant's voice across the satellites a million miles from anywhere that matters.

"She makes her people work on Sundays?" Rachel whispers, pulling some of my grandmother's old food from the fridge and sniffing it.

"Nah — weekends are optional. They only have to work them if they want to keep their jobs."

I watch a drop of water speed down the side of an orange juice carton on the kitchen table and wonder how long ago my grandmother's hands were on it. When did she pour her last glass? Or did she drink it straight from the carton, fridge door open as she took a swig? A Cherry Coke feeling fizzes in my stomach, bubbles rising alongside thoughts of my grandmother and the inevitable future: me wading through my own mother's final foodstuffs and wondering how things could have/would have/should have been different. The sadness of everything slides up my spine and grabs me, two cold hands around my neck.

"That's the last bag of groceries," I tell Rachel, pointing to the stuff I just brought in. "I need some air." My eyes are steady on the side door as I move toward it, tugging on the cool metal handle and flinging myself into the fading sunlight. I head around back, down the big hill, all the way over to the bleachers, turning back only once to look at the house and the tall rows of maples that guard it. Their branches and leaves scratch lightly against the chipped pillars of the wraparound porch and I know that they have the whole story, those trees.

But like the women in my family, they're not saying anything, either.

The evening sun is hot on my black tank top, but the underbelly of the bleachers traps the cool, gentle breeze off the water. Hidden beneath mostly deserted wooden rows, I look out at the lake that was such a part of my childhood summers and cry big, silent tears. I still remember the smells, like coconut oil and charcoal and hot dogs and fish. The moist air feels the same as it always has, and when I listen to the rippling water and the music and the kids laughing and splooshing and squealing, I become them. Five years old again, arms stuffed like sausages into inflatable swim fins, going in as far as my knees, then my hips, sneaking in inch by inch until Mom waves me back to the shore, ever-present and protective in those flippety, float-on-by days. Back then, I didn't yet miss the dad I never met. I didn't know that when I'd finally beg my mother to share everything she remembered about him, she'd look at me with exasperated eyes and give me the newspaper article and the whole, one-night story of them, saying only that she was sorry. That she wished there were more to tell.

AFGHAN BOY KILLS AWARD-WINNING BRITISH JOURNALIST; BOY'S FAMILY CALLS IT 'TRAGIC ACCIDENT'

KABUL—A twelve-year-old boy shot and killed *National Post* journalist Thomas Devlin on Thursday in Tuksar, Afghanistan. Devlin, thirty-six, was shot at close range in the head and chest after the boy returned from school and mistook him for an intruder. Devlin was at the house to interview the boy's mother [name withheld] for a story on paramilitary recruitment of children in the rebel-controlled village in northern Afghanistan.

Devlin, a London native and graduate of Oxford University, is best known for his extensive fieldwork in politically unstable countries with displaced civilians and endangered species. Last year, his *National Post* series, "The Elephant's Journey," earned him the esteemed National Journalism Award in Britain and international recognition for exposing major underground poaching networks in Kenya and Namibia. Both countries have since enacted stronger antipoaching and endangered species protection laws, crediting Devlin with raising national awareness of the impacts of poaching and worldwide compassion for the plights of orphaned elephants.

Devlin's recent work in Afghanistan was to be part of a larger *National Post* series on civilian life in rural areas of the war-torn Middle East. The family of the boy who shot him declined to be interviewed, saying only that the incident was a tragic accident.

Devlin, mourned by friends and colleagues at home and throughout the international community, left no surviving relatives.

Well, there *was* the woman from the bar he met on his last night in Philadelphia. No one knew about her, with the long dark hair and the little triangle of brown at the top of one of her otherwise hazel eyes.

He loved her laugh. He said so.

She loved his accent. She said so.

Shall we?

Yes, let's.

When Thomas (not Tom) Devlin boarded the plane back to London the next morning to transfer to the one that would take him on his very last assignment, he probably thought about the woman and her eyes and her laugh. She probably thought about him, too — the way he said her name. The way he smiled at her across the bar. That's how I like to imagine it. But back then, neither knew about the tiny little thing already setting up camp inside her uterus. If Thomas *had* known, maybe he would've thought about that tiny little thing before he saw the boy and the gun and opened his mouth to say, "God!" or "No!" or "PLEASE!" or *"Please?"* or — well, only the now twenty-nine-year-old Afghan boy and his mother know for sure.

The embryo of me aside, there was no one else, just as the article said. And now, other than me and Aunt Rachel, my mother has no surviving family, either. No one to tell the stories. No one to inherit the china in the dining room or the wavy chocolate-brown hair or the laugh that ends an octave higher than it starts. No one to tell us where we've been or who we are or whether any of it was even worth it.

Like so many of the hard things between us, Mom still won't talk about my father. Does she miss him? Does she resent him or the boy in Tuksar for making her a single mom? Does she ever think about him? I have his picture tacked up on my bulletin board — the headshot I printed from his online *National Post* bio — and sometimes I look at it for hours, searching the lines and shadows of his face for anything like my own. But the mirror tells me that I'm mostly my mother's daughter. Hair. Eyes. Skin tone. Teeth. All of them, a younger version of hers. So what is it, then, that makes me Thomas Devlin's daughter? Did I inherit his sense of adventure and twist it into my own form of recklessness? His need to uncover and expose the truth? His constant search for something more?

I never met my father, so it's not like I feel this big hole in my heart where all the stuff of him used to be: the scent of his cologne. The sound of his voice. The bend of his favorite hat. But there are times like now when I wish that he was here, that I could ask him what I should do, what I should say, how I should be. That he'd answer me. That he'd look at me and say the right words and kiss me on the cheek, and I'd believe him.

A seagull lands on the bleachers and my mind comes back to the present, fingers scratching and peeling a loose patch of paint from the row in front of me. As I drop papery gray flecks into the dirt below, I notice someone, two sections over, one down, stretched out on his back with a book pressed flat across his chest and a baseball hat pulled low over his eyes. I creep one section closer, hidden by the shadows, my hands on the bars beneath the bleachers as I watch the gentle way his lungs expand and contract, expand and contract in the setting sun.

"You're not going to sneak up and scare me, are you?" he asks.

"I...no. I was just...I'm...sorry?" I step backward and, in all my startled and graceless glory, whack my head on a support beam. *"Oww!"*

"I felt that." He sits up and puts his hat on the right way before sliding in under the bleachers to meet me, his face hidden by the shade. "You okay?"

"I didn't mean to interrupt." I nod toward his book and hope he'll stop watching me rub my stupid (and now throbbing) head. Hope that the breeze has sufficiently dried my earlier tears. Hope that he doesn't ask too many questions.

"Nah, it's cool," he says, flipping over *Catcher in the Rye*. "I've read it before. I just like coming down here. It's peaceful...*usually*." He smiles. "Hey, seriously. You okay?" He rubs the back of his head on the spot where the lump is undoubtedly forming on mine.

"Yeah. I'm...um..." I take another step back. "I was just leav —"

"Stay." He reaches for my hand but changes his mind. "I mean, you don't *have* to leave," he says. "Unless you want to. But it's cool if you want to stay."

I'm about to ask Mr. Holden Caulfield just who he thinks

he is, reaching for my hand under the bleachers, all up in my personal space like some kind of stalker. But then he turns his hat around backward and shifts so the light is on his face. As soon as I see those eyes up close — gold-flecked and amber and a little bit mischievous — all I can do is smile.

Chapter six

"Little *Ricky*?" I throw my arms around him; his laugh is the only confirmation I need.

"It's Patrick now, but yeah. It's me." He pulls away to look at me again, his hand sliding down my arm and closing around my wrist. "My dad told me you guys would be back today. Hey, I'm really sorry about —"

"Your parents still live here?" I ask, staring. His braces are gone now, and he's got six inches of height on me. The freckles of childhood have faded into smooth, tan skin, but otherwise, he's still the same Little Ricky Reese. I mean, *Patrick* Reese.

"Dad does," he says. "They split up a few years ago, but he kept the house. Mom's in New York now doing her off-Broadway thing. Trying, anyway."

"What about you?" I ask. "You're here?"

He sticks his hand out between the benches, turning it over in the sun. "I actually live in Brooklyn with her during the school year, but I come to Vermont in the summers to help my dad with his construction stuff."

"Your dad still has the remodeling business?" I remember the tools and workbenches and the mounds of sawdust in his garage next door. How Ricky always wanted to help, but we weren't allowed to play in there.

"Yep. Only instead of Handyman Jack's, now we're Reese and Son Contracting. When I turned eighteen a few months ago, he made me a partner. Which is a fancy way of saying he mailed in some forms, got new signs for the truck, and gave me a lot more work to do." Patrick smiles, readjusting his hat.

"I can't believe…I can't believe you're here, like *right here*," I say. "I was just thinking about when we used to come down here to look for stuff after the races."

"Me, too." He unearths a layer of dirt with his sneaker, still smiling beneath his cap.

"I haven't seen you in eight years."

Little-Ricky-now-Patrick nods and pulls his *Catcher* book against his chest. "Delilah Hannaford, you nearly broke my heart when you didn't come back that summer." He winks at me.

"I was eight," I say, following him as he walks out toward the docks. "I didn't get a vote."

"I know. That's why I've decided to forgive you. Well that, and you're still kind of adorable."

"*Kind* of?"

Patrick laughs and puts his arm around me, pulling me close in his old magnets-on-the-fridge way. "Hey, seriously, Delilah. I'm sorry about Nana. I was home when Dad...I mean, he called me over there and told me what happened."

"How did he know she was...you know. *Gone?*" I keep my eyes down as we speak, one foot moving slowly in front of the other along the planks that make a wide path around this end of the lake.

"We were helping her remodel the sunroom in the back. When she didn't answer the door yesterday, he went in, and that's when he found her."

I consider this as I recall the old sunroom, big bay windows looking out over the lake, all the sunlight shining through them nearly absorbed by the heavy wood panels covering each wall. I think about the matriarch of my family taking her final steps and final breaths, feeling again like I'm watching some fictional cop show with the tough-but-emotionally-wounded police escort giving details on the crime scene.

"Emergency response took her to Maple Valley so the doctor could confirm the cause of death," Patrick says. "He said it was her heart. He asked us if we knew how to reach her next of kin, so Dad gave him the number he still had for your mom, but it was an old one. They tried Rachel next. You know the rest."

"I'm not sad, really." The confession falls out fast, but Patrick's eyes don't falter as I rush to explain. "I mean, the whole *thing* is sad, but it hasn't really hit me. There's so much… I haven't been back since my grandfather's funeral. I don't remember them very well, you know?"

He nods. "That was the last time I saw you. You were wearing a light blue dress and you were just…" Patrick looks out over the lake, searching. "Inconsolable," he says. "You asked me to find you four-leaf clovers for his grave."

Clovers. I don't remember the light blue dress, but the clovers — of course. It's as if I was here last week, combing through the grass while Papa watched me from his wheelchair. *Look, Papa! A six-leaf clover!* I'd made it by tearing three leaves down the middle because I'd already found so many four-leafers that I was afraid I'd use up all the good luck in Red Falls. My grandfather kissed the top of my head and called me his lucky little rabbit's foot. It was like that every summer at the lake house — me. Papa. Little Ricky. The four-leaf clovers. I thought they'd last forever.

I lean on the rail over the water, watching the sun spark off the surface. A family walks behind us, the youngest of three kids riding his dad's shoulders and pointing at the sailboats in the distance. "Boap! Boap! Boap!"

"More tourists than I remember," I say.

"Yeah. They've really jacked this place up. Dad and I worked on some of that new construction over there." Patrick points across the lake to a row of gray and white cottage-style homes on a spot that used to be no more than a thicket of trees with a small dirt path leading into the woods. "They stopped the boat races because the motors were disturbing the out-of-towner fishermen and the sailboats. They said it was preventing an 'authentic New England experience.'"

I laugh. "Whose idea of authentic?"

"Exactly. It's not completely overrun, though. Besides, once the boat races stopped, the turtles showed up." He points toward the edge of the lake where two turtles bask on a large, smooth rock, their heads craning toward the sun. Behind them, a smaller turtle scrabbles up the side, slipping back into the water with a *sploosh*. Just as quickly as she fell, her head and feet poke through the surface of the lake for another try.

"I saw some new places on Main Street," I tell Patrick as the turtle finally summits the rock. "Trendy camping store. Nail salon. Coffee place."

"Luna's," he says. "The coffee place. I do shows there all summer."

"Shows? Like, 'To be, or not to be' stuff?"

"Um, *no*." He shoves me on the shoulder as we continue our walk, his deep smile showing off his dimples. *Oh no*. I remember *those*.

"I sing and play guitar," he says. "Acoustic."

"Seriously? You sing?"

He nods, taking off his hat to run a hand through his sticking-out-everywhere summer hair. "You should check it out next week. We usually get a pretty good crowd. I do a mix of originals and covers — people like to sing along, you know?"

"Patrick, that's so awesome."

"Oh, man, wait till I tell Emily about you!"

"Emily?" My chest tightens. "Is that your girlfriend?"

"No, nothing like that. Just a good friend. She works at the café. Luna is her aunt, actually. She's always at the gigs, either working or just hanging out. You'll see. You'll like her."

"Sounds cool."

"Next show is next week, Tuesday," he says. "Think you can make it?"

"Definitely." I skip the whole irrelevant part about my current state of semi–house arrest. Not to mention the part about my non-boyfriend, also irrelevant.

Our walk stretches on for nearly two hours, all the missing years smushed back together. As we near the bleachers again, Patrick buys popcorn from a vendor along the path and we take turns throwing it in the water, watching the seagulls bob on the waves and dive after the little white kernels.

"I still can't believe you're here," he says when the popcorn's gone. His eyes hold mine longer this time, and I let myself get a little bit lost in the honey color they take on in the low sun. When he smiles again and squeezes my shoulder, something swirls in my chest. I can't temper it, and it unhinges me a little. So I pull away from his touch and tie my humidity-prone hair into a loose ponytail, mortified to imagine how frizzy it must be but grateful for the distraction. "I should get back, Ri — I mean, Patrick."

"Sure," he says. "I'll see you soon, anyway. My dad stopped over there earlier. I guess your mom wants to talk about the sunroom and other house projects over dinner tomorrow."

"Dinner? You sure you want to come around?" I ask. "One house. Three women. Dead people. I can almost *guarantee* random, unprovoked cat fights and spontaneous bouts of crying."

"Well, since you put it like *that*…" Patrick's fingertips brush my bare arm so lightly the hairs on my skin have to stand up and stretch to reach him.

"See you then," he says. He flashes his dimpled smile once more and heads back to his spot on the bleachers, *Catcher* in hand. As I walk up the hill to my grandmother's house, my hand moves to my arm where the feel of his touch still lingers, warm and soft and familiar like my memories of Little Ricky racing around the lake, devising contests to dig up the biggest fish bones or jump off the highest dock.

You're still kind of adorable.

That thing in my chest lurches sideways and I take a deep breath, count to ten, and bury it, way down deep.

Chapter seven

It's silent back at the lake house.

The groceries have been put away and Mom's card table desk is tidy — pen-filled coffee mugs threatening to evict the rooster-themed tissue box behind them. Everything is still. Lifeless.

No one is here.

Upstairs, all of the doors are open but one — the room at the end of the hall that my grandparents shared. Mom's luggage is stacked in her old room; Aunt Rachel's in hers — the Purple Room. I fell asleep in there once, the Purple Room. There was a monster under the bed, something scaly with huge yellow eyes and an appetite for small children. Mom was working in New York City that week, and I remember screaming for Nana, who was less skilled at scaring away monsters than my one-legged grandfather but could definitely get to my room faster. Nana was at my side flipping on the light after the first scream, but in her haste, she'd forgotten to put on her hair. Unbeknownst to me, she didn't have her own — just a collection of wisps that hovered around her head in a cotton candy cloud. It took an hour for her and Papa to convince me that the banshee standing at the end of my bed was actually Nana, even after she got back into her wig. I'm not sure I ever really trusted my grandmother after that, even though I never again saw her without her hair (or slept in the Purple Room).

My bags are stacked in the bedroom I always had here in the summers. We never talked about it before, but as I drag my stuff across the floor toward the closet, I realize with a chill that this must've been Stephanie's old room. I sit on the corner of the daybed — the same one from before, minus the white lace canopy — and wonder whether this was *her* actual bed. *Her* actual canopy that I slept beneath. *Her* actual toys and dolls that I played with. Then, thought converted to action without my awareness, I'm on my knees, crawling partway under the bed as if I might find a clue. A sign. A treasure map. The missing diary, somehow overlooked for all these years in this most obvious hiding place.

It's bare, of course, the floor beneath the bed. Nothing more than dark brown slats of hardwood, blanketed with a

fine dust, marred only in the corners by the occasional movement of the bed and a single, deep carving near the left front
post:

$$SH + CC$$

SH. Stephanie Hannaford. *CC* must be the boyfriend Rachel
mentioned. I run my fingers over the grooves in the wood and
wonder what she was feeling that night. How long ago she
carved it. Whether she wanted it to be seen. When I finally
pull myself out from under the bed, the air is cold and I rub
my arms. *What else have you left for the living to find?*

Whether they once belonged to Stephanie or not, the dolls
that lined the shelves in this room when I was a child are
gone, replaced now with jars of buttons and boxes overflowing with ribbons and zippers and swatches of loose fabric. I
don't remember my grandmother sewing, but there's a Singer
nestled under a landslide of tissue-paper patterns, turquoise
fabric caught mid-stitch, spilling over the table like a water-
fall. This is the room I always had, but everything is different
now. Everything changes in the space of eight years — faces,
places, even memories — realities as different from our recollections as we are from our old selves.

The closet is jammed with winter coats and boots and dry
cleaning bags of laundered dress clothes, but most of my stuff
fits into an empty dresser. On the top there's an old mason
jar of colored, unmatched buttons that rattles when I open

and close the drawers: shiny, glass-hard bits of rainbow like the sweet-and-sour candy we used to buy at Crasner's. The bed looks just-made, and across from it there's a small table and chair beneath a window where I can sit and lean on my elbows and stare out at the seagulls gliding down to the lake.

Or, from the window over the bed, at Patrick's house. Lifting the shade, I see his old bedroom window from here, just like before. I wonder if he's up there now, reading the rest of *Catcher in the Rye* — maybe the part where Holden talks about the books Phoebe writes but never finishes, or when he calls a prostitute to his hotel room, or...

"Delilah?" Mom knocks softly on the doorway, entering without permission and taking a seat on the daybed. I open my mouth to order her out, but the part of me that wants to fight is outvoted by the part that remembers her in the yard a few hours ago, yanking out the grass.

"Hey," I say. "Where were you guys?"

"We took a walk into town to meet Bob Shane, the funeral director, to discuss the plans. Apparently Mom made the arrangements years ago, just in case no one was around to carry them out."

I join her on the bed, not sitting too close. "When are we having the funeral?"

"I was hoping to take care of it as soon as possible so we could focus the rest of our time on the house, but that's not going to happen. She wanted to be cremated, which Bob can

56

do this week, and buried in the plot next to Dad. But she also wanted some of her ashes scattered over the lake. Since Red Falls is so popular in the summers now, outdoor ceremonies require a special permit so they can rope off part of the lake for the scattering."

"Sounds complicated," I say.

"Between that and the actual service plans, realistically, we're looking at the end of summer."

"And don't forget about this guy," Aunt Rachel says, showing up in the doorway with an economy-size mayonnaise jar. "He was in the hall closet, just like Bob said."

Mom shakes her head. "I really hoped he was joking."

"Nope. Man, for a jar of ashes, this thing weighs a *ton*. Must've been a big dog."

I jump up from the bed, backing away toward the closet. "A dog? A dead dog is in there?"

"Little Ollie," Rachel says, setting him on the floor at her feet. "Her Saint Bernard. He died last year and she had him cremated by the vet. Bob told us that Mom wanted them buried together. It's against the rules, but he promised her he'd mix their ashes anyway. I have to run these over tomorrow."

"This family is insane," I say, flopping back on the bed. "I can't believe I'm stuck here for the entire summer."

Mom looks at my hands, but she doesn't reach for them. "Delilah, I know this isn't how you planned to spend your summer. None of us expected to be here, and it's going to take time to get used to these . . . *arrangements*. We've got just about two months to get this house in shape, organize an estate sale, and plan the funeral service. Plus, between Realtors anxious to secure the listing and people offering their condolences, I expect we'll be inundated with visitors over the next few days. It's going to be a zoo. We've got to stay on track and remember why we're here."

I look at my mother and her sister and the flowers embroidered on the bedspread and wonder whose version of *why we're here* she's referring to. Are we here to delve into the past? To talk about what happened at Papa's funeral eight years ago? To remember Stephanie? To say good-bye? Or are we just here to sell the house, get back to Key, and forget about Red Falls all over again?

"I understand being back here is tough on you," she continues. "It's tough on all of us. But I don't want you wandering off again like you did this afternoon. Considering your issues with following rules, you need to stick close to the house with me or Rachel unless I say otherwise."

I'm ready to make a case for myself, but Mom launches quickly into a monologue about my recent behavior, throwing in a few of her favorite miscreant catchphrases like *acting out, attention-seeking, impacting your future,* and *not without consequences*. I hear all the words, but only peripherally, like watching the sailboats today on Red Falls Lake — in front of me but distant, their speed and imbalance warped into something slow and graceful by the curvature of the Earth.

"Did you hear me, Del?"

I shrug.

"I spoke with Mr. Marshall at Kennedy the other day, and he —"

"What?" I ask. "You talked to the *guidance* counselor about me?"

"It's no secret that you barely passed this year. You've cut classes. Missed assignments. Shown up late. We're concerned you might not have a successful senior year."

I wrap and unwrap a loose thread from my shorts around my finger, watching the tip turn purple and white, purple and white. *She just lost her mother, Delilah. Let it go.* Purple. White. Purple. White.

"He also said that you skipped all the big pep rallies this year. The dances. That you ate lunch in the library alone a lot. What about your blogger friends? I thought you loved those girls. What happened?"

What happened? I'll her *exactly* what happened — all of it. How my so-called blogger friends are more concerned about scoring booze for the next creek party than they are about reporting the issues and spending time together. How ever since Libby Dunbar inherited the junior class blog, it's taken on its own demonic life, morphing from a cool and somewhat helpful academic resource to a gossip 'zine almost overnight. How the trendy new format launched Libby into pseudo-celebrity status where freshman girls clamor to carry her books and clean up her lunch tray. How the blog's most popular feature, "Kiss or Diss," invites people to publicly rate the looks of classmates. How the "Rumor Mill" message board publishes more atrocious lies than the stuff in the grocery store tabloids. And how last month on the "Free-4-All Graffiti Wall" someone anonymously uploaded cell phone pictures of me and Finn kissing behind the skate park, one of his hands up my shirt, the other on my ass. How every morning after that, I'd show up at my locker to find another printout of that awful pose taped at the top, guys calling out across the hall in front of the whole world, "When's my turn, Hannaford? Do I have to buy tickets or is the feel-up service complimentary?"

When I asked Libby to remove the photos, she told me I was overreacting, that the pictures weren't even that bad. She laughed and said that her blog would make me almost as famous as it made her. Then, after I e-mailed a final plea, she wrote back one last time, saying only this:

"Delilah, I'm not censoring anyone. I really thought you of all people would know how important freedom of the press is. Your father died defending it."

When I open my mouth to confess the whole sordid tale, the only words that fall out are, "Things are just different this year, Mom."

"Yes," she says. "Things change sometimes, and not always in the way we'd like them to. I understand that. But the whole situation speaks to the larger issue of your behavior, and frankly —"

I hold up my hand. "I don't want to talk about it."

Rachel shifts in the doorway and I catch her fidgeting with her pocket. The air is magically infused with essence of oranges, but I don't think any of it gets on Mom, and she presses ahead.

"I'm your mother, Delilah Hannaford, and I *do* want to talk about it."

"Are you kidding me? You never want to talk about *anything!*" I don't name the things that have gone unsaid between us for so long, but they're here, rising up like steam in the heat of this place. Tears creep back into my eyes, and it's a monumental effort to keep my butt on the bed, to keep my feet from carrying me right back down to the lake.

Before Mom can respond, Rachel is in front of us, clapping her hands together. "Too much negative energy. Let's all take a deep, cleansing breath" — she sucks in, waving at us to do the same — "now exhale."

We obey, repeating it three times.

"Much better," Rachel says. "It's obvious we all have a lot to work through, but we just got here. We haven't even unpacked. Someone has *died*, remember?"

Mom closes her eyes. "Rachel's right," she says, rubbing her temples. "I'm sorry, Del. One day at a time, okay?"

"Fine, Mom. But —"

"Let me do the cards," Rachel says. "They'll help clarify our thoughts."

I used to love Rachel's tarot readings on my D.C. visits,

but that was way back when my future didn't look so bleak. Now, I just don't have the emotional fortitude for those tricky little death cards and devils and half-naked girls prancing around in front of Nana's needles and bobbins and blouse patterns. "No thanks," I say. "Mom won't go for it, anyway."

Rachel laughs. "Hey, I got her to turn her cell phone off for the rest of the night. Stranger things, right?"

Mom shrugs. "After the weekend I've had? I'll go along with anything. Count me in."

Rachel turns over my last card, laying it face up on a square black cloth dotted with silver stars and moons. "This," she says, "is your final outcome."

"There are boys in tights in my final outcome? *Perfect.*"

"It's the Page of Cups," she says. "He represents the birth of something."

Mom picks up the card for a closer look, as if the answers to all of my problems are inscribed on the Page's golden chalice. "Please don't tell me you're pregnant, Delilah."

"It *can* mean a child," Rachel says, glaring at Mom, "but in this case, it's probably the birth of a new relationship or friendship. Kind of like an unexpected new beginning. It might mean a situation, but if it's telling us about a person, it's usually someone imaginative and artistic. Passionate. A dreamer. What do you think, Del?"

I avert my eyes from the house next door, splashes of blue

peeking in through the window. "What do *you* think? You're the fortune-teller."

"It's not fortune-telling," Rachel says. "The cards are just a way to pick up messages from the universe. I can only tell you what they mean in the positions they're drawn. It's up to you to figure out what they're trying to say. There's a lot going on in this spread, but it's not inherently negative."

I look at the card in the immediate future position: the Fool, a young boy playing the flute with his eyes closed, happily dancing toward the edge of a cliff. *Tra-la-la!*

"No?" I ask.

"No. I want you to pay particular attention to this outcome card," Rachel says, pointing to the page, "especially considering the Five of Cups in the crossing position. She's the spilled-milk card, whereas the Page of Cups signifies a time of emotional rebirth. With the Five here speaking to a loss, maybe the ending of a relationship, the Page is saying that it's okay to trust again. Don't shut yourself off to new possibilities. But be mindful of the Fool, and don't dive into anything with your eyes closed. Does any of this strike a chord?"

"I'm not sure," I say, glancing over the spread. "Is it about... well... being back in Vermont? Family stuff?"

Mom leans in for a closer look, but Rachel shakes her head. "I don't think so. Usually in a family spread for you, we'd see more of the mother cards, like queens or the Empress. This one's probably about friendships. It could be about your friends at school, or new friends you might meet here in Red Falls. Could also be about your relationship with yourself. That's for you to figure out."

I look back over the cards again, accidentally thinking of Patrick. Is he the artistic dreamer? Is the Page of Cups heralding a passionate... *no.* Another non on the non-boyfriend list is the last thing I need. The only card that rings true here is the Fool, because that's what I am for even *considering* this stuff right now, stuck out here in the middle of maple sugarville with all these secrets and a broken family that can scarcely go an hour without fighting.

Rachel puts the cards back together and shuffles the deck. "Now, let's see what the universe is trying to tell your mom."

Her first card is a woman, tied up, blindfolded, and surrounded by swords. "In your case," Rachel says, "the Eight of Swords likely refers to the burdens of a successful career."

"I don't feel burdened," Mom says, her fingers tracing the delicate gold links of her watchband. "I love my career. Things at DKI are great. I've worked for this kind of opportunity my whole life, and now I have it."

"Like I told Delilah, everything is open to your interpretation. See — this next one looks scarier than it is." The card depicts a woman being ferried across the water in a small wooden boat. Like the woman in Mom's first card, she's surrounded by a cage of swords. "They're in rough water," Rachel says, "but it smoothes out ahead. The swords don't completely surround her, either. This could be about forgiveness, or facing and overcoming a difficult situation."

"Interesting." Mom picks up the card, looking at it with squinted eyes.

"Definitely something to think about while we're here," Rachel says. She describes a few more cards, mostly about career and hard work and material comforts, and turns over Mom's final outcome.

"Ah," she says, her fingers trailing over the image of two children standing on a path in the sunlight, sharing large cups of flowers. "I was wondering when this would turn up."

"What is it?" Mom asks.

"Six of Cups. Funny that it appeared as your final outcome. The Six of Cups has to do with childhood memories," Rachel says. "It's the nostalgia card."

Mom looks at her sister, then the cards, then at me. She runs her hand along my ponytail and stands, crossing out of the room and down the hall, her bedroom door clicking closed behind her. Rachel silently reassembles the deck of cards and slides them back into their velvet drawstring bag, folding the stars-and-moon cloth into a small, perfect triangle, leaving me alone with the Hellmann's jar formerly known as Little Ollie.

Everything is open to your interpretation.

chapter eight

After last night's crystal-balling, the voices that float up the stairwell this morning seem exaggerated and unreal, my mind still stuck halfway in a nightmare in which a pack of mythical, two-dimensional characters imprisoned on laminated cards comes alive, rising up from the lake to warn me against impending doom.

But the voices remain sure and solid, growing louder as I open my eyes and stretch away the lingering sleep. Warm air blows in through the open window over the bed. My stomach grumbles.

Downstairs, Megan the Baker, along with an older woman and a girl about my age, are assembled around the table with

Mom and Rachel, all of them picking from a plate of cut fruit and the pastries we got yesterday at Crasner's.

"Delilah," Rachel calls, waving me over. "Come meet the rest of Megan's family. This is Luna, her mother. She owns the coffee shop we saw in town."

"I remember when you were just a little thing," Luna says, standing for a hug. "Hard to believe you're the same age as my niece."

"Hey," the girl says. "I'm Emily." *Patrick's Emily.* She smiles at me from behind a curtain of shoulder-length brown hair, big blue eyes warm and genuine. "I'm working at the café all summer. You should check it out — way better than all the corporate stuff at the other end of town."

"Definitely." I sit next to her and grab a maple walnut muffin from the plate. She smiles again and I let my shoulders relax, just a little. Maybe the summer won't be so horrible after all.

After Emily tells me more about the coffee shop and her time so far in Red Falls, Luna and Megan catch us up on eight years of missed news. No one seems to hold a grudge or question Mom and Rachel about why we left, though the conversation is dotted with the awkward pauses of those who aren't quite sure. Those who want to ask but can't find the words. Those who know part of the story but need the rest of the pieces to put it all together.

"We're glad you're here again," Luna says to Mom as Rachel puts on another pot of coffee. "I'm just sorry it's not under happier circumstances."

Mom covers Luna's hand with her own and thanks them for coming, but I can see behind her smile that she's anxious to start work on the house. To map out plans for the rest of the summer — plans that probably don't include entertaining guests from our past. But with no sign of moving toward the door, Luna accepts another cup of coffee and Megan refills the pastry plate from the bakery box on the counter, everyone jumping back into the conversation as if we have only today to make up for all the missing years.

We're halfway through the second pot of coffee when the first car rolls into the driveway, followed by another, then another. Emily and I step outside to see who's here, and from a row of boat-size Buicks, a parade of white-haired women bearing foil-covered trays marches in a crooked line to the porch, introducing themselves as friends of Elizabeth's.

"We are so sorry for your loss, sweat pea," they say, lowering their eyes and moving toward the screen door as if called to the house by the spirits within, ghosts old and new branding us a family in mourning.

One in need of many pounds of coffee cake.

Elizabeth Hannaford knew a lot of people. And those people sure love coffee cake. And they sure love talking. Rachel keeps their coffee and tea cups full as they share stories about my grandmother's famous potato salad and her volunteer work at the hospital and, oh my, look how big Delilah is, and it's wonderful to see you all again after so many years, but we sure are sorry it's for Elizabeth's funeral. They ask about plans for the service and if there's anything we need, and all of the outside parts of my mother seem to be smiling, seem to lean forward in her chair and welcome their kindness. But beneath it all, Claire Hannaford Speaking struggles to climb out and get to work. When she ducks into the living room and pulls the tin of pills from her purse, I offer to tell everyone that she has a headache so she can retreat to her room.

"Thanks, Del. Unfortunately, there's no time to lie down on the job today. The neighbors are coming later to discuss plans for the remodel. Rachel's cooking and I need to get some supplies ready before they get here. You remember Jack and Little Ricky, right?"

The side door on the porch opens and closes a thousand times today, groups of visitors rotating in and out from morning until late in the afternoon, clearing out only as the dinner hour approaches. Finally, I see the shapes of Patrick and his father walking toward the house from the sidewalk, and when I hear their footsteps on the creaky porch step, I rush to meet them. Patrick leans in for a hug through the open doorway, and in his arms I'm reminded of the *other* dream I had last night, which ... oh ... which I immediately stamp out of my mind, hoping that no one else noticed the temperature in the room shoot up about five hundred degrees. Could my subconscious *be* any more inappropriate?

"We ran into each other at the lake yesterday," Patrick says, answering the question on Mom's face. "We're old friends again. All caught up. How's your head?" he asks me.

My hand rubs the spot where I whacked it under the bleachers yesterday. "No bump. Guess I'll live."

Rachel smirks at me over her mug, but I ignore her, shaking off the lingering smoke of my dream. I know what she's thinking about — that "passionate dreamer" stuff is all over her face. Yes, there goes my favorite aunt, destiny-mongering around New England with her merry band of tarot characters.

Jack, Patrick's father, stands in the doorway with open arms. "Delilah! My God, you're beautiful. All grown-up."

"I remember *you*." I smile up at him, standing on tiptoes to reach him, the reunion of his arms like a warm blanket. Jack wants to know all about the last eight years, asking me about Key and school and future plans, but Mom clears her throat like she's got a bit of food stuck, standing behind me with an armload of notebooks, pencils, and sticky notes. We have never in my life run out of office supplies. If our house got blown down by a freak storm, I'm confident we could build a fortress out of mail sorters and thumbtacks with hanging folders for shingles and survive just fine, and here she is again, ready to avert another potential disaster with the click of her Bic.

"Thanks for coming," Mom says, all of us now at attention

around the table as Rachel dishes out her baked squash casserole and spinach salad. "Just so we all know what we're dealing with, the plan is for Patrick and Jack to help us prep the house for a listing. Since they've worked here before, they know the major obstacles and how each of us can best help."

Jack gives us an update on the work-in-progress in the sunroom. "I think we already have the materials, so that shouldn't be an issue. That's the only room that needed a major overhaul," he says. "We'll have to see what the exterior looks like. Might need to get some painters out here."

Mom makes a few notes as the rest of us eat, mumbling to herself about materials and painting estimates as her food goes cold. "Rachel and I will tackle the internal property and decide what to trash, donate, or tag for the estate sale," she says. "And Delilah will help wherever we need her. I'm hoping to have it on the market no later than early August so we can feel out the interest level before we leave. We may sell it furnished, but we'll probably need at least three estate sales to clear out the rest of the junk."

I think of all the stuff upstairs and wonder where it will end up — the fabric and thread and patterns, and from the closet, the coats and shoes Nana walked around in for all the winters of her life. Images of Mom's bedroom back in Key flit in front of me like gnats. I swat and blink them away.

"I'm going to do as much as I can," Mom tells Jack, "but as my sister and Delilah know, I'm somewhat chained to my desk. For major decisions or issues, check with me or Rachel. Otherwise, I trust your judgment. You've been doing this a lot longer than we have."

Jack nods.

"No problem, Miss H," Patrick says.

"Are we all on the same page, Delilah?"

The same page? I don't think we're even in the same *library*, but no need to bring that up. I nod.

"Great," she says. "Starting tomorrow, I think it would be helpful for you to follow Patrick around with a notebook to assess the exterior. Whatever he tells you to write, you write. I need you to stay close to the house — got it?"

"Sure, Mom." There are worse punishments than tailing Patrick all summer. Don't contractors usually work without shirts?

"Okay, then." Mom claps her hands together once — her version of *Go, team!* "Any questions?" Apparently, her annual bonus depends on our ability to complete this mission on time and under budget.

"No," Jack says. "But Claire — and Rachel and Delilah, too — I just want to say again how sorry I am about Liz." He pushes a casserole mushroom around his plate. "She was —"

"Thanks, Jack. We appreciate all you've done for her." Mom's gentle nod sugarcoats her interruption, but she's got the face. The *You're Skating on Thin Ice, Delilah* face. Only this time, it's meant for someone dead.

Jack nods and pops the mushroom into his mouth, eyes fixed on the now-empty plate before him as if he can't remember how it got that way.

"All right," Rachel says, clearing the dishes. "Who's ready for some coffee cake?"

chapter nine

"We'll start here and work our way around," Patrick says, propping a ladder against the back of the house. "The gutters are probably the worst of it — they look pretty nasty."

I stand near the ladder as he climbs, pencil poised to catch his running commentary. It's manual labor, but I'm glad to be out in the sun, away from the kitchen and day two of the seemingly endless paying of condolences by the coffee-cake bakers of Red Falls.

"Sorry about last night," I say, squinting into the sun to see him. "I mean, my mother. She gets a little demanding sometimes. Well, *most* times."

Patrick pokes around the gutters, dropping a pile of leaves behind him. "No biggie. My dad has his moments, too. Write this down — back gutters stable. Need cleaning."

I scribble down what he says. "Parents, right?"

"Tell me about it. So what would you be doing all summer if you didn't have the honor of inspecting gutters with me?"

"Oh, you know. Typical summer stuff," I say, avoiding all the taboo topics: Finn. Cell phone pictures. Seven Mile Creek. Google-stalking my father. I kick at the dirt with my flip-flop but don't get much traction and stub my toe on a rock instead.

"Such as?" Patrick asks, still poking around the muck of the gutter.

"Movies. Hanging out. Reading. Whatever. Not much going on in Pennsylvania."

"Yes, but in Pennsylvania, you've got a friend."

"Huh?"

"The slogan — you know?" Patrick puts his hand on his heart and sings, straight out of the old tourism commercials. "You've got a friend, in Penn-syl-van-ia!"

"What about Vermont?"

"It's 'Vermont, naturally.' No song, though."

"Naturally." I laugh.

"Hey, I didn't say it was good, *friend*. Look out," he says, dropping his shirt from high up on the ladder. "It's hot as hell up here."

He moves down a rung to check the second-floor windows, the muscles in his tanned shoulders and arms tightening as he grabs the sides of the ladder. I watch the way his bare back twists as his hands move along the wood frames searching for flaws and fractures. I'm just spotting him, of course, in case he slips. I need to assess his approximate weight so I can best position myself to catch him if he falls, so he'll land on top of me and...

I force my eyes back to the notebook. "Find anything?" I ask, head down.

"Windows in good shape. Glass solid. Looks fairly new. Write that down."

"Good. Solid. New. Got it. What about you? What do you do when you're not fixing stuff or breaking hearts onstage?"

"Write this," he says. "Exterior and shutters need work. Get estimates for paint or siding."

"Got it. So?"

"Breaking hearts? Not exactly. I do what everyone around here does," he says, climbing down to grab his Nalgene bottle. "Swim. Hike. Water stuff. Kayaking on the lake is fun — I'll take you sometime."

I close my notebook, my eyes involuntarily tracking the tiny rivulet of water trailing down his chin...his neck...his collarbone...

He steps closer and offers me the water bottle. "You'd like it, I think."

"Water?"

"Kayaking." He's right near me now, officially past my "just friends" space, smiling with his amber-honey eyes and those dimples, and I'm so hot standing out here on the hot grass in the hot sun next to the hot house...

"Patrick?" *Jack*. Patrick takes a step back, still smiling as I grab the water bottle from his outstretched hand.

"Man, it's funny to see you two like this," Jack says, a grin plastered all the way across his broad, tanned face. "You were inseparable as kids. Even after all day playing, you wouldn't leave each other's houses. Half the time we'd let you sleep over just to avoid the fight."

"Um, Dad?" Patrick shades his eyes from the sun and looks at his father. "Did you need something?"

"I gotta make another hardware store run. Those nails I got aren't the right size — wood's thicker'n I thought."

Patrick hands over the keys from his pocket and smirks. "You know it wouldn't kill you to walk, right, old man?"

"Maybe not. Wouldn't kill you to keep your clothes on, either." Jack's still laughing as he heads next door toward the green-and-white Reese & Son Contracting truck.

I look to Patrick's reddened face. "It's nice to know my mother doesn't have a monopoly on embarrassing her offspring."

"Oh, you think that's funny?" Patrick sticks his arms through the holes in his shirt and grins at me, a little bit of devil in his otherwise perfect smile. I drop my notebook and run, Patrick close behind, both of us laughing like the kids we used to be, laughing harder than I've laughed in months. I'm squealing and sprinting and dodging Patrick all around the house, nothing but happy and sun and warm all over me, and I feel a release, a free fall of carefree summer days with no end in sight. But on our second trip around, when we near the back corner of the house, I look up and notice them — the curved panes of the bay windows reflecting the lake, the windows Little Ricky and I used to curl up against to read when the rain kept us inside. Like a new movie starting in my head, I see a red cardinal and I stop, remembering the bird trapped in the enclosed sunroom, confused by all the windows. Papa was in his wheelchair and couldn't do much to chase it out, so he called Jack. Ricky and I stayed close behind Mom, watching from the height of her elbows. When Jack finally coaxed the bird to the open door, it shot out and sped away toward the lake, sailing over the trees beyond. All of us cheered and clapped and retold the story a hundred million times, so happy were we that the bird could reunite with his family.

Except for Nana.

I don't remember thinking my grandmother was miserable or bitter when I used to visit her, but those words, cruel and sad, come to me now as I remember the red cardinal. She was so flustered by it, so unimpressed that Jack set it free, so tired of hearing the story and how it made us all smile.

Papa always laughed. He taught Ricky and me how to play checkers and backgammon, told us adventure stories about his travels through Asia during the Vietnam War, and read the comics with me every Sunday over breakfast. I remember feeling *cared for* by Nana — she cooked for us, gave me a bedroom with toys and a lace canopy princess bed, sent Christmas presents, drank tea late at night with Mom and Rachel — but now that I think about it, she didn't *smile*. Her laugh? If she had one, I don't recall the music of it. And some days she'd go to her room after breakfast and stay there for two or three days, coming out only for the bathroom and to get the food Papa left on a tray outside the door.

Did I know she was hurting, even if I couldn't name it? Did I feel it, like when you can tell it's going to rain because the leaves get all shaky and silvery and your bones creak and you just *know* it's coming? Patrick said that Nana died of a heart attack, but I wonder how much of her life she could have saved — how much of our family history could've been rerouted — if only she'd been happy. If only she could've laughed the way Papa did when I told him my made-up stories, even after the death of their youngest daughter.

And just like my recollection in the bedroom yesterday, I realize now that the shock of losing Stephanie must have done that to her. It took away her laugh. Her joy. Her ability to know happiness.

"You okay?" Patrick stops the chase, his hand on my shoulder as he catches his breath.

"I don't know why she didn't try to get in touch with me. I hadn't really thought of it that way until just this second.

If your only grandchild is taken away from you because of some family fight, wouldn't you at least try to call her? Or send birthday cards or letters or something?"

"I wish I knew, Del. I have no idea."

As my aunt sorts through her mother's food and my mother buzzes around her desk inside, I remember the sad things about my grandmother and sit down in the grass to catch my breath with a boy with whom I've only just reunited. He was once my very best summer friend, and in the space between our lives, he's grown and changed as I have — separate, away, strangers who are still connected by some weird cosmic rubber band, stretched apart for nearly a decade only to be snapped back together in this moment on Red Falls Lake.

"Hey, baby. Don't be sad." Patrick puts his arm around me and pulls me close to him, my mouth near the skin of his neck. I feel like I should resist, but he's so warm and solid and real, like a memory that hasn't yet faded — one that I visit over and over when I'm scared or alone. It's the first time since Finn that I've been this close to a guy. It's funny to smell someone different. Different soap, different shampoo, different skin. His hand brushes my ear as he moves to squeeze my shoulder, and a shiver rattles its way on through. "She's still here with you, Delilah."

"Do you know what happened that day?" I ask him. "I mean, after Papa's funeral? Did your parents ever say anything about the fight after we left?"

Patrick shakes his head. "No one talked about it in front of me. I asked them when you were coming back. They said they didn't know. My mom tried to call your mom and Rachel, but they wouldn't tell anyone what happened, and of course your grandmother wasn't talking about it. Eventually, my mom stopped calling. I asked about you every summer for years after. They kept telling me it was a family situation. That it wasn't our business."

"But your dad's been here the whole time. He worked for her. She must have said *something* about it."

"Nope. And when she died and I knew you'd be coming back, I asked him again. He told me that Liz never talked about it. Maybe the whole thing was all her fault. Who knows?"

I look out over Red Falls Lake below. From here, it's just a giant blue hole, still and peaceful and immune to the constant flux of sailboats and people and babies below.

"I was thinking about the time the bird got trapped in there." I nod toward the windows of the sunroom. "Remember?"

"Yeah. My dad built that tunnel out of sheets to get him out — I totally remember! It was a cardinal, right? I haven't seen one in forever. Sometimes I see blue jays, but never cardinals."

"Same." I stand to brush the grass from my shorts.

Patrick turns his backside to me. "Get mine, too, all right?"

"That costs extra."

"How much?" he asks.

"I'll have to get back to you on that. My rates went up since eight years ago."

Patrick shakes his head, looking at me in his just-a-second-too-long way. "I think you're okay now, Hannaford," he says. "My work here is done."

Chapter ten

"All right, girls, where do we start?" Emily stands in the middle of the kitchen in her overalls, a red bandanna tied loose around her head. After a week of figuring out the house stuff and managing the constant stream of droppers-in, it's finally time to plan the estate sales. Mom had to run errands in town, so Em and Megan, self-proclaimed garage-sale queens, offered to help us with the first wave.

Rachel and Megan head for the basement, leaving me and Emily to sort the contents of the kitchen cupboards and drawers into piles: use while we're here, sell, donate, or trash. So far, trash is winning. Tupperware with no lids. Mugs with missing handles. Torn old picnic tablecloths that haven't seen the outdoors in years.

"Check this out." Emily holds up a pair of beige ceramic mugs printed with tic-tac-toe boards. "They're from Chances, the café before it became Luna's. Your grandma must've swiped 'em. Saucy old gal, huh?"

I shrug. "I don't really remember that much about her."

"Oh. I'm sorry, Delilah."

I take the mugs from her and set them in the sell pile. "This is actually the first time I've been back here since I was a kid."

"Yeah, Patrick told me. Hey, I hope this doesn't sound weird, but he really missed you. Don't tell him I said that."

That butterfly keeps banging around inside at the mention of his name. *Stupid insect.* "He did?"

"You should've seen his face when he first told me about you last week. Man, you guys must've been really close."

"We were," I say. "But it's been a long time. It feels so strange to be back here. I'm still trying to sort out some of the memories." I don't know why I'm so comfortable talking to Em. Maybe it's her smile, or the way she says everything so straight. No buildup or fanfare. No awkward pauses. Maybe it's her eyes, full and honest. Or maybe it's the three-act puppet show she performs with the oven mitts and pantry boxes.

"Oreo, Oreo, wherefore art thou Oreo?"

We spend hours sorting through the kitchen, chatting

about life and books and movies, about all the things that matter and all the things that don't. My sides hurt from laughing, and when Rachel and Megan finally emerge from the basement with their bags of trash, ready to call it a day, I look at the clock on the oven and wish we had a few more hours.

"You're going to Patrick's show tomorrow night, right?" Em asks.

"Yes." If I can't convince Mom to let me go out, there's always the window.

"Awesome. I finish work at six. See you there." She hugs me good-bye, and it's been so long since a girlfriend hugged me that it takes me a second to figure out what's happening and to remember how to do it back.

"You two seemed to hit it off," Rachel says when they're gone. "I'm glad. She's a sweet kid."

After dinner, I bring down the coats and boots from my bedroom closet for the use/sell/donate/trash evaluation. Cleared of everything but the cobwebs, the closet is roomy enough for me to hang up my summer jacket, my long dress, and a few of my sleep shirts that got crunched in the dresser. Even after I line up my shoes along the closet floor, there's still a spot for my empty suitcases. I try to shove the biggest one in the back, but it slips from my hands and lands hard on the floor, kicking up one of the floorboards.

Perfect. Hopefully Jack can fix it before Mom finds out I broke something. After the car damage last month, there's not much room left on my tab.

I yank the chain for the light and pull my suitcase back out. As I crouch down to replace the board, I see it — a patch of white illuminating the otherwise black hole in the floor. It's covered in dust, but I stick my hand in to retrieve it anyway, breath shallow in my lungs.

Here beneath the floorboards and cobwebs and spiders lies the formerly missing diary of Stephanie Delilah Hannaford.

I pull it gently from the hole, feeling the weight of it against my fingers. It's bound in cracked white leather, yellowed with age and etched with a single gold rose. The flimsy brass latch once locking the pages no longer holds them shut, and as I take it into my lap, the front cover falls open, loosing a cascade of crushed flowers and faded red maple leaves pressed between pieces of waxed paper. My heart pounds, unable to outrun the feeling that I was *meant* to find this diary, that Stephanie herself meant for me to find it, here, tonight, tucked safely under the floorboards of the bedroom closet since before her death, hidden through all of my childhood summers as I slept just five feet from its secret place.

I open the diary to the first page. It's covered with black letters, small and perfect. I trace the opening words until my fingers memorize their old grooves, the tiny loops of her handwriting bringing Stephanie closer to me than any passed-down story or photograph ever could.

"Thank you," I whisper into the dark space of the closet.

Dear Diary,

I'm sixteen today. Claire sent you to me and I know that I'm supposed to fill the pages with all of my collected wisdom, but I'm not sure how. I should feel more wise, right? More confident? Instead, eight hours into this new age, I feel neither. Am I alone in this? My sisters seem immune, as if together they are in on some secret that they just don't want to share. Were they ever as lost or alone? As unsure? Claire is already finishing up her second year of college, and Rachel, well... we're as close as ever, but I know that nothing lasts. She'll be gone soon enough, too. And though I know they love me, I can't help but feel as though they're leaving me here unprepared, alone to deal with Mom and her moods and Dad in his all-consuming quiet, shadowed by my mother's raging outbursts. I just don't have the armor for it.

But hope is not as lost as this dismal letter would have you believe! When I stretch my hands and reach into the faraway place of tomorrow, there's Casey Conroy.

Please don't tell my sisters. He's a bit insane, in the best kind of way. I don't think they'd

understand what I see in him — they're much
too practical!

Ah, well. Happy birthday, happy birthday,
happy birthday to me.

XOXO,
Steph

Casey Conroy — CC. There it is, in perfect black print, the name belonging to the initials carved under the bed. Now that I see it, now that my lips can form it, his full name hangs in my throat, stuck to the lump rising in the wake of reading Stephanie's words. The letter is so *usual*, so unsurprising, so much like something any girl my age would write, that for a moment I forget that she's dead. That this diary was hidden here before I was even born. That between the entry on her sixteenth birthday and the final page, so many of the stories for which I've been searching may be written.

And my mother and Rachel have no idea that it's here. That it wasn't lost or taken with Stephanie to the great beyond. That I have it, and that through her words, I've stepped into a piece of my family's elusive history.

I slip the diary beneath my clothes in the bottom dresser drawer and head downstairs for a late-night snack, heart racing, mind racing, the air around me crackling with the electric fear and hope that comes with the discovery of something new.

"You're up late," Mom says. She's in the kitchen reading the *Red Falls' Bee*. She doesn't look at me at first, and as she turns the pages of the town's weekly, the edges of my heart ache for her, wanting so much to tell her about the diary. To let her know that upstairs, tucked into the folds of my summer shirts, a part of her sister lives on — a part that she and Rachel can still know, even though she's not here. But as I watch my mother flip through the *Bee*, late at night in the kitchen of her childhood home, I lose all the words for it.

"Can't sleep?" she asks as I dig through the freezer.

"Not really. Are there any fudgesicles left?"

"Check behind the ice trays. Rachel's trying to hide them so she's not tempted."

I dig out the box. "Where is she?" I ask. "Sleeping?"

"She went out for a drink with Megan. She should be back soon."

"Oh. How was your day?" I ask.

"Fine. Met with Bob Shane again at the funeral home. Picked up the cremains."

"*Cremains?*" It's weird to think that someone can live a whole life — falling in love, getting married, having babies and grandkids and family feuds — just to end up "cremained" in a little box at the end of it all.

"That's what they're called," Mom says as if she's reading an article from *Funeral Directors Monthly*. "The cremated remains."

"I don't like that word. *Cremains*. Sounds like *Craisins* or something."

"Delilah, please."

"Sorry. Where is the...I mean, the...where is she?"

"There's an urn," Mom says, making the shape of a cube with her hands. "It's on the dresser in her bedroom. I guess we'll just keep it there until we get the permits cleared for the lake ceremony."

"You mean, she's *here*? In the *house*? *Upstairs*?" A layer of goose bumps rises on my skin.

"It's *fine*. It's put away in the bedroom. You don't need to go in there. Anyway, since you're here, let's talk briefly about tomorrow. I have a DKI call first thing, so I'll need you to be ready when Patrick gets here to clean the gutters at eight. Jack said there are tools in the shed and other supplies in the garage. You'll also need to —"

"Mom, do you miss it here?"

"Do I...*what*?"

"Do you miss it — you know, coming here? Now that we're back, I mean. Do you regret that we stopped visiting?"

"Delilah, I don't really want —"

"Why?" I push harder, a trail of cold chocolate running onto my hand as I think about the diary hiding upstairs and Aunt Stephanie and how I would trade anything to know my father for even one day, while my mother cut her own family away like the scraps from a paper doll, sweeping her entire

90

childhood into the trash as though it was the least important part of anything.

I grab a paper towel from the roll. "Why, Mom? How could you act like she was basically dead all this time? How could you do that?"

Mom is frozen. I can almost see the memories trying to fight their way up her spine and out of her mouth like some dormant alien pod, but she swallows them back again, her eyes opening and closing, lids as wrinkled as pecan shells. Beneath them she regards me, equally repulsed and fascinated, as though I'm some unidentified fungus or gruesome crime scene or challenging crossword puzzle that she could probably figure out if only she had more time.

But she doesn't, because: "Del, I'm sorry. I don't want to get into this now. It's late, and..."

And blah blah blah, e-mails to answer, clients to service, marketing plans to market, and, of course, there's the pinnacle of *my* summer vacation, cleaning out the gutters with Patrick.

"Get some sleep," Mom says, folding the newspaper into a neat rectangle. "We've got a long day tomorrow."

I want to crawl into bed and cuddle up against my anger at her, my frustration, my helplessness. The three are familiar companions, but when I lay my head on the pillow and wait for the blackness of sleep to seep in, curiosity stands at the foot of the bed, staring, waiting for me to flip on the light and pull the diary out from the drawer.

Dear Diary,

I decided to tell my sisters about C. At first, they freaked out, but then Rachel got over it and started asking me all kinds of questions and made me promise her that I wouldn't rush into anything, and that if I did, I'd at least be safe. Claire, of course, is still trying to convince me what a bad idea he is, but she doesn't know him. I think she'll come around. I'm glad they both know now. I hate keeping secrets, especially from my sisters.

Well, not that I tell anyone about the things C whispers to me late at night, under the stars at the lake. We go there when the entire town is asleep — I climb out the window and down the maple tree and he waits for me near the hill, and together we lie on the dock and he traces the veins in my arms and tells me how life is going to be when we can finally leave this town, this place, this tiny speck on the map of our lives. I want to see the whole world with him, and when he smiles and his eyes light up like the stars, I know that he means every word he says, and I know that I will love him until the day I die.

Even after.

My sisters may have a lot of the world figured out, but when C chases me in front of the black water while the entire state of Vermont is deep in their dreams, I close my eyes and spin around and wonder if they will ever get a chance to feel this way.

But… but… yes, there's always a but. Sometimes, when I'm not thinking about C and I'm alone in my room and the night outside is still, I feel this… hole… pressing against my heart. I can't name it; can't trace it. I don't know why it's there or where it came from, just that it is. Sometimes it hurts, like something's missing and I just haven't discovered what it is yet. Other times it's just this low undercurrent of wrongness. I don't know. I haven't been sleeping all that well — maybe my brain is shutting down! Guess I'll try to think about it more and write again. I don't know. It's just plain… weird.

Anyway… Claire is coming home this weekend! Rachel and I are making this huge surprise dinner. Mom and Dad don't even know about it yet. Can't wait to see her.

XOXO,
Steph

I read a few more entries about Mom's visit, about Stephanie introducing her sisters to Casey, about her sisters actually *liking* him. And I try to imagine them not as they are now, aged and lost and dead and unknown, but as kids. Still mostly happy. Still looking forward to an entire life together.

I don't keep a diary, but if I did, I wonder if I'd write about Finn. The way he calls me Lilah. All those times in the woods. Other than that, I don't have much to say about him — we haven't even spoken since the night Mom caught me sneaking back into the house just before we left for Red Falls. The story of me and Finn certainly doesn't warrant an entire diary, but as I flip through the rest of Stephanie's, I see Casey's name on nearly every page, spelled out in full on some, just C on others. I wonder how long they stayed together. Was he there at the end? At the funeral? What happened to him after?

I slide the diary back into the drawer and crawl into bed, my late aunt's words a new weight, a new thing to chew and worry and slip in between the layers of my dreams. My mother lost her baby sister. Then her father. Then her mother. She's not close with Rachel, and I'm not making things better for her either.

Most of the time, I want to hate her. But tonight, I can't. All I can do is close my eyes and promise the stars twinkling through the windows that I'll try. That I'll work with Mom, Rachel, Jack, and Patrick to finish up the house, sell the rest of my grandmother's things, and get us all back to our regular life.

But as I drift off to sleep with Stephanie's words rolling like ticker tape through my mind, I wonder if any of us even knows what a regular life *is*.

Chapter eleven

"I think I'm gonna be sick." I hold my nose as Patrick kneels in the grass and digs into a moldy pile of leaves and old garden clippings near the front corner of the house. "I'm serious, Patrick. This is foul."

"I brought you a pair of rubber gloves," he says, smiling. "Might want to put them on before we get to the *really* nasty stuff."

"It gets worse?"

"Gloves, Delilah."

I do as he says, trying hard not to breathe through my nose as I hold open a black outdoor trash bag.

"So, Emily seems really cool," I say, turning my face away from the mess. "I love that she's not shy."

Patrick laughs. "Yeah, she's definitely not shy."

"Um, what do you mean, gutter boy?"

He laughs. "Not *that*. She's just really outgoing, that's all. I met her last year while her family was staying with Luna for a few weeks. This year, her parents sent her alone to work with Luna for the whole summer. She wants to own her own café one day."

"I know. That's awesome. I would love to have just one single thing in my life figured out like that. I break into hives whenever someone even mentions SATs."

Patrick stands and ties off the first bag, tossing it alongside the house. "I know what you mean. I don't even want to *think* about the future."

"Aren't you going to work with your dad? Reese and Son?"

He shakes his head. "Dad and I . . . he's really into the whole 'and son' thing. Don't get me wrong — I enjoy the work and the money's great and Dad and I are pretty close, so I always have a good time working on projects with him. But this stuff isn't where my heart is."

I follow him to the back of the house where he's already set up two ladders and a garden hose. "Where is it?"

"Music," he says as we climb our respective ladders. "It's all there is for me. I think about notes and scales and lyrics, even in my sleep. I see something like the lake in the winter or the Brooklyn Bridge lit up when no one's around or seeing you again after all these years, and I want to write a song about it. To find the melody that tells that story, you know? And then I wake up in the middle of the night, just because I can't stop thinking about it, like whatever is inside wants to come out, and I know I just *have* to do it, no matter what anyone says or how it shakes out with my dad."

"Wow."

"I want to perform," he says, running a gloved hand through the gutter above the back windows. "And I want to teach."

"Patrick, I can totally picture it. You'll be incredible."

He drops a pile of leaves to the ground and reaches in for another handful as I do the same. "You think so?" he asks.

"Without a doubt. So why don't you just explain it to your father? If he knew you were so into music, I'm sure he'd support you. No?"

"Well . . . *no*. Not only is he stuck on this partnership thing, but he has *major* issues with artists and musicians. Mom basically left him for her acting. Seriously. It's like this unspoken rule in our house — I never ask him to come to the Luna's gigs, and I never talk about Mom's shows. He's still not over her, Delilah. I don't think he'll ever move on. I know my dad always looks like he's smiling, but on the inside, it's like his life was frozen on the day she left. He doesn't know how to unfreeze it."

I think about Patrick's father and it reminds me of Stephanie, the words of her life captured and frozen in the pages of the diary the way Jack's life is frozen here, waiting for a wife who will never return — a life that will never pick up where it left off.

"I have to tell him soon," Patrick continues. "I promised Mom I'd do it this summer. I'm already enrolled at a school in Manhattan. I start in the fall. He has no idea. And every time I work up the nerve, I see his face and his smile and I think about when Mom left and how heartbroken he was, and then I just close my mouth and pick up the hammer and keep on banging away."

Beneath my bright yellow rubber glove, a spider crawls out from the gutter onto the roof, disappearing under the eaves as I climb back down to solid ground. "I know that face," I say. "I see it on my mother whenever I want to talk about anything. She and I used to be really close. But now, it's like she's constantly running. She runs to work. Runs from one meeting to the next. Runs to client sites. She's been doing it for so long that it just comes naturally now. She runs away from me and I'm her own daughter."

"My mom's not around much either," he says, bagging up the leaves on the ground. "Lots of auditions. Any one of them could be 'the big break.' Everyone thinks it's so awesome that I have all this freedom, but honestly, it kind of sucks. I'd rather have my mom around once in a while to bake cookies or bitch at me to turn down the music."

I nod. "Exactly. But in the meantime, she's not. And I'm supposed to be figuring out my life and I have no idea where to start. I'll probably end up like her. Get a desk job. Hang up a few motivational posters. Become a responsible corporate citizen-slash-zombie. Gross, right?"

"Ah, I can't see you in a job like that," he says. "There's too much life in you. That kind of gig would suck it right out of you, and then I'd have to go kill someone, and then you'd spend the rest of your days trying to bust me out of jail."

"Um, as promising and well-thought-out as *that* sounds... got any other ideas?"

Patrick laughs.

"What's so funny?"

"I have one idea," he says, shaking his head. "But your mother would *definitely* not approve."

"Well, what is it?"

"You don't want to know." He laughs again. I pick up the hose, squeeze the trigger, and douse him.

"No more laughing, gutter boy," I warn. Soon we're both covered in a thick, grimy paste of water and dirt and stuck-on leaf parts, mud masks cracking around our eyes and mouths. When this most horrendous project is complete, Mom grants me official permission to go to Luna's for Patrick's show, saving me the effort of an elaborate window escape. When she sees us up close, two swampy creatures from the depths of Red Falls Lake, her smile is broad and deep, like the time when I set off that fire extinguisher in Connecticut.

De-guttered and pink after a hot shower, I slather myself with Rachel's homemade vanilla sugar body butter and wrap up in Mom's summer robe. It smells like her — Coco Chanel. The first time she bought a bottle was after she landed a full-time marketing manager gig at DKI, complete with a 30 percent salary hike. We went to the Chocolate Bar to make dinner out of our desserts, and right after the double fudge mousse and hand-dipped white chocolate strawberries, we headed to Four Corners Mall so she could splurge on us. I got an iPod and she got the perfume, and for that whole first year, Coco was the smell of celebration. Of success. Of happiness. She was still around back then, taking me school clothes shopping, watching movies with me, baking cookies, bitching about loud music, just like Patrick said. And she smelled great doing it.

Now, several promotions later, buying a new bottle of perfume is just another errand on her assistant's long list, and Coco Chanel is the smell of nothing but a woman leaving; a door clicked closed after a casual "Don't wait up — I'll probably be late again tonight."

"Hey, you," Rachel calls from the porch. "Come sit with me."

I join her outside, rocking the porch swing with my foot, lavender aromatherapy candles floating in a bowl of water nearby.

"Where's Mom?" I ask. "I thought she was done for the day."

"Nope," she says. "Had another meeting. She's in her bedroom."

"Of course."

"It's okay, Delilah. Really. She's done a lot with the estate already. It's going much better than I thought."

"But you're upset."

"Just...pensive," she says, tucking her legs beneath her. "I pulled the nostalgia card again today. Then I found these old pie tins in the basement. The cheap kind you're supposed to throw out after, you know? And I had this memory of picking blueberries with Mom...I must have been ten or twelve. We spent the whole day together, just the two of us. The berries were everywhere, so sweet and warm from the sun, and we ate them straight from the bushels. Later we baked a pie and ate most of it while it was scorching hot out of the oven, hours before anyone else got home. Amazing what we think we've forgotten, huh? All that from a hunk of tinfoil."

"I know what you mean," I say, my thoughts floating back to the red cardinal and the four-leaf clovers.

"There's a lot of research on scent and memory, too," Rachel says. "I read this article...some scientists think that odor is a more powerful emotional trigger than visual cues like photos. I believe it. That's how I am with real maple syrup. One whiff, and I'm right back here again, right back to the days when Mom used to make her own maple sugar candy."

I close my eyes and pull my wrists to my face, breathing

in the cuffs of Mom's robe. *Don't wait up — I'll probably be late again...*

From an open window, the electronic warble of the printer-scanner–fax machine pierces the air. Rachel and I listen as Mom comes downstairs, retrieving and reading her fax aloud for the caller on the other end of her earpiece. Muffled by the papery rustling of maple leaves in the breeze, her words blur into a series of indiscernible sounds, chopped and broken but urgent as always.

As Aunt Rachel tells me about the junk she uncovered in the basement — used gift wrap, refolded and stored; unopened shampoos and conditioners undoubtedly bought in bulk; board games from her childhood — my own broken recollections of my grandparents mesh with hers, our voices entwined in a thick, slow-cooked stew of memories and events and scents and sayings. Pictures of Nana come more clearly now, aided by Rachel's vivid descriptions of her mother's cooking and clothes and habits and all the little things that make each of us who we are. If Mom can hear us, she doesn't make it known, busying herself instead with the constant shuffling and reshuffling of paperwork.

"I wish Mom would talk about this stuff," I say. "I know she wants to block it all out, but I don't. I want to know about Nana. I want to know what happened."

Rachel closes her eyes and inhales the air over the candles. "Del, our mother said a lot of hurtful things at Dad's funeral.

Things that can't be unsaid. And now that she's gone, we'll never resolve it. It's like everything from that time in our lives is just...I don't know. Frozen, right where we left it."

Frozen, just like Jack in the house next door. Just like Stephanie on the pages of her white diary.

I don't want to believe my aunt, because believing her means believing that my relationship with Mom could become irreparable. That I might never be able to work things out at school. That nothing is ever truly fixable.

"Bad things happen," I say. "But why does it have to erase all the good? You and Mom used to be close. Same with me and Mom. I don't know how everything got broken."

She looks at me for a long while, but Mom is in the kitchen doorway now, a five-minute break between meetings, asking if anyone wants a snack.

"No thanks," I say, more to Aunt Rachel than to Mom. "I need to get dressed, then I'm heading to Luna's. See you later?"

"We have an appointment with the estate lawyer tonight," Mom says, "but I expect you back by ten, got it?"

"Got it."

The screen door bangs closed behind me, and through it I hear the familiar rasp of whispered accusations. Low voices mingle and clash, and I quickly dress, slipping out the front door before the Hannaford tide sucks me into its raging undertow.

Chapter twelve

Luna's — along with Crasner's Foo nasty and the rest of the Main Street stretch that we drove through on our first day — is just a ten-minute walk from Nana's house. The sun is still out, it's not too hot, and for the first time since our arrival, the anticipation of something good buoys me above the dark waters of all else.

Walking through the café doors is like stepping into one of Rachel's tarot books. The walls are painted in dark purple and fuchsia, accented with swags of velvet and sparkly silver moons and stars. The smell of fresh coffee and cinnamon wafts over the mismatched furniture as tourists sip their cappuccinos, floating like rafts in the easy laughter of summer vacation.

"Hey, Delilah," Em calls from behind the counter. "Perfect timing. Patrick's about to be harassed by his fan club." She nods toward a honey-haired, C-cup Jezebel seated at a nearby table. "This oughta be good. Watch."

Patrick sees me and smiles, but before he can cross the room, Jezebel tackles him in some sort of Oh, How I've Missed You embrace, and that stupid butterfly bangs into my ribs with a limp wing.

Patrick blushes as he struggles to break free of her lingering and somewhat annoying (to the average onlooker who might care, which, for the record, I don't, but that doesn't change the fact that it's annoying) hug. When he finally succeeds, she looks at him with big cartoon eyes and promises to be back for his show. Then she chews on the straw of her frozen coffee drink and says good-bye with another hug, only instead of using the word *good-bye* like a normal person, she says, "Ta!" *Ta?* When she finally makes her exit, it's a grand show, Jezebel walking so slowly that it's impossible *not* to notice the glittered HOTTIE printed across the ass of her pale pink shorts.

"So you have a fan club?" I tease Patrick when she's finally gone.

"You say fan club, I say stalker."

"Right. It must be tough having beautiful girls throw themselves at you like that," I say. "Poor thing."

"Yes, they're just throwing themselves, aren't they? You should see the collection of lace thongs and hotel room keys I have at home."

I know he's kidding, but it gets under my skin. I try to think of him as Little Ricky with braces and freckles, but that only strengthens the invisible pull I feel toward him, the sense of entitlement rising in me as though knowing his past gives me some claim to his future, some connecting string between now and the days we played hide-and-seek under the willows when his parents were fighting and he didn't want to go home.

"I'm sure the older women love you, too," I say.

"There *are* a lot of them, huh?" Patrick laughs, twisting his coffee cup inside its eighty-percent-post-consumer-recycled heat sleeve.

"Red Falls wasn't crowded like this when we were kids," I say.

"We didn't have Luna's. There wasn't anything to do here but watch the boat races and eat maple sugar candy."

"I wonder what they'll finally do with Nana's house?" I ask, thinking of the new cottages Patrick pointed out across the lake.

"Probably turn it into a hotel for rich people who think 'rustic' means you have to wipe your own —"

"Hey, those rich people come out to see your shows, right?"

"Good point. I guess I should be a little more humble. Emily! Another coffee?" he shouts across the counter, waving his empty cup. Em gives him the finger. I think I might love her.

"Humble," I say. "Good start."

Patrick needs to finish setting up for the gig, so I find an open computer on the back wall, checking my e-mail for the first time since we left Key.

There are no messages.

I torment myself instead by clicking on Libby Dunbar's e-mail about the blog pictures on the "Free-4-All Graffiti Wall," trying to think of a decent response.

> Delilah, I'm not censoring anyone. I really thought
> you of all people would know how important
> freedom of the press is. Your father died defend-
> ing it.

When I read Libby's message now, I realize that most of the anger I'd been harboring over the photo situation is gone, a tiny sailboat tossed on the waves of way more important things. Why respond at all? That stuff about my father... she'll never get it. She'll never understand the embarrassment of parent-teacher conference night when my mother asks to do hers over the phone. She'll never know the sinking feeling of seeing my report card — back when it was still decent — unopened on the counter for weeks.

"You're lucky," my friends used to say. "No one bugs you

about grades and homework. My father is all over me about that crap."

No, my father never bugged me about grades or homework. He never scolded me for accidentally stealing lipstick or denting the car or sneaking out with Finn. But I still look at his picture at the top of all of his online news articles, tracing the deep lines in his face and imagining that I put them there, even now, all these years after his death.

I sign out of my e-mail and Google Thomas Devlin again, but it's the same old list of links and articles, memorializing him for all eternity in little blue letters on a bright white background. *Frozen.*

"I just finished my shift," Emily says when I grab my iced latte and meet her back at the counter. "Let's find a table before they call me back in."

The café is filling up, but Em and I find a spot right in front of the stage just as Patrick starts the sound check. Emily tells me more about her family — about moving to Vermont from New Hampshire a few years ago, her little brother in middle school whom she loves even when he's driving her nuts, her parents sending her up to Red Falls for the summer. She asks me about school and my family and what I do for fun back home, picking up the conversation where we left off at the house the other day. I tell her about Mom working a lot, just like she's doing at the lake house. I tell her that my dad died before I was born, but I keep the conversation light. Flowing. Moving on before the seeds of curiosity about my father's death take root.

At a round table not far from the stage, an older guy sits with two kids waiting for the show to start. He laughs with them and points at invisible things outside so he can sneak bites from the pastries on their plates.

Usually, I don't miss my father. But times like this, I wonder. I play those pointless games — What If and Maybe. What if the *National Post* didn't give him that assignment? Mom wouldn't have had to raise me alone. Maybe she wouldn't have gone to work full-time. Maybe she wouldn't be unhappy. What if Mom could've had with Thomas what Stephanie had with Casey? What if they got married? Maybe he'd be here with us now, helping Mom and Rachel with the estate, or sitting here at Luna's, giving us a brief history of the British Invasion as we await Patrick's performance.

"Wait till you hear him," Emily says as Patrick plugs in another amp. "He's amazing. I'm not just saying that because we get better tips on show nights, either."

I stir the slush of my drink with a straw. "I can't wait," I say. "It's so funny to see him up there."

"Why? What do you mean?"

"The last time I saw Patrick before this summer, we were jumping off bleachers and rolling down the hill to make ourselves dizzy. Everything's *so* different now. In a good way, I mean. It's cool."

"Definitely," she says. "He's been practicing all week for you. But as usual, I didn't tell you that." She smiles.

"What do you —"

"How you all doin' tonight, Red Falls?" Patrick's opening chords interrupt, alighting the Luna's crowd in a blaze of cheers and whistles. I wave away the question and sit forward in my chair, ready to clap and cheer and join in on the big Red Falls welcome as Patrick dives into the first song.

And oh my *God*.

Patrick can *sing*.

I don't mean *la-la-la* sing. I mean, *sing* sing. Goose-bumps, holding-our-breath, lumps-in-our-throats, tears-in-our-eyes, all-we-need-is-*love* kind of sing.

He belts it straight out, his voice like milk and honey and everything rich and warm and good. I want to drink it. To take off my clothes and slip into his music like a hot bubble bath. One song leads into the next, graceful, flawless, Patrick holding back just enough to build up the anticipation in us, thick and heavy and stretching into every corner and shadow. Luna's is packed, all of us singing along as we learn the words, hands and fists and coffee cups pumping in the air, chanting and whooping and clapping with every note. Jezebel the stalker-slash-fan-club-president is back again as promised, right next to the stage, whistling and cheering in a sequined halter top with no bra, watching him as her girl-friends snap pictures with their cell phones, and I don't even hate her anymore, because now, I *get* it.

Patrick's voice finds its way through the crowd, over the cheers and the hum of his guitar, right into me, right down through my feet. He's beaming and crazy and so natural up there. He was *made* for this, the way some people are made for motherhood or medicine or art. In his face, there is nothing but music and life and the radiant light of cam-era flashes as the whole crowd claps for him. When he winks at me during the last song, watching me through it all, it's like he's let me in on a precious secret, mine and his, and I'll never forget it. I'll never give it up, not even if another eight or eighty or eight hundred years pass before I see him again.

"Okay, when you told me you could sing, you didn't tell me you could *sing*." I shake my head, eyes feeling big inside of it as we walk toward Maple Terrace after the show. "Not like *that*."

"Thank you," he says. "I'm glad you were there."

"Patrick, I mean it. You're amazing."

"I know you do. And thank you. I mean that, too." He smiles, stopping beneath the moon at the end of our street and turning to face me. "I'm glad you're back. I'm..."

He lets his thought fade as his eyes sweep over mine, down to my mouth. His hands cup my face, and the ground — in the sneaky way that grounds have — drops from beneath my feet. I can't hear anything but the sound of my own breath, needy and hot and a little suffocated. I feel my body pulling to him, everything uttered between us building to this, magnets on the fridge, and I don't consider the possible complications, because his eyes are right now on my face, closing, eyelashes casting half-moon shadows on his skin, and —

Bzzzz.

"Oh!" My phone vibrates in my pocket. "It's me. Sorry! It's my phone."

Let it go, Delilah.

"I should get it."

Are you serious?

"Just because, I don't know, it might be important. Or something."

Oh my God! You're just like your mother! Stop! Stop now!

"One second." I ignore the succession of voices in my head and flip open my phone without checking the caller ID. "Hello?"

"Lilah."

"Heyyy…" It's a breath more than a word, everything in me rushing out on a feather of a sigh.

"What's up?" Finn asks. It's the first I've heard from him since I left Key.

"Just…out for coffee. This place near where we're staying. You got my text about Vermont, right?"

113

"Yeah," he says. "Sucks that you're all alone in the middle of nowhere, huh? I could be good in this situation."

"I'll be okay." I try to ignore the guilt bubbling in my stomach because Patrick and I aren't even together and Finn's not my boyfriend, so why should I feel bad for talking to him? "How are you?"

"Wishing you were here," Finn says. "Seven Mile is just a creek without you."

"I think we'll be here pretty much all summer. My grandmother died. There's a lot of stuff to take care of."

Here's the part where you say, "Delilah, I'm so sorry to hear that. How are you handling everything?"

"Shit, seriously? Well, just call me when you get back, okay? I just wanted to say hi. I gotta jet. Party tonight. You know how it is."

"Um, yeah. Sure. I —"

But the conversation is over. "Bye," I say into dead air. I snap the phone closed and slip it into my pocket. Patrick doesn't ask about the call, or try to pick up the threads of where we left off. It's like he's a different person now, like five minutes ago someone else possessed him and left and now the magic is gone and here we are.

I don't say anything as we continue our walk home. I just keep smiling at Patrick and shaking my head and mumbling words like *amazing* and *unbelievable* over and over, and he laughs and puts his arm around me and makes me promise

I'll come to Luna's and cheer for him always, for as long as he has a guitar and I'm here in Red Falls.

"I promise," I say, waving when I reach the door of the lake house. He waves back, turning up the path to the blue-and-white Victorian.

Chapter thirteen

At the end of the upstairs hall, the door to Nana's bedroom is shut, undisturbed as far as I can tell since Mom returned from Shane's with the urn. I took her advice and stayed away from it, but tonight is different. Maybe it's the universe Rachel's always talking about, trying to send me another message. Maybe the ashes are calling to me, or maybe my heart is just full of love and hope and nostalgia after hearing Patrick sing, because tonight, I don't want to read Stephanie's diary. I want to be with my grandmother.

The door isn't locked; it opens easily when I turn the knob. There's no creaking or moaning or shifting shadows to warn of poltergeists or haunting doom, and when I flick on the light switch, I find only a regular bedroom with regular bedroom stuff, two big windows, and the lingering scent of medicine, hand lotion, and perfumed powder.

The room is wallpapered as I remember it — same neat rows of tiny yellow tulips on a white background. The beige carpet looks new, but the fluffy yellow comforter and curtains are the same, faded now from years of washing and warming in the sun beneath the windows. A glass of water sits on the night table next to one of those plastic pill boxes with individual compartments for each day of the week, S M T W T F S, and it occurs to me that this is where she took her last breath.

On top of Nana's oak dresser, the urn rests as if it's always been there: a simple black box etched with pink-gold flowers and vines. Two china dolls with shiny black silk for hair and painted-on eyes guard the box, watching me as if I owe them an explanation.

Can we help you, Miss Hannaford?

I ignore the dolls, resting my hand atop the black box, fingers tracing the grooved vine at the edge.

It's cold. I pull away.

In front of the dolls, the dresser is piled with randomness: Receipts. A watch that doesn't work. Four gold bracelets. A mini-book about the U.S. first ladies. A silver sculpture in the shape of a hand with costume rings stacked on each finger and a glass bead bracelet draped over the thumb. A small hinged metal box with pink glass jewels on the outside. A loose photo of a Saint Bernard lolling in the front yard with his tongue out — Ollie, I guess.

I slide open a dresser drawer, so hoping that I'll find letters or *her* diary or photographs or keys to a hidden chest that holds all the answers — so expecting it, even — that the plain ordinariness of her socks and stockings, tucked neatly into rows of white and black and beige, surprises me. The next drawer is lined with slips and underwear in the same basic palette. The next is for clothes — sweatshirts, T-shirts, nightshirts. Pants. Shorts. Back on the top, behind the dolls and the black box, there's one more drawer, small and neat. I tug on the center handle, careful not to disturb the urn. The drawer is mostly empty. Just some pastel-colored hand lotion samples. Loose change. A box of Q-tips. My grandmother's prescription cache.

The bottles are see-through orange with printed labels from a chain pharmacy in town. I recognize the names of most of the drugs from the commercials that show people talking to their doctors and then dancing or swimming or fishing with their grandkids. There's a pill for cholesterol and one for blood pressure, and another I think for calcium and bone density.

But there are others, too. Three bottles half-empty, their forebears probably already allocated into their appropriate slots in the S M T W T F S box near the bed. And as my mind again connects the names with the commercials, the symptoms with the side effects, the befores with the afters, I understand.

My grandmother was being treated — medicated — for clinical depression.

Through the translucent orange of the pill bottles, some of my memories clarify, while others shift slightly out of focus. I think about my grandmother that day with the cardinal — how little she was affected. I remember during some of the summer festivals and parties, Nana would make excuses to retire early from neighborhood gatherings or dinners with friends.

Not now, Delilah. Why don't you and Ricky go outside so I can rest?

I roll one of the bottles in my hand, fingers rocking it against my palm as the pills slide back and forth inside the plastic. Imagining her here in the bedroom, alone at night, taking a dozen pills before bed, falling asleep with nothing but her blue regrets — well, considering she never tried to get in touch with me after that family fight, I shouldn't even care. But I do care, and all the soft parts beneath my ribs squeeze together when I think about it.

The china dolls still watch me. Next to their long, lace-and-velvet dresses, I'm practically naked in my white tank top. I unfold a thin beige sweater from a shelf next to the dresser and pull it over my head, static crackling through my hair.

There's a pile of books under the table next to her bed. I sit on the floor in front of them, pulling out several horror novels — *Pet Sematary* and *Thinner* by Stephen King. *Flowers in the Attic* by V. C. Andrews. I read a few random passages aloud, convinced that a combination of particularly haunted phrases will summon her ghost and induce a message from the other side.

None comes.

Still wearing her sweater, I move to the vanity table and sit on the small wicker stool in front of it. I rummage through her makeup and jewelry, hoping to catch a side-glance at her through the mirror — the looking glass to the great beyond. I clasp a delicate necklace around my neck — a tiny silver heart suspended from a wire-thin chain — and dab a bit of her talcum powder on my face with a soft, pink poof.

"What would I say to you, anyway?" I ask the air in front of me, staring in the mirror at the silver flash on my collarbone.

"Maybe you'd tell me what you're looking for?" A voice speaks from the hallway.

I jump up from the stool, knocking it over.

"Mom, you scared me half to death!"

"I was hoping you'd leave this room to me and Aunt Rachel."

I look down at my feet, which, along with everything around them, are covered in the talcum powder I dropped when I thought my grandmother was scolding me from the great beyond.

"I just thought —"

"It's all right, Delilah." Her voice is limp and wilting after the long estate meeting. "We were planning to start on it this week, anyway."

I reach for the chain around my neck and hold it up to show her the heart. "I found this with the jewelry," I say. "I wasn't going to steal it, if that's what you're worried about."

"Cut it out." Mom sighs. "That day at Blush was just... look, I realize that I can't be home with you very much. I know we don't spend time together like we used to. And I'm sorry, but you know how much time and energy my job requires. I need to be able to trust you to take care of yourself so that I can go to work to earn money and plan for our future."

"I know. It's just that —"

"No, Del, I don't think you realize how much pressure I'm under at DKI. Corporate budgets are being cut everywhere, and we need to work even harder to keep clients and win new business. That means a lot of hours for my entire team. What kind of message does it send if I have to constantly leave the office to follow you around and make sure you aren't getting yourself into more trouble?"

"I'm sorry. I know. I —"

"And you have so much to look forward to this year. Your SATs are coming up in the fall, and soon we'll be looking at schools and filling out applications...you really need to stay on track. I know this trip isn't the ideal place for it, but I'm hoping we can use the time to regroup. Take a break from life back home and return at the end of the summer for a fresh start. I'm willing to forgive and forget and give you that second chance, but only if you're willing to take it."

She lifts my chin with her fingers, smoothing my cheek with her thumb.

"I love you, Delilah. I just want you to be happy and safe, okay?"

"I know."

"Let's go," she says. "Keep the necklace. It's pretty on you."

"What about the mess?" I find the empty makeup pot and try to scoop some of the talcum powder back in, sending up clouds of white dust.

"Just leave it. I'll vacuum tomorrow." She reaches for the light switch, waiting for me to follow her out. Maybe it has to do with being in my grandmother's room, here among her ashes and the common things of the dead that become sacred, wanting so much for my mother to like me, to understand me, to mean what she says about me being happy and safe... I don't want her to turn off the light. I don't want us to go.

"Mom?" I look at her, my hand hovering near my hip, searching for something to hold. "Well... what happened at the estate meeting, anyway?"

She pauses for a second. Her body leans forward as if to come closer, but her feet don't cooperate. "Nothing to worry about," she says, sliding out of her taupe suit jacket. "Just...

you know what, Del? I'm exhausted, and I still need to check my e-mail before I call it a night. We'll talk about it tomorrow, okay?"

"Sure, Mom." I don't believe her any more than she believes herself, but I nod and follow her out anyway, ducking back into my room to dust off the lingering powder as she pulls Nana's door closed with a soft *click*.

Chapter fourteen

I didn't tell Mom about finding Nana's prescriptions last week.

We didn't talk about the pills or the estate meeting or Patrick's show or the way Aunt Rachel is pulling away from us, hiding in the basement to sort through Nana's stuff by day, out with Megan for drinks at night.

I didn't tell Mom about the diary either, the entries growing more intense and personal as Stephanie falls headlong for Casey and begins to lose some of herself in the process. When I think about Patrick's show last week, hearing him sing as if it was for me alone, I understand how easy it would be to lose yourself in the heart of another. It's frightening. Exhilarating. An ocean with no lifeguard. Stephanie was in deep with Casey, and knowing that as I do now, seeing it written and feeling it crackle in the air around the pages as I read the words... I can never share it with my mother. It would just about kill her, the intensity of Steph's life on the pages a sharp contrast to the cold, unchangeable reality of her death. How can anyone accept that someone once so vibrant, so alive, is never coming back? The right to read the diary is more hers than mine, but even if I thought it wouldn't wreck her... Love? Passion? Life? Mom and I just don't talk about such things.

I'm so used to avoiding her now that when she knocks on my door this morning as I'm pulling on my painting clothes, it takes me a minute to remember the words to invite her in. When I do, she says she wants to talk. *Needs* to talk. And I wonder what I did this time.

"Um, okay," I say. "What's going on?"

Mom sits on the edge of the bed and smoothes out her robe, though it's not wrinkled.

"I thought we could talk about... I meant to tell you about the estate meeting," she says. "I was so tired the other night and then it just slipped my mind."

"It's cool. I kind of forgot about it, too," I lie.

"Apparently the town declared the house a historic point of interest last year. It's one of the only remaining original settlement homes of its size in Vermont."

"What does that mean?" I ask, lacing up my old sneakers. "We have to turn it into a museum or something?"

Mom shakes her head. "No, nothing like that. Just more paperwork. They also think we can find a private buyer without listing."

"Oh." I stand to look out the window. Patrick and Em wave from the backyard, ready for our painting party. "Okay. Well, we're doing the shed today, so —"

"Wait — there's more," she says. "My parents had some money saved — they were smart with their investments and still had a lot of Dad's veteran benefits."

"That's good."

"We won't have any issues getting the house renovated and getting it on the market. Her funeral services are covered, too."

"Cool. Thanks for the update. Can I —"

"Delilah, she also left quite a bit of money for you. For your education."

"*What?*"

"It's in a trust. It's enough to cover a good chunk of your college expenses. Maybe a little extra."

Mom's gaze slides to the jar of buttons on my dresser, tears gathering in her eyes.

"But...I don't understand, Mom. She had nothing to do with me since we left Red Falls. Why would she leave me anything?"

She smiles, looking back to me. "I don't know, Honeybee. I guess she wanted you to be taken care of, despite...well, despite a lot of things."

"But if she cared about me so much, why didn't she try to call or write? All those years, I never heard from her. Now she's trying to make up for it by paying for college? Who cares, Mom? You have money saved. I don't want hers." I rub the silver heart necklace on my collarbone, wishing I could trade all those thousands of dollars for the lost eight years between us.

"Delilah, it was generous of her. We don't know her motives. She's gone. We'll never know —"

"I don't remember her, Mom," I whisper, my throat tightening. "I keep trying to see her face or to hear her voice, and I can't."

Mom puts her arm around me and pulls me against her chest, but she doesn't say anything, and soon I feel the unevenness of her breath on my hair and wish that we could just go back to Key, back to the day before Blush Cosmetics. I'll remember to pay for the lipstick and I'll convince her to stay home from work and disconnect the phones and we can order pizza and watch movies, just the two of us. We'll ignore Aunt Rachel's call and we'll never know that any of this ever happened and then we won't have to be here now, sitting in her dead sister's old room, wondering what the hell we're supposed to do next.

"All right," Mom says, rising from the bed and wiping her eyes with the back of her hand. "It's going to be a beautiful day today, and you've done a lot of work already. You guys should enjoy the lake a little before the July Fourth crowd gets here. The shed can wait. Consider it a day off, okay?"

Mom starts to move toward me, but stops midstep, distracted as if she suddenly realized she left the car running. She puts her hands in the pockets of her robe as she backs out of the doorway, our eyes locked until she turns away toward her room.

Outside, Patrick and Emily sit with their backs against the shed in the shade, paint cans and rollers and tarps piled on the ground around them.

"Day off," I call out the window. "Let's go kayaking."

Mom and Aunt Rachel don't hear me as I approach the kitchen, but I hear them, bits and pieces of a whispered conversation floating to my ears.

"Claire," Rachel says, "instead of getting angry with me, why...talk to her about it?"

"You know I can't," Mom says. "It's way...complicated and..."

"Because you complicated...the longer you...worse..."

"Don't you think...?"

I take one more careful step down, straining to hear them through the wall of the stairwell and the chopping of Rachel's kitchen knife against the cutting board.

"No, I don't," Rachel says. *Chop chop chop.*

"...bring it up here," Mom says. "...expect me to say?"

"...no idea," Rachel says. "You...I didn't agree...handled it...Casey?" *Chop chop chop.*

My ears perk up at the mention of Stephanie's boyfriend.

What does he have to do with anything? Do they know where he is? I wish I could hear what they're saying, but one more step down and they'll see me.

"...only sixteen," Mom whispers. "The situation... extremely... won't understand."

"...not an eight-year-old kid..." Rachel says. "Talk to her...truth."

I wait another minute, but there's no more talking, just Rachel frantically chopping vegetables. I take the last step down and face them in the kitchen, both of them going as white as the curtains over the window.

"Delilah?" Mom says, clearing her throat when the last part of my name sticks. "Are you... I thought you were going out for the day."

"I was upstairs getting ready. What were you guys talking about?"

"What do you mean?" Mom looks at Rachel.

"I heard you."

"Heard us what?" she asks. "We've been talking about things all morning."

"Come on, Mom. Just now. Rachel's was trying to convince you to tell me something. What's going on?"

She looks at her sister again, but Rachel's on a mission to dice up those carrots and doesn't respond.

"Your aunt and I were just discussing some of the details of the will," Mom says. "I told her that I let you know about the college fund. We need to clear up a few more points with her lawyers in order to access money for the remodel and the headstone. Nothing for you to worry about."

I can't connect the dots of complicated and Casey with will details and headstones, but Mom's not going to share any more, and Rachel might as well be out drinking with Megan for all *she's* contributing to this conversation.

"Fine," I say, grabbing an apple from the bowl on the table. "I'm going kayaking with Patrick and Em. I'll be back before dinner."

"Veggie chili tonight," Rachel says, as if her announcement deserves applause. "A favorite at Sundance."

"Sounds good. See you later."

"Delilah?" Mom calls as I reach the door. "Don't forget to wear a lifejacket out there," she says. "I don't want you getting hurt."

chapter fifteen

"Do you guys know anything about Casey Conroy?" I ask as we walk to the dock where they rent out kayaks and paddle-boats.

"Never heard of him," Em says. "Then again, I'm new here."

"I don't think there are any Conroys in Red Falls now," Patrick says. "I don't recognize the name, but I could ask my dad. He'd know."

I tighten a blue-and-yellow life vest over my T-shirt. "No, don't say anything to him. It's just a name I've heard a few times lately. I think he knew my mom and Rachel." I don't tell them about the diary, the bits of conversation I picked up in the house today, or the initials carved under the bed. "You know me. Obsessive as always."

Patrick smiles. "Good. While you're obsessing, we're getting the boats."

As Patrick and Em untie the kayaks and drag them toward the shore, my mind drifts from Mom and Rachel to the other morning news: Nana's trust fund. For eight years, she didn't have a granddaughter. Yet she socked away enough cash to pay for my entire education? That's tens of thousands of dollars. Why not leave it to the town or the forest or the National Saint Bernard Foundation instead? Was it her fault that we left Red Falls, and paying me off is her way to absolve the guilt? And what if I don't get accepted into college? What if I decide not to go? Do I have to return the money? Will she come back from the dead and haunt me?

And what does Casey Conroy have to do with any of this?

This is the song that never ends ... it just goes on and on my friends ...

"Delilah?" Em asks. "You coming?" She and Patrick bob on the water in their red and blue boats, waiting for me to push off and join them.

"Sorry, guys." I shake away all the what-ifs and grab the sides of my yellow boat, leading it off the sand and climbing in, one foot at a time. After several shaky attempts, I manage to get inside and stay upright long enough to position the paddle across my legs.

It's the last time I'm vertical for our entire kayaking adventure.

"Not bad for my first time out, right?" I ask Patrick, leaning on him as I limp into Alphie's Pie in the Sky, the pizza place around the corner from Luna's.

Patrick cocks an eyebrow. "You didn't *drown*, if that's what you mean."

"Don't worry, Del," Emily says, pulling out a chair for me. "It gets easier. Next time will be better."

Patrick laughs. "Who says there's a next time?"

"Hey! I'm certainly not the first person to get hurt trying this, am I?"

"No," Patrick says. "People get hurt kayaking all the time. They aren't ready for the roll and get water up their noses. They drop the boat on their toes carrying it up to shore. They over-extend their shoulders paddling too hard. But in all my years of living on this lake, every single summer for my entire life, I have never seen someone come away with a knee injury caused by the water, twenty feet away from any kayaks, docks, or people."

"The waves knocked me down!" I say. "I didn't see it coming. I totally could've drowned. Emily? Back me up here."

Em smiles. "Del, you were only in up to your shins. I honestly don't know how you wiped out."

"And you managed to dump yourself out of the boat about, well, eleven times," Patrick says, setting a Coke in front of me. "Not that I'm counting."

"I was testing my balance."

"You failed!" Em and Patrick say together, laughing as I prop my leg up on a chair.

The three of us share a cheese pizza and a large Greek salad, and even though my knee is throbbing, I keep laughing, keep encouraging the jokes as we recap our day, because being the star of the punch line is the only thing that keeps me from being swallowed up by the sinking realization that, without question, my mother is willfully hiding something from me. Something *about* me. Something major.

And Rachel knows about it, too.

"What happened to your knee?" Mom asks as I limp through the side door with Patrick and Emily.

"Just a scrape." I grab some peanut butter granola bars for dessert, inspecting the army of porcelain figurines lined up on the kitchen table, flanked by the dolls from Nana's dresser.

"What's all this?" I ask.

"We had an appraiser come in," Rachel says. "He agreed that we should try to sell the house furnished so we don't have to sell the furniture individually. Most of this other stuff will go at the estate sale, but there was one surprise in the lot. We can take it to auction if we don't find a private buyer." She holds up a blue-and-white china creamer in the shape of a cow.

Patrick moos.

"This hideous thing is early seventeen hundreds blue Delft china from Holland," Rachel says.

Em picks up the cow for a closer look. "She's not that hideous," she says. "I think she's kind of cute."

"Yeah, so does the appraiser," Rachel says. "Four thousand dollars kind of cute, hiding in the basement in a box of Christmas ornaments."

"Four *grand*?" Em sets the cow back on the table, far away from the edge.

I open the trash can to toss out my granola bar wrapper and spot the bottles from Nana's dresser, see-through orange, tipped into the trash with the organic eggshells and coffee grounds.

"You went through Nana's entire bedroom today?" I ask.

"Most of it," Mom says, wiping down the kitchen counter with a velocity the average household germ would never see coming. "I left the books and jewelry if you want to look through them. Nothing really valuable up there, though." The dolls on the table look offended, but like everyone else in this family, they don't say anything. And as I let the trash can lid slap closed over the pill bottles, neither do I.

Later, after Patrick and Emily leave and Rachel walks to Crasner's for more fruit, I pour two glasses of iced hibiscus tea and sit next to Mom on the porch, rocking the swing with my foot.

"Did you have fun on the lake today?" she asks, taking a sip from her glass.

"It was great. Patrick is teaching me how to kayak."

"How's your knee?" She leans forward to take a look.

"It's nothing. So what were you and Rachel fighting about earlier?"

I watch the lines of her face change as she leans back in the swing and looks out over the driveway. "What do you mean? When?"

"Today. Before I left."

Mom shakes her head. "Nothing. I told you. Just legal stuff with the will."

"Sounded like you were arguing."

"She said something that upset me."

"Was it about what happened eight years ago?"

Mom turns to face me, her fingers white around her iced tea glass. "Del, you are *so* hung up on this," she says. "I understand it was hard for you when we left here, and maybe I should've handled it differently, but you need to hear me on this. There's no big mystery here. Families fight. They tear each other apart. Sometimes there aren't any happy endings or logical explanations and we just have to accept that and move on. Sometimes it really *is* that simple."

"But I know you're keeping something from me," I say, pushing away my own guilt about keeping Steph's diary hidden.

Mom covers my hand with hers, but it's cold and firm. "Delilah, really. There's no need to dig up the past. Just focus on getting your own stuff back on track. That's what I need you to do right now. That's what we all need to do."

She pushes off from the swing and heads for the kitchen, back to her desk and her laptop, before I can press further. I follow her in and sit at the kitchen table, looking over the odd lot of my grandmother's things.

Let it go, Delilah. We just can't go back there again. That's what Mom said to me every time I asked about Nana after that fight. Every time I packed my suitcases for another summer in Red Falls and cried as she silently unpacked them. Eventually, I stopped packing. I stopped missing Nana and Little Ricky and the cardinal and the fireflies around the lake. I stopped asking. I stopped wondering. And I let Nana and Papa and the whole sleepy town of Red Falls fade into the long Hannaford history of Things We Just Don't Talk About.

As I stare at the back of Mom's head, hands smoothing her hair as she replaces the cell phone earpiece, I begin to think I had it all wrong. Mom is right. Families fight. Maybe it really *is* that simple. And maybe I should stop digging for a truth that's been shattered and shoved so deep into the earth by so many different hands that no one even remembers where the pieces are buried.

Mom lets out a long, slow breath over her desk and all the air in the room changes, electrified like the air before a storm. She clears her throat and I wait for the lights to flicker; for the power to surge and pop and fizzle and throw us into days of darkness.

But nothing happens.

"Hey," she says into the earpiece. "It's me. Thanks for sending that e-mail. The project files are on a disc in my office. Should be four still images and the video. Right."

I turn back to the trinkets on the table.

"Moo," I whisper to the cow. She doesn't answer back.

Chapter sixteen

"One large house blend and one iced chocolate hazelnut latte, extra whip," Luna announces. "These are on the house."

"Thanks, Luna." I take my drink from the coffee bar, grateful Mom and Aunt Rachel have another estate meeting tonight. In the apocalypse of last week's overheard and then promptly dismissed Casey conversation, we've managed to avoid any more direct hits. Out of guilt or distraction or genuine second chances, Mom has loosened the restrictions on my free time, the two of us reverting easily to our ships passing in the night routine. Tonight, I'm grateful to be out, away from the awkward silence that permeates the walls of the house. Away from the pages of the diary, still calling from my dresser drawer.

Away from the urn and the ashes of my grandmother and her departed dog. Away from the past, if only for an hour.

Across the café, I look at Patrick, clipping the ends of the new strings on his guitar, and Luna, asking me to take home the leftover scones. I think about Emily, open and free and completely without expectation. And Megan, showing up almost every day to help Aunt Rachel. The people I've met in Red Falls, thrown into my life by the weird and tragic circumstances of this summer . . . they *know* how crazy the Hannafords are, and still, they don't judge. They don't demand. They don't assume. They're just . . . *there*. Wanting to know us. Wanting to be with us. There's a word for these people. Sometimes I think I'm on the edge of some great understanding, looking up at all the answers I just can't reach, like apples too high in the tree. But tonight, I stretch my fingers toward the sky, and I think I have the answer. The word.

Friends.

"Do you mind if we hang out a little longer?" Patrick asks Luna from the stage, strumming a few chords on the new strings. Luna's already turned off the OPEN sign — Patrick and I are the only ones left. "I'm working on a new song and I don't quite have it," he says.

"Stay as long as you want," she says. "Just lock up when you go."

The coffee shop falls silent when she leaves, save for the low hum of the refrigerator and the buzz of the overhead lights. In the absence of the usual crowds, everything takes on a new life, a new intensity. The burnt-chocolate smell of coffee infusing the air. The silver moon and stars hanging overhead, spinning softly, reflecting flashes of light. And Patrick's eyes, clear and intense as he works on his music. Here. Now. Just the two of us. Alone.

"What are you thinking about?" he asks.

"Friends."

"Do you miss them?"

"Back home? No, I really don't. It's funny. I have these people there. You might call them friends. I always did. We hung out together, went to the same parties, that kind of thing. Always something to do on the weekends. But things changed this year, and now that I've been away for a few weeks, calling them friends...it doesn't feel right anymore. Like they were just there to pass the time. They haven't earned the right to be called *friends*. Does that make any sense?"

"Perfect." Patrick nods. "I went through that stuff last year with an old friend from school in New York. We didn't have a fight or anything, but junior year, it just felt off between us. We started hanging out in different crowds, and the few times we got together, it didn't fit anymore. It sucked, too, because he used to be a really a cool guy."

"So what happened?"

"Eh, we grew apart. Went our separate ways. I'd run into him sometimes, and we were friendly. But we didn't jam on the weekends anymore or meet up after school for a bike ride."

"Were you sad?"

"I was, but then I realized that I was holding on to something that didn't exist anymore. That the person I missed didn't exist anymore. People change. The things we like and dislike change. And we can wish they wouldn't all day long, but that never works."

"Nope. I've tried it."

"And friends," he says, "I mean real, true friends... I used to think certain people in my life were the real deal. That we'd stay tight forever. Now, the older I get, I keep coming back to something my dad said: In your entire life, you can probably count your true friends on one hand. Maybe even on one finger. Those are the friends you need to cherish, and I wouldn't trade one of them for a hundred of the other kind. I'd rather be completely alone than with a bunch of people who aren't real. People who are just passing time."

"I'm starting to see that," I say, thinking of all the acquaintances that have passed through my life, and all those who might still come and go. But when Patrick smiles at me, the sadness of it leaves my shoulders and for now, everything is fine.

"So check this out," he says, ducking behind the stage. He dims the café lights and flips on a set of round, colored stage lights that shine up from the front and sides of the platform to illuminate the main event.

"Luna had these installed last weekend. What a difference, huh? It's a small place, so the sound fills out pretty well without cranking the amps. The tough part is when the crowd is distracted. It doesn't happen often, but it sucks trying to sing over that — not just because it's hard to hear, but because you know no one's listening. The lights should help focus their attention. Then I just have to work harder to make people care."

"Patrick, I've heard you sing. How could they *not* care?"

"Not everyone who comes to Luna's on gig nights is here to see me. Some people are actually more interested in the coffee. Or the scones. Or in hitting on Emily."

"Oh, I didn't say I *wasn't* here to hit on Em," I say. "Just that hitting on Em and enjoying your music aren't mutually exclusive."

"Is that so?"

"It is."

"Then I'm glad we had this little chat. I'll have to let Em know I'm stepping up my game. She's tough competition, especially in the looks department — *way* cuter than me."

I laugh with my head down to hide the fact that my face is probably *completely* pink. I mean, Em *is* cute. And awesome and hilarious and sweet. So why isn't he into her like that? Is he?

"Don't you have to practice something?" I ask. "Let's hear it."

"All right, Hannaford. You win. Come here." He motions for me to sit in front of him and passes me his guitar pick, using his fingers bare against the strings. Our knees touch; his Martin guitar and the rising tide of music all that's between us.

When Patrick sings, his eyes close and his face goes simultaneously intent and content, like he's taking a long, beautiful journey but has to concentrate very hard on the path. It's just the two of us, alone on the stage, and even through his unpolished practice lyrics, his voice rolls over my skin and gives me goose bumps. The currents of the melody carry me away from all of life's disappointments and hidden things, and I'm left with only wonderment and possibility, endless and pure. I don't even realize my eyes are closed until the music stops, and in the soft echo of the last note, a kiss lands and melts against my lips like a snowflake, cool and amazing and completely unlike anything I've ever felt. Patrick pulls me closer, and the silver heart on my necklace clinks soft like a raindrop against his guitar strings.

Our kiss deepens, Patrick finding his way past my lips. My racing mind slows, fear and worries fade as I fall headlong into it, feeling and tasting and inhaling every bit of it, just me and him and the world outside holding its breath, waiting for us to finish, waiting to see what happens, waiting to see if I remember how to walk after this.

But when Patrick shifts to slide his guitar out from between us, the spell breaks. I realize how close we are now, too close, no-air-left-in-the-room close, nothing to keep him from getting any nearer to the real me.

"Sorry," I blurt out. "I, um...I should go. I need to go do this, um, this thing. It's just that I told my mom that I'd help her later and I really should go now."

"Are you sure she can't wait a few minutes?" Patrick asks. He's smiling, but his eyes hover on disappointment.

"Yes."

"Good. Come here."

"No — I mean, *yes*, I'm sure she can't wait." I stand to dust off my shorts and put some much-needed distance between us before he convinces me to stay. "You know my mother."

"You okay, Del? I hope I didn't...I'm...are you —"

"No, I'm good, I'm fine. I love the song. Very Bob Dylan." If my words were footsteps, I'd have tripped over them and broken both legs by now. "I just remembered the thing with Mom, that's all. Bad timing."

"Nah, don't worry about it. I'll walk you home," Patrick says. "Let me just pack this up and —"

"That's okay. I'm fine. I need to go before she freaks out. I almost totally forgot and now I'm kind of late. I'll see you tomorrow, okay?" I don't let Patrick answer or catch me in the net of his confused gaze before I'm through the door, the summer-sticky air condensing instantly on my skin. Outside, it takes a second for me to realize that I'm just standing here, shivering despite the humidity.

It's one foot in front of the other, Delilah, remember?

Chapter seventeen

Later, certain that Mom, Rachel, Patrick, and the rest of Red Falls is asleep, I tiptoe down the stairs and out the side door on bare feet, skipping the creaky third step. I walk down the street with Stephanie's diary, away from Nana's house, past Patrick's house, all the way to the other end of the road. Under Maple Terrace's only street lamp, I stretch my arms out and pretend that the light is a force field, illuminating me like a star-angel to keep the dark things out. When it's everyone-else-is-in-bed quiet like this, the Vermont summer crickets outnumber me, *surround* me, getting louder and louder and louder with each breath until they're all part of the heartbeat in my ears, the same soft thud, the same hum, the same low buzz of everything all at once that keeps the world spinning on its axis.

Sometimes I wonder if my whole life will pass by this way: me waiting in the shadows, waiting for something to happen. Waiting for someone else to *make* it happen. Something new or different or crazy and amazing. I've been there for so long, letting everyone else figure it out for me, floating along without much direction or conscious thought. Reacting. Attention-seeking, Mom calls it. Impulsive. Reckless.

I think about Finn and all those times at the creek. I think about Patrick. I think about Stephanie and Rachel and Mom and my dead newspaper dad and it squeezes my insides. It makes me want to leave, to run, to get on a plane with a little black notebook and wander in and out of cities and villages and people's homes until I find out *exactly* how my father felt that day in Tuksar, looking down the barrel, pen pressed to paper, fate in the hands of a boy who wasn't even old enough to grow a mustache.

I sit on the sidewalk beneath the light and open the diary over my knees.

> *Dear Diary,*
> *It's four a.m. and I've been awake for two days, my mind buzzing, my cells buzzing, everything around me buzzing. Mom is driving me INSANE and I need to leave. I need to get out of this town. I need to go somewhere. Anywhere. Else.*

*C promised me that he would take me away
from here. That we could go soon and far and
never look back. And when he said I promise you,
I promise you, Stephie, you can have the whole
world if you want it... I kissed him and I knew
that he MEANT it and I told him that I would
love him with everything I had in me until the
very end of everything, and I meant it, too, and
the old man selling popcorn from a cart on the
wooden path near the shore smiled when he saw
us kiss.*

*So how much longer? How much longer until
we can walk the streets of some new place with
new faces and see them smiling just to see us so
in <u>love</u>??*

— Steph

Back home, when people see me with Finn, they don't smile. They *stare*. And I get all wood-elf-princess-warrior like the first time I was with him, walking out of the woods at a creek party with leaves in my hair and one shoe missing and everyone whispering. Finn never asked me about secrets and mothers and the nature of friendship. He didn't care. Being with him was about one thing. And I was *fearless* with him. Crazed. Alive. And a little bit *Oh yeah? Say it. I fucking* dare *you.*

I bet Thomas Devlin was like that. It got him killed, but

at least he *felt* something. I can tell from his stories — always from faraway places, always fast and breathtaking, words spilling out on the page like ninjas, sneaking up on the rest of us for the stealth attack. Was that his legacy for me? My genetic inheritance? *Crazed. Alive. And a little bit...*

When I got home from that creek party after the first time with Finn, I found a renegade pine branch stuck in my hair. I saved it in a shoe box under my bed so that I'd never forget that moment; that instant when Finn looked at me across the bonfire, nodded almost imperceptibly toward the woods, and raised a single, questioning eyebrow.

Shall we?

Yes, let's.

But that isn't love — not the kind Aunt Stephanie had with Casey. What I have with Finn is more like what my parents had, which is surreal and gross to consider, but true. I'm not in love with him. I'm in love with the way he erases things. That's why I saved the pine branch. I don't remember that night out of longing or any sort of dreamy hope-chest wishes. I remember it to *forget*.

But now, when I try to lose my mind in the fog again, Patrick's voice cuts through it, singing with his eyes closed. Instead of graying and vanishing, my thoughts multiply, intensify, run together like tributaries in a stream, meandering and braiding and ending up always in the same inevitable river — that *kiss*.

I close the diary and take a deep breath, holding the

late-night Vermont air in my lungs as the crickets continue their low hum and I think about my aunt and wonder if she was okay while she lived and then…then I sing softly the words of Patrick's songs, the ones I remember, over and over, rubbing my thumb on his guitar pick, safe in my sweatshirt pocket.

Forgetting is no longer an option.

Chapter eighteen

"Tomorrow's the Fourth," Mom says, pouring a cup of coffee and plugging in her cell phone charger.

"Is it?" Last year, I spent the Fourth at Seven Mile Creek, all of us piled on blankets and chairs in the woods while Mom was on business in Chicago. We couldn't even see the fireworks. No one cared.

"You guys should go to the Sugarbush Festival," Mom says. "I'm sure they still do the carnival — remember? You'd eat too much cotton candy and get a stomachache on the Ferris wheel. Patrick always got stuck next to you."

"Thanks for reminding me."

"It's true. And he stayed by your side, even when you were throwing up. Poor kid."

A tremor passes just below the surface of my skin as I think about last night. *Don't worry, Mom. I think he's over it.*

"I remember that one," Jack calls from the sunroom. I didn't even realize he was here. "We had to throw out his T-shirt."

"Awesome. Thanks for sharing," I call back.

"Anytime, Delilah. Anytime." The drill starts up and I have to shout for Mom to hear me.

"I'll see if Patrick wants to check it out tomorrow," I say.

"You should. All right, I have to get to work. Office is closed tomorrow for the holiday, but that just means twice as many e-mails on Wednesday. You all set for today?"

"I think I'm supposed to help Rachel with estate sale stuff," I say. "Patrick's coming over to work on the sunroom floor with Jack. They're going to talk about —"

Bzzzz.

"Sorry, Del. Gotta take this upstairs where it's quiet. But I really appreciate your help. We're making excellent progress here."

I don't tell Rachel about the kiss exactly, but she's going on about the Lovers tarot card she pulled when she asked the universe about me last night, and when the sound of Patrick's voice sends me bolting for the basement, she doesn't need a crystal ball to figure it out. She flashes me a conspiratorial smile as I pull open the cellar door and leave her to invent a good cover story.

Patrick is in and out all day, and with Rachel's help, I manage to avoid being seen for most of the afternoon, ducking into the basement to rearrange boxes of trinkets whenever he gets too close to the house. But just before dinner, as I'm carrying up a box of random camping supplies, there he is, all amber-gold eyes and playful dimples, guiding me back to the bottom of the stairs, moving the box from my hands to the floor so there's nothing between us but air and dust.

"I've been wondering about you all day," he says, so close that his breath tickles my lips. "I was worried about you last night. I hope I didn't freak you out."

I shake my head, looking at the floor so that my hair falls in front of my smile.

"So we're okay?" he asks.

"We're good."

"Glad to hear it." He lifts my chin until our eyes meet and his lips brush over mine, soft at first, dandelion seeds blown against my mouth like a wish, and then... completely. Hungry. Suffocating and desperate and I don't want it to stop. I've never been kissed like this before — not by Finn or the celebrity crushes in my head. Not even in my craziest dreams.

A door opens and closes upstairs, and Patrick pulls away, leaving me bewildered and shell-shocked, back against the wall to keep my body from evaporating in a long, hot sigh.

"Gotta run to the lumber yard with Dad," he says, "but I'll meet you tomorrow for the Sugarbush, okay?"

I can't even speak anymore, so I just nod. I'll probably have to devise some elaborate alternate communication method now, like writing in symbols in the dirt or tapping out letters in Morse code on my head, because I've obviously lost control of whatever brain parts are responsible for forming words.

"See you soon, Delilah." Patrick smiles, picks up the box of camping stuff, and disappears up the stairs. I hear him talking to Rachel and Jack in the kitchen, chitchatting about the estate sale, blathering on about nails and drill bits, small-talking about the weather, and blah blah blah and ha ha ha and here I stand alone, unable to remember even how to say my own name, which at this point I can only say for sure begins with a *Dee* and ends with an *Uhh*.

The next day, Patrick meets me outside as promised, looking exactly as before, except for those eyes. They're the same amber-gold, but somehow, they look deeper. Clearer. And when he sweeps them over my face and stops to gaze at my lips, my skin electrifies, buzzing for our entire walk into town.

"Where's Em?" I ask, feeling her absence more acutely in the wake of whatever this new thing is between us.

"She and Megan are helping Luna with her booth," he says. "They're giving away frozen drink samples on the fairway, so it's gonna be mobbed."

"All day?"

Patrick laughs. "All night, too. Afraid to be alone with me, Hannaford?"

"No." *Yes.* "Just wondering about Em."

"She can't save you," he says, pulling me into another kiss as we slowly make our way to Main Street.

The annual Fourth of July parade and Sugarbush Festival is everything the banner in town foretold...and more. Log rollers in ceremonial flannels falling into the lake. Kids winding sticky fingers into the manes of brown-and-white ponies trotting in a circle. Baton-twirlers and trumpets and American flags waltzing together down Main Street. And all foods maple, including the world-famous drizzlers: vanilla ice cream cones drizzled with real maple syrup and topped with a piece of maple sugar candy in the shape of a leaf. Patrick makes the mistake of asking me to hold his while he throws baseballs at milk bottles stacked in weighted pyramids.

"*Aaaand* we have a *winnerrrrr!*" a man shouts into the mic in a singsong carnival voice as I lick the last of Patrick's ice cream from my fingers. "Pick out a prize for the beautiful girl."

"For you," Patrick says, kneeling in front of me with a moose in his outstretched hands.

I pull the stuffed animal to my chest. "Thank you. I shall love him always. I shall call him Holden Caulfield."

"From the book?"

"Yes, from the book. You were reading it when I saw you my first day here."

"You remember that?"

"It's one of my favorite books," I say.

"You were totally checking me out."

"Patrick! Not in front of Holden Caulfield!" I cover the moose's floppy ears with my hands, hoping neither he nor Patrick sees the red flooding my cheeks.

"Come on." Patrick puts his arm around me and leads us toward the giant Ferris wheel. "It's got the best view," he says. "You can see the whole lake — remember?"

The last time I rode a Ferris wheel was here, eight summers ago. Spinning around in a circle, hundreds of feet in the air, suspended over the pavement in a rickety metal box with no walls or seat belts or parachutes...it was just like Mom and Jack remembered.

"Delilah, are you all right?" Patrick tries to uncurl my fingers from the so-called safety bar pressing loosely on the tops of our legs.

"Fine. I'm fine." What was it Rachel said about deep cleansing breaths? *In...two...three. Out...two...three.*

Patrick gives up on my china-white fingers and puts his arm around me. "The thing about seeing the best view in Red Falls is that you kind of have to open your eyes to do it."

I laugh, forgetting my fear for a second but not long enough to open my eyes.

"Look. If we fall from here, at this speed and distance, we'll be dead for sure. We won't even feel it."

"Well, when you put it like that..."

"Trust me, okay? We're fine. Look, Holden Caulfield isn't worried."

I open my eyes and let out a deep breath, concentrating on Patrick's arm protectively over my shoulders. With his free hand, he holds up the moose so I can inspect its sewed-on smile.

"Check it out." Patrick points in front of us as the wheel crests the summit, stopping to let other riders board. Below, a throng of people winds and stretches its way up and down the fairway like a giant snake. I hear them squealing on the rides that spin and twirl and defy gravity. There's music everywhere, and the smell of barbecue as men swing strong-man hammers and kids lick pink-and-blue cotton candy from their fingertips.

Farther out, past the main crush of the carnival, Red Falls Lake shimmers beneath the late-day sun. We can see the town volunteers checking the fireworks setup on a huge, flat boat in the middle of the lake. Up here, we're giants, locked into our steel cage while the ants work below and the seagulls hover and dive all around them.

"I think I can get a cool shot of us," Patrick says, reaching for his cell phone. "But you have to lean this way a little. And keep your eyes open. And smile."

I do as he says, keeping my hands on the safety bar but leaning back into him. He flips open the phone and snaps just before the wheel starts moving again, whirring us around and around and around until I can't tell the difference between the afternoon sky and Red Falls Lake, both equally blue and beautiful and bright, almost close enough to touch.

Suspended at the top of the world with Patrick's hand on my knee and Holden Caulfield tucked under my arm, I look out across the fairway and pretend that I can see Mom and Rachel from here. That they're walking with Nana, pushing Papa in his wheelchair and looking up at me to take my picture. Rachel's eating baby blue cotton candy. Papa is dropping curly fries into his mouth like long spaghetti noodles and Mom snaps the picture, waving with her free hand while she laughs and laughs and laughs.

The wheel whirls; the imaginary Hannafords disappear. But Patrick's still here, watching me, both hands moving to my face as he closes his eyes and kisses me, our lips warm and maple-sweet and tangled up entirely for the rest of our descent.

After we ride all of the regular rides and half of the kiddie ones, after I eat my way up and down the fairway six times, after we visit Luna's booth and help Emily hand out free drinks, after I lose most of my money on the water gun game and Patrick commissions a caricature drawing of us with Holden Caulfield, the sky begins to darken and we find a good fireworks-watching place overlooking the lake. When the show starts, the children of Red Falls run between the blankets, twirling glow-in-the-dark necklaces and squealing as the sky cracks and whistles and explodes, white lights pop-ping into weeping willow starbursts.

"Those are my favorite," I say. "They remind me of the trees. Remember when we used to hide under them?"

"The weeping willows? Yeah," Patrick says. "I still do that sometimes. Just lie there and stare up into the branches. It's another world up there."

"I have an idea." I stand and tug at him to follow me. We duck behind the crowds, behind the carts selling light-up silk roses and hot dogs and fried dough and more maple driz-zlers. We curve around to the side of the lake and climb up a low hill until I find the huge weeping willow grove I spotted during last week's kayaking misadventure.

"Here," I say, pointing at the biggest tree in the grove. Its branches touch the ground like a big, soft parachute, round and puffed out around the trunk. "For old times."

Patrick smiles and parts the branches for me, holding them aside until I pass through. I have to duck to fit beneath the outer layers, but inside, the branches open into a wide velvet canopy, lush and full and welcoming. The tumble of leaves muffles the crowd beyond, but there's enough light from the festivities and fireworks to cast both of us in a pale, green-blue haze. Beneath the branches, I sit back against the trunk.

"That's not how you do it," Patrick says. "Remember? You lie back, like this." He lies in the grass, stretching out with his hands behind his head. I copy him, giggling when our elbows bump and his foot falls into mine at the other end of us.

We lie side by side for a long time, the willow's branches cascading down around us like long, wavy hair in a gentle breeze. It's not cold, but I give myself over to a shiver, a gentle rolling that starts in my head and rumbles down through my heart, out my hands and feet. Patrick feels it and moves closer, his leg warm against mine. I keep my face toward the willow branches, trying to see all the way to the very top where the squirrels climb and the birds fly and the bright green leaves stretch to touch the sky. I feel him shift onto his elbow to face me, his hand drifting lazily to my hair. His fingers brush through it, lightly tracing my jaw and neck as I try to keep breathing, knowing and wanting more than my own life what will come next.

Patrick's hand continues to follow the lines of my face as I close my eyes, his fingers running through my hair and onto my shoulders and back again, brushing the soft edges of my ears, my eyebrows, my cheeks. Soon, his touch is warm on my neck and collarbone, and when his fingers float across my lips, I open my eyes. He has to kiss me. He has to kiss me right now or I will die a thousand deaths in a thousand little firecracker explosions under the biggest weeping willow in all of Vermont.

I tug on his arm until he folds and crashes into me, kissing me soft and hard at the same time, both hands in my hair. Outside, the grand finale blazes on, booming and popping and whiz-banging in the sky: a temporary, explosive celebration of whatever temporary, explosive thing we have. Both beautiful and breathtaking and full of the white-hot, double-dare summer intensity that's meant not for a lifetime, but for a short and shimmering burst.

As the final fireworks pop and whistle and sizzle down to the lake, we slowly unglue and lie back under the tree, me nuzzled against his chest while his hand rests under the blanket of my hair and everyone outside cheers, as if for us.

Chapter nineteen

Patrick walks me home to a dark house. After confirming that Rachel is out and Mom is tucked away in her room, I sneak him upstairs, locking my bedroom door and tiptoeing in the dark to the bed. We try to pick up where we left off beneath the willow tree, but it doesn't feel right, Holden Caulfield looking on, Nana's sewing stuff watching from the table, the weight of Stephanie's frantic diary entries like an invisible force in the room. So instead of kissing Patrick, I lead him to the closet, leaning in to whisper about the diary and show him the hole where it used to live.

"Hey. There's something else up there," he says when I

yank on the chain for the closet light and bathe us in a soft, white glow.

"What do you mean?"

"Shoved in the back. Looks like an envelope or something." He stretches to reach it, pulling out a thick manila envelope, yellowed sides tearing at the seams. "Pictures."

Together, we sit on the floor and spread them out between us — photographs of my family that my grandmother must've tucked away after each member died. Or in our case, left.

With Patrick strong and warm beside me, I flip through all of them, my mother and Rachel as girls with another who looks like a younger version of me — Stephanie. I hold her up to the light and look into her eyes and wish she was here with us now, looking at the photos, telling me where they were taken and sharing the thousand words each of them is supposed to be worth, cashed in so I could finally know. There are school pictures and drawings and a photo booth strip of a teenaged Stephanie and Megan. There are shots of my mother asleep on the couch with books and papers and Rachel pulling Steph in a little red wagon and my grandfather, standing for his wedding photo, before they took his leg and confined him to the wheelchair. There is more Hannaford family history on the floor between us than I've ever seen in my life, yet there are still missing years. No photos of Stephanie in her late teens, near the end. None of Mom and Rachel during college or even from the holiday breaks when they must've come home. None that could be Casey — just a few of Stephanie with someone ripped or scratched away. Removed. Erased. More questions.

I know I told Mom that I'd stay focused, that I'd stop asking questions that don't have answers, that I'd stop delving into the past. But now, with snapshots of all that's left of our family swirling in front of me on the hardwood floor of Stephanie's old bedroom, I know that I can't keep that promise forever. And my mother shouldn't ask me to.

I pull the diary from the drawer, and though I don't let it out from between my hands, I tell Patrick about Casey Conroy and some of the things I've read. Some of my suspicions that my late aunt, like my grandmother, may have suffered from some form of depression. Even in a whisper, voicing it feels almost like a betrayal, my throat tightening over the words as I realize how protective I've become of the two people in the diary — people I've never met. People who, like my father, would have been part of my family if only they'd been around long enough.

"Hey, Del, don't look like that," he says, brushing his fingers on my cheek.

"Like what?"

"Like you feel guilty for reading it."

I run my hand over the worn leather, the rose etched on the cover not unlike the gold flowers on my grandmother's urn. "But I *do*."

"She's not here anymore. And the diary has been hidden

164

under there for, like, seventeen years. There has to be a reason no one else found it before. Maybe you were meant to."

"That's what I thought at the beginning."

"I would've read it, too. You're just looking for a connection with your family."

I hear Aunt Rachel on the porch, coming in through the kitchen door. As she makes her way up the stairs, Patrick and I remain absolutely still. Her footsteps pause outside my door and I breathe deeply as if I'm asleep, the glow from the light in the closet as soft as a nightlight, no brighter than the moon through the window. Soon, Rachel's footsteps move away, carrying her to the Purple Room where she closes the door tight behind her.

I lower my voice from a whisper to a faint breath, inching closer to Patrick as I continue.

"I just wish I knew more about her life," I say. "About Casey. What happened after she died. Where he ended up."

"Your family doesn't talk about it, huh?"

"Nah. I guess it was just too hard for them. So far, there's nothing specific in the diary about depression or medication or anything like that. But some of her entries are all over the place. And others are really flat, like she didn't even want to get out of bed that day. Plus, she was a total insomniac. And she was *so* into this Casey guy. My mother and Rachel would question her about him, about whether she was sure, that kind of stuff, and she'd get really pissed. I read an entry the other night where she didn't speak to Rachel for two weeks just because Rachel asked her if she'd ever thought about dating around."

"Are you going to tell your mom about any of this stuff?"

"I don't know. Sometimes I think my mother wouldn't even care. She doesn't have time for it all, you know? She hates being back here. For her, the sooner we get everything packed up and sold, the better."

"Maybe she hates being here because she doesn't know about any of this," Patrick says, flipping through another set of pictures. Black-and-whites, this time.

"I've thought about it. But I told her I'd stay focused on all of the house stuff and stop asking about the past. She doesn't want to talk about it. And part of me hates her for it and thinks she's being crazy and selfish."

"What about the other part?"

"The other part looks at these pictures and the diary and I can't even imagine how horrible it must have been when Stephanie died. What it must have done to their family. And then I feel like the selfish one for wanting her to relive it all just so I can find answers that might not even exist."

Patrick hands me a photo from his stack. "Honestly, Del? I think you should try. At least show your mom the pictures, even if you don't tell her about the diary."

I take the photo from him and hold it in front of my face. It's us — my mother and me. She's smiling with me on her lap as I blow bubbles into the summer sky, my hair in pigtails and undoubtedly warm from the sun and the touch of her hands. Looking at it now, I can feel them on my small shoulders. I remember the picture. I remember when Papa took it because he had to do it more than once — I kept turning around to show Mom the bubbles. My grandfather made cow and frog and pig noises to get my attention. He ultimately won with the pig, and when I stopped giggling, I looked right at him and blew the biggest bubble Red Falls had ever seen.

I look at the picture in my hand, the woman with the laugh and the wavy chocolate hair and the little girl in pigtails and wonder how the two could ever become such passing ships, black pirate flags waving under the shadow of a constant storm.

"This is insane," I whisper, the words scratching inside like tiny pieces of glass. "How could they not talk about her? Did your father ever say anything?"

"No, Del. We never talked about Stephanie. I was only a year old when she died. You weren't even born yet."

"I know I'm getting neurotic about this... I just have this feeling that Stephanie's death, Casey Conroy, and whatever happened after Steph's funeral have something to do with the fight eight years ago."

Patrick squeezes my shoulder. "*Maybe*. I don't know. Your family has been through a lot. That fight could've been about a million other things. Stephanie wasn't even alive eight years ago."

"But why else wouldn't they want to talk about her now?" I press. "Why don't they ever talk about her? There were never any pictures of her in the house — not that I remember. Why are they all here in the closet like this? Even the pictures of Meg — *wait*."

"What is it?"

"Megan. She was Steph's best friend."

"I guess it's worth a try," he whispers, kissing me once more before it's time to sneak him back downstairs and out of the house.

I stay up another two hours to finish the diary. The entries span her later teens and become more sporadic with each passing page. Sometimes, she goes weeks or even months without writing. Other times, she writes frantic and messy, two or three times in one day.

I'm no longer unclear on whether Stephanie suffered from depression.

Saw the doc again today — Mom's doc. More pills. He says they'll stabilize my mood, get me back on track, but I feel like they just change my personality. And if my personality changes, then I'm no longer me, and the friends who like the old me and the man who loves the old me say good-bye.

They make me feel fuzzy, and they keep me up at night, but I guess the doctor knows what he's doing so we'll see.

In the meantime, it's almost graduation. Dad

said I could get whatever dress I wanted. Claire and Rachel are coming home for it. It's exciting to think about new beginnings and all that, but it's also frightening. Where are we going? When are we leaving? Casey is supposed to look for work in New York this month. If that doesn't work out, we might just go all out and head to California. Why not? Sometimes I think I'd be much better at loving Mom from a nice long distance.

OK. She has her moments. Today was a good day. Tomorrow, we'll see. And if doctor what's-his-name can promise that his magic pills will keep me from turning into my mother, I'll take the whole bottle.

Ah, here comes the sun. Better try to get some sleep. Casey's taking me out late tomorrow night.

— S

And then, a few days later…

Mom keeps calling from downstairs that I'm going to be late for school. Whatever. Not going anywhere today. Haven't slept in a million years. This sucks.

— S

There are more like that, leading up to the final entry. According to the date, it was written just a few months before she died.

I don't care. I can't care.

No matter what my mother says to me . . . no matter how loud she yells or how long she goes without speaking to my father and me, I always have C. And no matter how far away my sisters are, no matter how infrequent their visits and letters, no matter how many times they promise and forget and life goes on, there is always C.

In my life, in our years together, Casey Conroy is the only person who hasn't let me down. Who hasn't judged me or screamed at me or ignored me or completely forgotten my existence. He is the one I always come back to, the face burned into my heart that wakes me from the nightmares, carrying with him the rising sun, chasing away the dark. He has my heart and I his and when the world ends, the promise of him is all that matters.

But should the world end, he and I will no longer exist as he and I. And that's what scares me the most. That's what no one understands when they throw words at me like daggers, words like OBSESSION. If I'm obsessed with being loved,

well, so be it. I'm obsessed. I'm obsessed with
not ending up in a coma of misery like the rest of
the world, so let them throw at me all the words
they can invent. The words are useless, and I've
no more use for them. I'm all out.

And so it is here, tonight, that I say good-
bye, dear diary. Good-bye.

— *Stephanie Delilah Hannaford*

That's it; the final entry. There are a dozen or so more pages, but they're all blank. Nothing appears to have been torn out. She just…stopped writing. Said good-bye to the diary, just like she said she would. Then she stuck it under the floorboards and went on with her life, however little of it she had left.

The diary leaves me with almost as many questions as answers. What happened in the months between her final entry and her death? Did anyone know how sick she really was? Did she stay on her medication? What caused her heart to fail? Did Casey know? Did he stay with her through the worst of it, or did he disappoint her in the end like everyone else?

And if Stephanie was sick, and her mother was sick, what about Mom and Aunt Rachel? What about me?

I slide the diary back into the drawer and push my hand through the photos on the floor again, stopping at a large black-and-white of Mom and Rachel. They're young — six or seven, maybe — and they're dressed up, maybe for a wedding, or for Easter Sunday. They're standing on the path leading from the sidewalk to the front of the house, and it's lined with pots of flowers. They're smiling, facing each other with big handfuls of flowers from the pots, and as I see the happiness in their eyes and the flowers and the sunshine, I recall the card from Mom's tarot reading on our first night back in Red Falls.

The Six of Cups . . . childhood memories . . . it's the nostalgia card.

I scoop the pile of pictures back into the envelope, tucking them into the drawer with the diary.

Tomorrow, I need to find Megan.

Chapter twenty

The day after Fourth of July, while the rest of the non-vacationing world returns to work, I stake out the Crasner's parking lot and wait for Megan's shift to end. She smiles and waves when she sees me, crossing the lot to my sidewalk bench.

"Hey, Delilah! Good timing." She tips an open bag of chocolate macadamia cookies toward me. "Just made them. What's up? Grocery day?"

I take a cookie. "Actually, I was hoping we could chat."

"Everything okay?" she asks.

"Everything's okay," I say. "Just tired. I was up late last night. Do you have time for a coffee?"

*　　*　　*

"I found some pictures in Nana's closet," I tell her after Em delivers our drinks at Luna's. "Pictures of my mom and Aunt Rachel, and some of Aunt Stephanie."

"I always thought your grandmother got rid of them," Megan says, tears glazing her eyes. "She didn't leave any on the walls after she died. Wow. You know, sometimes losing Stephie feels like a lifetime ago. Other times like it just happened yesterday. Today's a yesterday kind of day."

"What was she like?" I ask, eager for a perspective less personal than the diary's.

"Stephanie was... *intense.* That's the best word to describe her, Del. The best one."

Megan has a lot of stories about my youngest aunt, some hilarious, some heartbreaking, others tame, two girls walking through town, watching a movie, laughing at something at school, eating French fries.

"What about later?" I ask. "Just before...I mean, when you guys were my age. And after."

Megan looks out the window, tracing the rim of her coffee mug as a pair of moms passes by out front, two women wearing pink Vermont T-shirts, pushing strollers, laughing in the sunshine.

"Sweetie, how much do you know about Stephanie's death?" Megan asks.

"Not that much. Just that she died from cardiac arrest at

nineteen. I was so young when they first told me about it, so they left out most of the details. And now, they just don't like to talk about it."

Megan covers my hand with hers across the table. "That's true, Delilah. She died from cardiac arrest. But she also had depression. She was on different medications. For a while... I don't know. Stephanie was my best friend. But near the end of her life, we drifted apart. Even though she was seeing a doctor, she just wasn't right. I don't know if she was mis-diagnosed or not taking her medication properly or what, but she was not the Stephanie that we used to know. She became intensely fixated on her boyfriend. Barely graduated high school. Didn't know what to do with her life after that — it was all about him. I don't know. Sometimes I think I could have been more supportive. More open-minded about her relationship with Casey instead of worrying about how much time they spent together. I should've known that she was sick. I should've been able to help her. It still haunts me, Del. I didn't know how to be her friend anymore. As much as I wanted to love her, I had no idea how to do it."

I wish I could show Megan the diary, but I know it would only make it harder for her, seeing how scattered Stephanie had become. How little she mentioned Megan or her other friends. How possessive she was about Casey. Obsessed, just like her last entry said.

"Whatever happened to her boyfriend?" I ask.

"Casey stayed with her all the way through it. He wasn't a bad guy or anything. Her death really knocked the wind out of him. He left town soon after the funeral. Went to Los Angeles, last I heard. None of us really kept up with him."

Tears move across my eyes like storm clouds over the lake, spilling to reveal what's in my heart — disappointment that Megan doesn't know more about Casey. Sadness for my aunt Stephanie. Sadness for my mother and Aunt Rachel and their parents.

"You know, after everything," I say, wiping my eyes with a napkin, "I can't believe Mom and Rachel would leave their friends here in Red Falls, even if they were mad at their mother. I mean, *you* were here. And Jack and everyone else who knew us. It doesn't make any sense."

Megan squeezes my hand. "I don't know why you guys left, Delilah. I never knew the details of that night. Even now, Rachel doesn't want to talk about it, and we've spent a lot of time together these past few weeks. You have to remember that once your mom and Rachel left Red Falls for college, I really only saw them on their school breaks. I was always closest with Stephanie, and when she got sick, everything changed. After her death, I still spent time with your mom and Rachel during the summers — especially after you were born. But when they didn't return that year, we simply lost touch."

"But why? Why couldn't anyone pick up the phone or send an e-mail?"

Megan shrugs. "It's complicated. I think when bad things

happen — whether someone dies or people argue or split up — you get to a point where it's just too hard to go back. There's so much lost. So many versions of the truth. So many versions of how things might've turned out differently. We all long for what *could* have been, Del. For some people, it's just easier to move forward and try to forget."

"But you didn't do anything wrong. Why did they stop talking to you?"

Megan takes a sip of her coffee, looking back out over Main Street. "Unfortunately, when families fight, lots of people get caught in the tide. It was just one of those things. Your grandmother was a tough old bird. She made it known that she wasn't going to talk about it, and that was that. We lived here in Vermont with her. I'm sure if I was in Pennsylvania with you guys, I would've stopped talking to your Nana instead."

"There's still something I don't understand. I know Stephanie died of cardiac arrest, but what made her heart stop in the first place? Was it the medication?"

"I'm not sure exactly." Megan finishes the rest of her coffee. "I'm sorry, Del. I really think you should talk to your mom about this, you know? It's not that I don't want to talk about Steph, but I feel like I might be trespassing a little bit here."

I nod. "I understand. I didn't mean to put you on the spot. It's just that my family is really great at burying things and pretending to move on."

Megan smiles. "Maybe you think they've buried things, but remember, everyone has a different way of coping, and as simple as it might look on the outside, there are usually a lot more layers to a story. Take us, for example." She lowers her voice, nodding toward Luna behind the counter. "When we lost my dad a few years ago, Mom completely threw herself into this coffee shop. We all accused her of being in denial about his death — of avoiding her own grief. Then one night she sat us down and showed me this notebook where she and my father had sketched out a business plan and pages of notes and figures and maps. The two of them had been saving for years to open the shop together. It was something they always dreamed of and now, after his death, she finally had the money. She opened it in his memory. We had no idea. We just thought she was crazy."

I look over at Luna, wiping down the counter and the nozzles on the steamers, chatting with customers, making the schedule, and I wonder how much we don't see. How much of our lives we witness and accept as truth when the rest of the iceberg — the heaviest, bulkiest part — is buried and invisible.

"Just something to consider, Del," Megan says. "You know, her birthday is coming up. She would've turned thirty-seven this year."

"I know. It's this Saturday." I think about that first diary entry, written on the night of her sixteenth birthday.

"Yep. Maybe that's a good opportunity for you to talk to your mom. Give her a chance, okay?" Megan smiles. She remembers when things were still okay with my family.

So do I.

We all long for what could have been.

chapter twenty-one

On the morning of what should've been Stephanie's thirty-seventh birthday, I wake from a nightmare, the image of my late aunt's face haunting me even in the bright white of day. All of Red Falls was there in my dream world, all gathered around the lake, everyone digging holes in the sand. When I got closer, I saw that they were burying the things we set aside for our estate sale — Nana's trinkets and clothes and Ollie's chew toys. The lake was black sludge and smelled like tar, and Mom stood on a huge platform above it with a torch. She lowered it as the people cheered, the lake igniting like an oil field in the desert, black smoke rising around her as the flames shot up to the sky. Then she appeared on the shore, walking over the mounds of Nana's things with a bundle of papers. She gave it to me and told me to throw it in the fire, and when I did, I saw the Stephanie pictures. I tried to pull them from the flames, but they were burning too fast, the edges curling and melting as the girl in the photos screamed for me to save her and the townspeople looked on, clapping.

I shake off the nightmare, pulling my clothes on and blowing away the invisible smoke. From the drawer with the diary, I take the envelope of pictures into my hands, carrying it down the stairs, one step at a time, hoping the words come to me before I need to speak them. When I reach the kitchen, Mom and Rachel are already near the door, Mom holding her car keys and Rachel a pot of small pink roses.

"Are you going to the cemetery?" I ask.

"Yes, hon," Rachel says when Mom doesn't answer. "We're going to see Stephanie."

"I know it's her birthday," I say.

Mom finally speaks. "We were just going to drop the flowers off and...I don't know. Say a few words, maybe. I'm sorry, Delilah. I didn't think you'd be up this early. We won't be gone long."

"I found some pictures upstairs." I sit at the kitchen table, setting down the envelope as Mom and Rachel pull up chairs.

"What do you mean?" Mom asks. She and my aunt share the same sharp and shallow breaths, in and out like a seesaw. "What pictures?"

I swallow down the lump in my throat as I take the envelope in my hands, releasing the flap and spilling the photos across the table like water. Stephanie waves from her bike on top of the stack, brown hair blowing out behind her like she's moving even now, flattened into a picture in her dead mother's kitchen.

"I'm sorry...I just...I want to know about her. I want to talk about her. You guys are all so young and happy in these pictures and now she's gone and Nana and Papa are gone and it's just us and I want to know where we came from."

My hands are shaking as Mom grabs them across the table, resting them on the photographed candles of Stephanie's tenth birthday cake. Her fingers crush hard into mine but there's no anger in her eyes, only sadness and a new uncertainty. She doesn't speak.

"There are only three Hannafords left, Mom. No one else knows what happened and no one else will remember us."

Mom nods, her eyes fixed on pictures spread across on the table. "Would you like to see her?"

"Can I come with you?" I ask.

She pushes her chair from the table, stands, and holds out her hand. Rachel takes the flowers from the counter, still clutching a photo against her chest as if Stephanie, waving from an inflatable orange raft on Red Falls Lake, might feel her sister's heartbeat as her own and come back.

I go with them in Mom's Lexus, still *black sapphire pearl* with *cashmere* interior, still beeping with the freakishly calm GPS woman as if nothing has changed between Key and here over the last four weeks. I go because I want to give them another chance, an opportunity to tell me who Stephanie was and why they kept her buried. I go because I want to know.

None of us speaks. Rachel holds a tissue against her nose while her sister stays focused on a spot beyond the windshield — *eyes on the road, mind on the goal, and everything will be okay.* We glide down Main Street, past the Foo nasty and Luna's, past the hardware store and all the places I've seen on our journey back in time to Red Falls. We cross over the edge of town that bleeds into the woods, and then through a black iron gate, letters looping across the top of it: FOREST LAWN CEMETERY.

All around us along the wide, dirt path, white stones stick out from the grass like loose teeth in a bright green mouth, chomping at the earth. We drive through the younger section where the stones still shine, some whose names have not yet been carved. The cemetery seems endless, rows and rows of markers signifying the end of hundreds of lives, thousands of years combined into a vast, underground soup. I read the names as we pass — Martin and Kowalski and O'Connor and Dannon — and wonder. Who were these people? Who have they left behind? How many layers of stories and riddles are buried here like icebergs moored in the dirt?

When we reach the part with more trees and fewer graves, Mom pulls over and gets out of the car, motioning for us to follow down a long row of smooth, blue-white stones.

"Here she is," Mom says, kneeling down and running her hand along the arch of a pale stone that stands about two feet high. Her fingers trace the wings of a small bird etched into the rock.

"It's a cardinal," she says. "Stephanie loved them. They seemed to be drawn to her. She had a collection of red feathers."

"A cardinal?" I think again of the bird trapped in the sunroom so many years ago — how upset Nana was to hear the story again and again.

"They still remind me of her," Mom says. "I don't see them much anymore."

Rachel kneels beside her, setting the pink roses next to a potted arrangement of white tulips already there. The stone on the left belongs to Benjamin Hannaford, and an empty patch of grass on his other side waits for my grandmother. My heart hurts to see Papa's name carved here, a man whose laugh could fill an entire hall, silent and asleep for eternity next to his young daughter.

"Stephanie Delilah Hannaford," Mom whispers, tracing the carved lettering with her fingers. "Our baby sister. She was only nineteen. So, so young..."

Mom and Rachel exchange a glance, and when Rachel nods and reaches for her sister's hand, Mom takes a deep breath. "Delilah," she says. "When Stephanie was in her late teens, she was diagnosed with depression. Rachel and I didn't know about it right away — we weren't living at home at the time. We found out months later on one of our visits. She told us she was on medication and that she was seeing a doctor."

"Of course we were worried," Rachel says, "but she seemed okay. Dad said he was monitoring her medications and that Stephanie seemed to be making progress. Mom wanted us to take the semester off, but Dad talked us out of it. He didn't think it was necessary. Lots of people have depression. Lots of people manage it. But after a while, she just...her light went out."

"At some point," Mom says, "Stephanie got her hands on sleeping pills. Her doctor didn't prescribe them, and we never found an actual bottle, so we think she got them from a friend, or maybe stole them out of someone's medicine cabinet. The doctor told us she could've been taking them for a few days. Maybe a week. Then, one night, she took too many. Five. Six, maybe. It was enough to interact with the other medication in her system and cause a reaction. She went into cardiac arrest. It was basically an overdose."

"Oh my God, Mom. Did she...I mean, how do you —"

"To this day we don't know whether she took her own life," Rachel says. "Five pills? That seems intentional. But when someone's depressed and they just want to take something and sleep...it could've been a desperate accident. One pill didn't work. Two didn't work. She didn't leave a note. Up until that night, she was still making plans with her boyfriend to move away."

"We'll never know," Mom says. "My mother was the one who found her the next morning, lying on the floor in the sunroom. She must've wandered down there at night, after she took the pills. By then it was already...she was...*gone*."

Mom runs her fingers over the stone again, resting her hand on top. "My mother believed that Stephanie took her own life. She blamed us for not seeing the signs. We weren't there to see the subtle changes. The day-to-day. I guess I'll always wonder if taking that semester off would've made any difference."

I sit on the ground before the stone and I think about Stephanie's diary, hidden for years under the floorboards of the darkest corner of the closet, all of her written thoughts deepening, intensifying, blackening in the shadow of Mom's words.

"It's so hard," Rachel says, her voice shaky. "To think that she may have taken her own life...I hated her for leaving us. For not trusting us to be able to help her. And if she didn't do it intentionally, then I blame myself for not being here. For not...I don't know."

I picture the rose etched on the diary and I wonder if they could have saved her — Mom and Rachel. If they had found it and read through her final sentiments in time to change things.

*And so it is here, tonight, that I say good-bye,
dear diary. Good-bye.*

Mom looks over the green expanse beyond us, dotted with
white stones. "When Stephie died, my mother took down her
pictures — stopped saying her name. Dad never believed it
was suicide. Until the day he died, he always said it was an
accident. A mix-up. I didn't know what to believe. And now,
even with Mom gone...I still don't know. It's harder to dig
up the old bones and sift through the dirt than it is to let
them rest in peace." Mom doesn't cry, but her voice is thin,
words trailing to my ears on a tight metal wire.

"I always thought she got rid of all the pictures," Rachel
says. "Especially after we left. I'm glad you found them, Del."

I finger the soft velvet petals of the tulips, losing myself in
a swirl of thoughts and memories and hurt and yes, anger. I
never met Stephanie, but I'm mad at her, too. All those things
in her diary...all the people she loved...did she really take
her own life? Why didn't she talk to her sisters? Why not
Megan? Casey? Why did she stop writing? If one person had
known how she was feeling, maybe she would be with us
now. Instead, here we are, the only remaining Hannaford
women, crouched over Stephanie's grave with heads bent
together like wilting flowers, unable to climb out from the
burden of our pain as it continues to knit the broken pieces
of us together in a misfit patchwork quilt.

"Here's something you probably don't know about your

grandmother," Rachel says. "She loved tulips, but she could never get them to grow. She tried everything, every kind, every color, every bulb she could get her hands on, but they just wouldn't sprout. The spring after Stephanie died, Mom's garden had full blooms for the first time ever — but just the white ones. They grew back every year on the same day. Probably still do. These here must be from Megan," she says.

"There's still so much I don't know," I whisper. "Stephanie. Nana. The fight."

And it's out there, just like that, a branch snapping in the silence to scatter the birds from the limb.

My mother reaches for my hand and pulls me up. "It doesn't matter anymore," she says, her hand resting on my face. "We're here now, the three of us, like you said. Together. Moving forward."

Rachel offers Mom a gentle smile. "We'll be okay."

I look again at the letters of my grandfather's name carved into the stone next to Stephanie's, but nothing is revealed; everyone taking to his final resting place the secrets he kept in life.

I try to think about Megan and all the layers of our lives, but it's too much. It's too much to ask, too much to drag out of the mud into the bright light of day. I don't want to know about Stephanie anymore, about why she stopped writing in her diary or why she took the pills or why we stopped coming here or why my mother and Rachel are still running away. I just want to go home.

I leave the sisters at the graves of their departed family and wait inside Mom's Lexus, curled into the *cashmere* seats for twenty minutes before they finally return to the car, Rachel walking several paces behind her older sister, eyes turned down as if they're closed.

Chapter twenty-two

Patrick and Jack say you just don't find original, hundred-and-fifty-year-old plantation shutters like this on New England houses anymore — not functional ones that close over the entire window, not in such good working condition, and most certainly not thirty of them.

Thirty. And we have to remove them all because the painters are coming to do the house tomorrow. After the cemetery and the flowers and the silence in the car on the way home, removing thirty original, hundred-and-fifty-year-old plantation shutters seems like the most pointless thing in the world.

"Why don't they just do the shutters the same color as the house?" I ask. "Then the painters can do everything in one shot." It's eighty-five degrees, sweat is running down my back, and I still can't erase the image of my nightmare, the rot of it made more real by our cemetery visit.

"Shutters are complicated, Del," Patrick says. "You can't just paint over the hardware or it'll stick and they won't work anymore. Did you get the baggies?"

"Yes, sir." I hold up the box of Ziplocs.

"Don't you ever see the bright side of things?" Patrick asks as I mope against the bottom of the ladder.

"Easy to see the bright side when you're getting paid by the hour."

"Delilah, I will gladly give you my full wage plus a month's supply of your iced choco-nut whatever lattes if you trade places and clothes with me right now."

"You're not wearing a shirt."

"That's the deal, Hannaford," he says. "Take it or leave it." He jimmies a shutter free from its weathered, paint-stuck prison, scraping his shoulder against the outer wall of the house.

"No deal, Reese." I laugh, but my smile fades fast. Everywhere I look, I see the eyes of the girl who looks like me, her words loud in my head, haunting and pleading and begging me to save her from the fire in my dream, from her illness, from her grave beneath the stones of Forest Lawn Cemetery.

It takes us the rest of the morning to remove the shutters,

laying them in order on tarps across the lawn. I remove, label, and bag the hardware, and when we're finished, the yard looks like a piano keyboard stretched across the grass, almost as far as Patrick's house.

"It's not so bad," Patrick says. "At the end of the month, when we're done with all the work, the house will be like our magnum opus."

"Right. Except they're selling it, so I'll never see it again."

"Um, bright side?"

"The bright side is... I need to get out of here. Can we go out on the water? Just us?"

Mom's on her laptop when I go inside to change, phone attached to her ear, right back in step with whatever spreadsheet she left off to wish her departed sister a happy birthday this morning. I don't bother telling her where I'm going — just a note, scratched on a Post-it and stuck to her wall calendar.

"Going out with Patrick. Be back later."

Patrick rows in front of me, the muscles in his back tensing and relaxing as the paddles break the surface of the lake and propel him forward. I copy his motions — tense, relax. Tense, relax — pausing only to notice the stillness of everything, muffled and miniaturized by our distance from the shore, far away from the parents on the beach and their babies pointing up at the seagulls. Far away from the cemetery. Far away from my mother and Rachel and the Hannaford ghosts.

Kayaking has gotten easier since the first time he and

Emily took me. As I slice through the lake, water laps softly against the boat like a puppy learning to drink and the sun heats up my banana-yellow kayak, reflecting like a million stars on the water. My shoulders burn on the outside from the sun and on the inside from paddling, but I don't want to stop. Here, away from everything, I could almost keep on going.

When we reach the shore, Patrick climbs out gracefully, one foot at a time dipping into the water over the side of his red boat. He drags it out of the lake, watching as I tug my kayak by its nose onto the sandy shore.

"How do you feel?" he asks, his eyes golden and content. "Shoulders holding up okay?"

I look at him and shake out my arms. "I'm fine. A little tired, but okay."

"What about the rest of you?" Patrick looks harder into my eyes, his dimples vanishing.

I shrug. "Still processing, I guess. I showed them the pictures this morning, and they took me to the cemetery to see her. It would've been her birthday." I tell him the story. The roses and the tulips. The pills. The uncertainty. "And after talking to Megan and reading the diary and seeing my mom and Rachel at the cemetery...now I just keep thinking... what if...what if it runs in my family?"

"Hey," he says, reaching for my hands. "Your mom and Rachel are okay, and you are, too. Don't do that to yourself."

"But how can you say that? How can any of us even know that? I'm sure Steph thought she was fine for a long time, too. My mom needs pills to get through her day. What if she wakes up one morning and decides she doesn't want to go to work anymore? Or that she doesn't want to be a single mom? And she just..."

"Delilah, that's not going to happen."

"What about me? What if I just —"

"Not possible. You are *way* too stubborn to go out like that. Did you see how you handled that kayak today after what happened last time? That boat got *dealt* with."

I smile. "I did kind of own it today, didn't I?"

"You got here without falling, right? I think we need an award for this momentous occasion." Patrick laughs as he pulls our bags from the boats and leads us to a clearing surrounded by a grove of maple trees.

"I can't believe it's so quiet out here," I say through a mouthful of grapes.

"You can drive here, but you can't really see this spot from the road," Patrick says. "Most of the tourists don't know about it. Locals like it, though. I'm surprised we have it all to ourselves. Must be the clouds."

I look up and squint at the sky. The afternoon sun still burns bright down to the sand, but fat, gray clouds linger on the opposite shore.

"What's this place called?" I ask.

"Brighton Beach."

"Thought so. Rachel told me about it. She said my

grandfather used to bring them when they were kids, back when he could still drive."

"Yep. My parents grew up coming here, too. They brought me a couple times, but now I usually come by myself on the kayak. It's a good spot to get away and think."

I look out over the water, my thoughts helplessly drifting back to my family. "One thing about Stephanie that *does* make sense...it kind of explains how someone as control-freakish as my mother could get caught up in a one-night stand with a random guy she met at a bar. In my entire life, I don't remember her ever having a boyfriend outside of her laptop. She doesn't even have time for speed dating. Seriously. She must've been a train wreck back then."

"I'm sure she was. But really, the only thing that made it a one-night stand between her and your father was the fact that he got killed right after. You can't know what might have happened if he'd missed that flight or gone to the wrong house in Afghanistan or taken a different assignment. Maybe they would have met up again. Fallen in love. Maybe your mom would've moved to London. You could have been born British, you know?"

"Then I never would've met you," I say. "On the other hand, I'd have that cool accent, so maybe it would've been a good trade-off."

Patrick throws a grape at me, and before I can retaliate, he takes off with the whole bunch, throwing them at me one at a time until I chase him straight into the water. He grabs me and pulls me in with him, soaking us both and losing the rest of the grapes to the seagulls.

After the dip, we stretch out on our backs on sun-warmed towels, side by side, arms touching from shoulder to pinky, talking about birds and clouds and the gigantic enormity of things.

I turn to face him, resting my cheek against the towel. "You know the worst part? The whole thing is just one more mystery between me and my mother. One more thing she never told me about. As much as they explained their reasons for not talking about Stephanie, I feel like there's more to the story. I don't want to be selfish and keep asking them to talk about something that's obviously so painful — I mean, I can't even *imagine* losing someone like that. But as soon as we got back to the house, Rachel was down in the basement working on the sale stuff, I started on the shutters, and Mom was on her computer like everything was just fine. But it's really not, Patrick. Their little sister may have killed herself. How can anything ever be fine again?"

Patrick wraps his fingers around mine and sighs into the sky, neither of us saying anything for a long while. We watch the clouds gathering steam at the other end of the lake as the seagulls circle and cry above us, and I can't stop the replay in my head. I'm no closer to answers than I was the moment in the Foo nasty parking lot when Rachel first told me about shopping for school stuff with her sisters, and as much as I want to do like Mom says and move on, let go, stop digging...

I can't quiet the endless thoughts, fast and strung together in a long line of impossible question marks.

"Look," Patrick says, pressing a smooth, flat stone into my hand, perfect for skipping.

I hold it to my face for closer examination, turning it over in my fingers. There's something etched into the surface, blocky and deep.

PR + DH

"Amazing, right?" he asks. "I found it just like that. It's a sign from the universe. Ask Rachel. She'll totally back me up." His lips are just a breath away from mine, his hair flopping over his forehead. His honey eyes look at me like I'm the water that keeps him from dying of thirst.

"Delilah?" He's even closer now, whispers falling on my skin like feathers as his fingers trace my eyebrows. "You're beautiful, you know that?"

When he kisses me, I'm lost. The sun is fading as the clouds roll closer and I know I should feel the chill, but lying here in just my swimsuit, the bare skin of my stomach and legs is warm under the weight of Patrick's body. The taste of orange soda on his lips mingles with the grapes on mine, and I don't want to leave this beach, ever. I pull him closer to me, wrapping my arms around him as he kisses my neck. Nothing else in the whole entire world should matter, but when I open my eyes and see the stone lying next to me, the carved initials remind me only of those scratched into the wood floor under the bed.

SH + CC

"We should probably head back," I say, turning away from him. "I'm sorry. I just...I can't stop thinking about her."

"It's okay. Come on." He brushes the hair from my face and kisses my forehead, standing so we can shake the sand from our towels.

We pack up the bags and push off quickly from the shore, silt scratching the bottoms of our boats as we follow the same path back through the water — tense, relax. Tense, relax. Tense, relax. As we cross the center point of the lake, my shoulders and arms burn with the effort of rowing. The clouds shift to blot out the remaining sun, and I know before the first drop hits my face that the rain is coming, anxious to wash away the remnants of the day. But when it finally arrives, it doesn't wash away anything. It just falls sideways and heavy, chilling my skin as we quicken our retreat across the water in silence.

Chapter twenty-three

The weekend of the first estate sale arrives with grand, annoying fanfare, Rachel standing over me at six in the morning in her *Everyone Loves Cowgirls* T-shirt with a price gun in one hand, a cup of coffee in the other, and a look in her eyes that in my morning delirium can only be described as...*crazed.*

"Look what Megan borrowed for us from the store," she says, stickering my forehead. "They don't even use these things anymore."

I sit up in bed, taking the coffee from her outstretched hand and peeling the price tag from my skin.

I'm priced to move at $1.00.

"This coffee better be strong, Rachel. Because as soon as I get up, I'm going to harm you."

Rachel stickers me again. "I don't think so, Del. Your card today is the Eight of Pentacles."

"So?"

"It's the apprentice card. Attention to detail. Working hard. Applying yourself under the guidance of a mentor. Guess who?" *Click click*, says the price gun.

"Is there a kill card?" I ask. "Just curious when that might turn up in the spread."

"Very funny. Meet me outside in fifteen minutes." She blows on the end of the price gun and jams it into her waistband. "Time to make five tons of one woman's useless junk another woman's undiscovered treasure."

Patrick and Em are supposed to stop by later, but for now, it's just the two at us, stickering and setting out such historical Hannaford pieces as twelve porcelain kittens from the kitten-of-the-month club of 1983, an all-season collection of elastic-waist polyester pants, fourteen leaf-shaped muffin tins, and eight slightly chewed dog food bowls from the renowned "Ollie" collection. Claire Hannaford Speaking, of course, has a "make or break" conference call with her vice president of sales and some big-deal retail client.

"She's going to be locked up in there most of the day," Rachel tells me as she props a huge OPEN sign on an easel at the end of the driveway. "I guess this call is pretty important."

"Important." I look over the folding tables that hold all of my grandmother's possessions and think about the diary. The cemetery. The pills and the secrets and all the lost years. "They're *all* important, right?"

Rachel sighs. "Del, I know things are still tense between you and your mom, but we're all hurting here. Getting angry and bitter isn't going to help. You need to find a more positive way to deal with this."

"Maybe I should start drinking with you and Megan every night, since you're so awesome at dealing with things."

The gentle smile on my aunt's face falls. She digs into her pocket for her frankincense and orange oil, silver bangles tinkling down her arm, and my stomach bubbles with guilt.

"Rachel, I didn't mean —"

"You've got a customer." She spritzes the air around me with a few pumps and leaves me to tend to an old woman with dyed red hair, outfitted in a T-shirt appliquéd with fuzzy dogs.

"Did you find the sweater?" the woman asks.

I point to a rack across the lawn. "We don't have all the clothes out yet, but I think there are a few sweaters over there."

"No, not those." She looks around to confirm no one is listening before lowering her voice to a whisper. "*The* sweater. Ollie's sweater."

"They make sweaters for Saint Bernards?"

"Not *for* them. From them. You save the hair from their brush, and you can have it made into sweaters or scarves or whatever. It's softer than wool, and just as warm."

"You're...kidding?"

"Certainly not. I made it myself." She says it in a high, proud tone as though I'm just not getting it. Which, admittedly, I'm not.

"I didn't know people could do that." I try not to make a face at the idea of getting rained on in a dog hair sweater. "Well, if it's not on the rack, it's probably in the house. We're still getting organized."

"Do keep your eye out for it, would you? You'll know by the little label inside. It says 'Handmade by Alice' and there's a heart on each side. Don't you want to write that down? Actually, I'll give you my card."

Alice, weaver of dog hair, sifts through a bag that I originally thought was a cool faux but is more likely a shih tzu–poodle blend.

"Do you have any pets?" she asks, handing me a worn card with "Alice's Creature Creations" scripted on the front. I run my thumb over the raised foil hearts surrounding her name.

"No pets," I say. "But thanks for the card. We'll definitely let you know when we find it."

"Thank you, sweetheart. By the way, when is the service

for Liz? I understand you're planning something at the lake?"

"It's next month — the seventeenth. The time isn't set yet, but we're having it at Point Grace."

"Thanks," she says. "I guess I'll see you then, unless I hear from you about the sweater first."

I slide her card into the cash box under the tens.

"Man, people will buy anything," Patrick says, slipping a few fives into the box after his sudden arrival. "I've been here thirty seconds and some guy handed me fifteen bucks for a bag of old cassettes. Do they even *make* tape players anymore?"

"They make anything," I say. "Just ask Alice." I nod toward the redhead at the aptly labeled "Random Treasures" table now haggling with Aunt Rachel over a set of wooden cutting boards shaped like barn animals.

"Ah yes, Alice Bradley, CEO of Creature Creations. She moved here last year from Boulder. Big hit with the animal rights people. Lucky for you, I haven't started my Christmas shopping yet. Are you a Labrador or German shepherd kind of girl?" Patrick rests his hand on my shoulder and leans in close, whispering in my ear.

"Miss me?" he asks, his breath warm on my skin.

"It's only been a day." *I mean, yes.*

"Only a day? Ah, seems like years since I heard you complain about painting those fence posts."

203

"The fence was yesterday, and I wasn't *complaining*. I was just *saying* that painting is hard work." I try to swat his hand, but he grabs mine and holds on. From her table on the other side of the lawn, Rachel flashes me her "I saw this in your tarot spread ages ago" smirk and I smile back, melting the earlier tension between us.

The long hours of the morning pass like seconds, a steady flow of customers ambling down the driveway to rummage through Nana's old staff. Most of them offer sympathies, and many have long, elaborate stories about the objects on the tables — the fall wedding they attended together when they all got those crocheted maple leaf potholders. The bolts of leopard print fabric divvied up after the community theater's production of *Cats*. The skeleton door knockers the neighborhood kids sold for a school fundraiser one year. They pat my shoulder and frown and ask about the service. The plans. And, by the way, would Mom and Rachel prefer that they bring breakfast or lunch dishes to the house after the burial, or should they just pass around a sign-up sheet?

By the time Em arrives, Rachel's got Patrick lugging boxes up from the basement while I manage a busload of retirees who spent their first twenty minutes here sniffing the encyclopedias.

"Busy, huh?" Em asks. "Awesome."

"Awesome if you like book sniffers."

"I *love* book sniffers! Hey, speaking of freaks, where's Patrick? He said he'd be here today."

"You rang?" Patrick steps out from behind a clothes rack in the driveway with a serving tray in his hand and an old tuxedo jacket buttoned tight over his chest, but before we can fully appreciate the costume, Rachel directs him back to the basement. I watch him cross the lawn, suddenly aware of Emily's eyes, wide and giddy before me.

"Oh my God," she says. "I know that look."

"What? What look?"

"You! *That* look!"

"What are you talking about?"

"Patrick." She lowers her voice to a whisper. "Delilah, are you in love with him?"

"No!" I pull my ponytail over my face.

"*Yes!*"

"I am not. I mean, not like *that*. Just...I don't know... Em, this is totally freaking me out!"

"What? Why?"

"Because it's so intense, you know? And I promised myself I wouldn't get attached like that. Ever."

We pause the girl talk long enough to sell three of the twelve kittens, January through March. Emily tries to make a case for not separating them, but the woman only needs enough for three birthday gifts.

"Delilah," she says after the woman collects her bag of cats, "you can't promise yourself that you're not going to fall in love with someone. I'm not exactly a relationship expert, but I don't think it works that way."

"Em, Patrick lives in New York and I live in Key. That's already one issue. And he's going to college in the fall, and I have no idea what to do with my life. And then...God. There are so many reasons why this is a bad idea."

"You've really worked on this list, haven't you?" Em smiles, and I lower my voice as Patrick makes another trip across the lawn with an overloaded box of sports equipment.

"I look at my parents' situation and it scares the hell out of me. Remember I told you how I never met my father? Well, my mom barely knew him. They met in a bar one night, and they got together, and no one knows what would've happened later because he died overseas on assignment a few days after. He was a journalist."

"Wow, Delilah, I'm so sorry."

"I sigh. The thing is, Mom doesn't talk about it. So I don't know if it was just a one-time thing, or love at first sight, or what. I'll never know. I just know that he's dead and she's alone and all she does is work and I never want to end up like that, ever."

Emily considers my story, rearranging the kittens on the table. "So you'd walk away from someone you're totally in love with because it didn't work out with your parents? Because your father died and your mom is a workaholic? Because you're afraid something bad might happen one day?"

I shrug. "I know it's neurotic, but things in my life are just...*chaos*. That's the best word for it. School. Mom. Stuff at home. I can't deal with a broken heart, Em. Not from someone dying or cheating or living too far away...I just can't. I need to focus on getting my life back together. Stability, you know?"

"Stability?" Emily laughs as Patrick makes a he-man show of setting another of Rachel's boxes in the driveway before disappearing back inside. "Somehow I don't think that's your style."

"I don't know what my style is."

"What about the guys back home?"

I laugh. "There's this one guy Finn, but he doesn't really count. I call him my non-boyfriend."

"Ooh, I had a *non* once. Convenient but meaningless. Extremely short-lived."

"Exactly. But that's what I wanted. And Finn's pretty intense, too, but it's not serious between us. There's no timeline or expectations or promises. No rules. No what-ifs. Just what it is, moment to moment."

"That's cool. I mean, if that's what you want. No strings."

I shake my head. "I always thought I wanted it like that. But when we got to Vermont and everything was so crazy with my mom, it started to put things into perspective. I convinced myself to not think about Finn so I could deal with this family stuff...I mean, things have been kind of messed up at home for a while — not just because of my grandmother dying. I really wanted to...I don't know. Work on things with my mother. I know it sounds all *Oprah* and everything, but it's true. She and I used to be a lot closer, and when I see her now, the way she looks at me sometimes, it just sucks."

"I totally get it. Why do you think I'm up here this summer with my aunt instead of with my parents?"

"I thought you were doing an internship thing."

"I am," Emily says, "but that was just an added benefit. My mother thought it might do me good to be away from home. I get along great with her, but Dad and I have some issues. Actually, 'issues' is putting it mildly." She laughs, directing a man to the rest of the outdated music collection on another table. "So how is the *Oprah* stuff going?"

"It's a total roller coaster with Mom and Rachel," I say. "As far as boys...I was doing okay not thinking about Finn, or any other guy, but then I met Patrick, and everything flipped upside down. Ever since he kissed me, things —"

"Oh my God, he kissed you? Why am I the last to know these things?"

"Shh! Don't let everyone hear you!" I laugh, lowering my voice to give her the highlights version of that night at Luna's.

"Okay, best first kiss story *ever*," Em says. "Even though you bailed right after. It still counts. What happened next?"

"The next day was Sugarbush," I continue, "and things got even more intense."

"Did he kiss you again?" she asks, blue eyes lighting up like the lake on a sunny day.

"Um, yeah. There's pretty much been a *lot* of kissing since that night. And now, even though I had all these rules for myself at the beginning of the summer, I can't stop thinking about him. I don't know what to do."

"This is not a bad problem to have," Emily says, rubbing my knee. "First, what about Finn? Are you done with him?"

"Who's Finn?" Other than the first few days here and the one time when he called, I really *haven't* thought about my non-boyfriend since I left Key.

"Good answer," Em says, both of us laughing until the middle-aged man standing before us clears his throat, Papa's fishing tackle box in one hand and two ladies slips in the other, beige and black.

"It's a long story," he says as if our laughter demands an explanation from him.

I bag up his purchases and he tells us to keep the change and Emily and I are near hysterical when Patrick emerges in a pair of fake alligator heels, a gold lamé housecoat, and a curly, gray-haired wig studded with neon butterfly clips.

"Welcome to Red Falls," Patrick says in a husky voice. "I hope you're enjoying your authentic New England experience."

"What were you saying about stability?" Emily asks, wiping the tears from her face as the last customer cashes out without saying a word.

"I think we're done for the morning," Rachel says, snapping a picture with her cell phone before pulling the wig from Patrick's head. "We're going to end up in the town jail for disturbing the peace."

"Don't worry," Em says. "I don't think there is a town jail."

Rachel laughs. "Either way. I think I've seen enough of the good people of Red Falls until after lunch. You guys want eggplant parm? Big hit at the Telluride Film Festival. Those people know their veggies."

"I actually need to head out," Em says. "I have to pack. I'm taking the bus to Montreal first thing tomorrow to visit my . . . this . . . some friends. That I know there."

"When are you coming back?" I ask.

"Saturday. I won't be at Patrick's gig on Wednesday. Take good notes if his fan club does anything to embarrass him, okay?"

"Of course." I hug her good-bye and unfold a pale green sheet to spread over the "Random Treasures" table, covering the rows of crystal salt dips and gray Spackleware dishes. On the other end of the table, between the demitasse cups and miniature Matchbox cars, the noon sun reflects from the center of a small metal box — the pink jeweled one I saw on Nana's dresser that night I was in her room. Something calls me to it now, different from the last time I saw it, like maybe there's some long-buried memory attached to it. I *know* this box. Not from the dresser, but from before. I hold it up to the light. The memory continues to evade me, poking at me from a faraway place but refusing to make itself fully known.

Will I ever get any closer to the story of my family than I am right now?

I slip the box into my pocket, stuffing the requested three dollars into the cash box as Rachel flips the OPEN sign to the BE BACK SOON side and heads in for lunch.

Chapter twenty-four

Thanks to the post–July Fourth vacationer's exodus, Luna's isn't as crowded for Patrick's Wednesday gig, but his fan club is assembled at the front of the stage — Jezebel and the Tube Top Committee and a few other people from last time.

"Does Em have off tonight?" I ask Patrick.

"Montreal, remember? She'll be back this weekend."

"Oh, right."

"You gonna be okay?" he asks, his hand cupping the side of my face. The skin tingles where he touches me, and I hear the echo of Emily's words...

Are you in love with him?

"I'm great," I say. Satisfied, Patrick heads to the stage, and I smile to reassure us both.

When the house lights finally dim, the stage lights bathe Patrick in a rainbow glow, all heads turning toward him as he strums his first notes. I recognize the song — the one he played for me the night we were alone on that very stage, chords and lyrics finally perfected.

Watching Patrick perform is like watching marathoners or cyclists hit their stride, just when the adrenaline kicks in and keeps pushing them and they know everything is going to be okay, ever more excited, ever more out of their own bodies. Patrick *becomes* the music, fingers melting into guitar melting into him melting into songs, and for a time I envy him, freely throwing himself into the deep end of his passion.

The Luna's crowd is small but powerful tonight, people cheering and dancing as Patrick plays their favorite songs. I love being part of it all, seeing how much he's changed, and how much he hasn't — everyone falling instantly and hopelessly in love with him as always, stage lights or not, right through his voice and down to his soul — and when he looks out over the crowd and winks at me, I know that of all the girls shouting and blowing kisses and dreaming about him tonight, I'm the one he'll seek when the music fades; my hand is the one he'll reach for when the lights go dark.

＊　　＊　　＊

"You were stellar tonight," I say as we walk home side by side, a stack of song sheets folded under my arm. "Seriously. How do you do it? Don't you get nervous in front of all those people?"

"Doesn't matter how many people are in the crowd anymore, Delilah. Ten or ten thousand, I'm still only singing for one." He squeezes my hand as the crickets hum their own music around us, and I stop and pull him into a kiss.

"I wish your dad could hear you sing, Patrick. I know he'd understand. If he came to Luna's and —"

"He can't, Del. He just can't." Patrick smoothes the spot between my eyebrows with his thumb, erasing the lines. "Hey, I've got you. I've got this guitar. It's summer. We're here. What else, right?" He smiles, but the sadness in his eyes gives it all away, and on we go.

When we reach the lake house, the lights are out and the car's gone from the driveway. Jack's not home, either. Patrick looks from the dark windows at his house to the ones here and back to me, smiling mischievously as we walk together to the blue-and-white Victorian.

The hairs on the back of my neck are electrified. Upstairs, Patrick closes the door to his bedroom and I instantly feel it — that edge of forbiddenness. I've been in the *house* a few times since our Red Falls arrival, but never upstairs. Never here. Not since the days when we had the same size Converse

214

high-tops — mine turquoise, his red — and we swapped the left ones so we'd each have different color shoes. It takes a moment for my heart to relax, its quick hop finally slowing to a normal beat like eyes adjusting to the sudden dark.

Patrick's bedroom smells like soap and guitar polish and New England summer air, sweet and clean. I look over the pale blue of the walls, the books on the shelves, the concert posters wallpapering the perimeter. I don't remember his room from the last time I saw it; being here before was about games and toys and bug collections. There wasn't the overanalyzing. The aching, needful search for photos or flowery trinket clues about others who may have entered during the long stretch between my last summer in Red Falls and tonight.

But I don't see any. No photo-booth strips of kissing, funny-faced girls stuck in his mirror. No stuffed animals or dried flowers or phone numbers scrawled on little pieces of paper. Just the posters and clothes and an orange-yellow coffee can from Café du Monde in New Orleans, full of loose change. He empties the contents of his pockets into it as I pretend not to notice.

Patrick turns the stereo on low and pulls his shirt off over his head, tossing it onto the end of his bed and digging through a folded pile on his dresser for a new one.

"Hey, how did you get that scar?" I nod toward his arm and the long, light ridge cutting down from shoulder to elbow like a seam. "I've been meaning to ask."

He turns his head to look at it. "Oh, it's a really gross story involving a rusty nail and a clumsy step on the ladder last year. The important thing is that I was up-to-date on my shots."

"I stepped on a piece of glass in the kitchen last summer." I sit on the edge of the bed and slide my foot out of my flip-flop to show him a thin, white scar on the bottom of my heel. He tosses the clean shirt over his shoulder, takes my foot in his hand, and traces the line with his finger.

"That's nothing," he says. "Check this out." He lifts the cuff of his shorts to reveal a wide, jagged ditch of a scar cross-wise on his upper thigh. "A souvenir from Colorado two summers ago. We were white-water rafting and got dumped. I slammed into a hunk of limestone. It cut down to the bone."

"Whoa." I stand up to get a closer look.

"Medevac, forty-nine stitches, and a blood transfusion," he says. "Top that."

"Well, I bit through my bottom lip in sixth grade falling off the parallel bars in gym class. Two stitches, but you can't really see the scar." I make a pout to show him.

"Are you serious? Come here." He grabs me by the shoulders, pulling me an inch from his face, looking very intently at my mouth. "I don't see anything. Oh, wait…" He squints to get a better look, taking my face in his hands and tilting it toward his. "I think I see it now."

I try to swallow, but it's impossible with my head upturned, the soft pale of my throat stretched out before him, the silver heart of Nana's necklace hot on my skin.

"Yes, right there," he whispers, his finger sweeping delicately across my lips, and then...

I lean into his kiss, pulling him toward me, wanting to feel him around me like a hot bath. The longer we kiss, the deeper I fall, headfirst into this roiling sea. His hands move slowly beneath my shirt, light against my stomach, smooth and warm, buttons coming undone, sun-touched skin heating up and pressing together as we lie back on his bed. With his bare chest against me, he unhooks my bra with one hand and breathes into my ear and I feel my toes stretch and curl, my back arching to meet him.

There is no more denying my feelings for him, no more lying to myself about control, no more weighing out the pros and cons, no more comparisons and warnings and walls. I'm tumbling and turning somersaults in the water, no way to know which end is up, which means certain death, which promises all the air I need to breathe. It reminds me of that last day in Connecticut with Mom, when the sun finally came out and we got to swim in the ocean. No lifeguard. No way to see or feel or sense the bottom. Just us and the water and the exhilarating knowledge that it could crush the bones of our hearts, swiftly and completely, should the tide turn.

"What was that?" I ask, pushing against his chest.

"What?"

"Sounded like the front door."

"Are you —"

"Patrick? You home?" Jack's voice echoes up the stairs as he drops his keys on the table in the front hall.

"Shit!" Patrick leaps off the bed in search of his shirt. I pull mine on so fast that when Jack opens the door, I've got a pink-and-white striped demi bra shoved under my legs and my arms are crossed over my thrown-on, inside-out top as if I'm cold.

"Oh, hey, Delilah. I didn't know you guys were up here." Jack looks from me sitting on the edge of the bed to Patrick wiping his guitar case with a rag on the other side of the room. I feel the cooler air rush in from the hall and wonder if this is the part where the oxygen sucks in against the fire, just before the whole room goes up in flames.

"You kids hungry?" Jack asks, giving Patrick a "we'll talk about this later" glare.

"No, thanks," I say. I'm still afraid to move my arms. "I should go. Mom and Rachel will probably be back soon." I return his smile and wait for him to leave so I can fix my shirt and wriggle back into my bra.

"I don't know what's more difficult," Patrick says when Jack's finally gone, slipping his arms around me again. "Not seeing you for eight years while you're hundreds of miles away, or finding you again, seeing you every day, thinking about you constantly, knowing that you're sleeping fifty feet from my window when all I want to do is *this*."

His mouth covers mine and I fall for another minute into the hot press of his lips. I hear Jack calling again and push my hand against Patrick's chest, both of us nearly out of breath.

"For the record," I say, "I won't be sleeping tonight."

"Perfect." Patrick grins and pulls me into another kiss, his next words muffled and undecipherable as they crash like unguarded ocean waves against my lips.

Chapter twenty-five

As July stretches and slides into August, I slip into a state of near-constant daydream, my physical body complying with the endless estate sales and manual labor at the lake house while my mind wanders from the shadows of Stephanie's death to the diary, from my grandparents to Mom and Rachel, from summer memories of honeysuckle and fireflies and maple sugar candy to that night in Patrick's bedroom.

When no one is watching and our work is done and my mind is still, we draw each other close again — his lips brushing mine on the far side of the house; my hands in his hair under cover of the big weeping willow out front; tiny bits and pieces mixed into the hours of work or the free time we share with Em. It's almost enough to make me forget the weight of all that lies ahead: burying my grandmother. Selling the last of her belongings. Selling the house. Saying good-bye.

It's late one rainy night when I drift downstairs for a cup of hot tea with Patrick's copy of *Catcher in the Rye*. He left notes for me in the margins of all the best parts, and we vowed to do the same after Red Falls, marking up and exchanging our favorite books so that through them we can still know each other, even if I can't visit him as often as I'd like. After all my time muddling in the past, the future seems like a foreign land in which I understand neither the language nor the culture, wanting nothing more than a one-way ticket back to the present. There's still a month left. I don't want to think about the fall and the distance between Key and New York City just yet.

Rachel is out with Megan tonight, late as always, but when I reach the living room, I realize that I'm not alone in my nocturnal wandering.

"Mom? You're still up?" I sit next to her on the couch. "I thought you had an early call tomorrow."

She nods, pulling her robe close around her neck. Her eyes are shot with red, and I follow their gaze to the photograph on her lap. It's the three Hannaford sisters, Mom and Rachel on either side of Stephanie, arms tangled around one another, Stephanie whispering in Mom's ear as she giggles beneath her long brown pigtails.

"How old are you guys there?" I ask.

221

"Ten, eight, and six," she says. "Give or take."

"You look like triplets."

"Everyone used to say that," she says. "God, look at her. Look at those eyes. All those freckles. She seems so happy, doesn't she?"

She sighs, her Claire-Hannaford-Speaking smile locked in the desk drawer for the night. It's the same frail woman from our first day in Vermont. The same one from the cemetery on her sister's birthday.

For so long, Mom and I worked around our mutual distance as if it was just another part of the family. As much as I wanted everything out in the open, now I feel the hollow between us: a deep, fresh wound where the ghosts of the past used to live. I did that. I opened it and let them out, digging and scraping and clawing, insisting that there was more to the story of my family than Mom was willing to share.

Stephanie was depressed, like her mother. And though she loved Casey and her sisters and her friends, love wasn't enough to save her. Whatever was going on in her head in the time that followed her last diary entry, the things and the people in her life were not enough to save her. She ended it, and whether it was accidental or intentional, the result was the same. She's gone. Like Papa. Like Nana. Like the eight missing summers we didn't spend in Red Falls. Maybe Mom and Megan were both right. Maybe some things really are that simple, and other things have a lot more layers, and the only thing that's ours to accept is the fact that we don't always get to *know* the answers.

I look at Mom, slumped on the other end of the couch, longing for what could have been… It doesn't matter what caused the fight eight years ago. It really doesn't. We stopped coming here, and now there's no one left in our family to visit. Soon the house will be gone and Red Falls really *will* be a memory. All we can do now is move on.

"I'm sorry, Mom."

She turns her head slowly to face me, her eyes widening.

"I'm sorry about your sister, and about everything that happened this year, and that I pushed so hard about all the stuff with Nana and the fight. I didn't mean to bring up the past again. It was selfish." I think about that trip to Connecticut Mom and I took, and celebrating her promotion, and the picture with the bubbles, and how even after everything that changed, I still love her; I'd still be willing to trade it all in for a new start if she'd take the offer.

"Like you said," I continue, "it's all in the past. It doesn't matter anymore. I don't want things to be like this with us… all this fighting and tension and weirdness."

Mom takes a sharp breath, pulling me into a hug.

"I miss you, Mom." My throat clenches around the words like a child's fist around a dandelion bouquet, tears rolling hot on my cheeks, and I finally understand that it has never been about the secrets or the truth or the ghosts. I just miss my mother. I miss knowing how to make her smile. I miss being important in her life.

Mom doesn't say anything, but she's crying, hugging me tighter and tighter like we'll break into pieces if she lets go. Then, she's shaking. Really shaking.

"Are you okay?" I ask. "What's wrong?"

"I didn't want it to be like this," she says. Her voice is barely audible.

"Me neither, Mom. Things were just so weird... I couldn't remember what happened here, and my mind invented stories and I just kept getting more scared that someday we'd end up the same way that you and Nana did. I didn't want —"

"Oh, Delilah!" She pulls away from me, hands digging into my shoulders now, eyes narrowed at mine. Something urgent rises in her face, the presence of it suddenly large and forceful, chilling my skin. I've never seen her so shaken, so sorry, so used-up. It scares me. It scares me more than all the times I had to sit in the living room as she told me about the school principal calling her at work. More than when she picked me up from the security office at Blush Cosmetics and more than when she caught me sneaking back in the window the night she found out Nana died.

I wonder if Thomas can see all of this — all of us. I wonder if he still thinks about my mother and whether he likes the woman she became after he died. I wonder if he really knows about me. If he does, he doesn't say; no message or sign to fill up the cold spaces in the room.

I meet her intense gaze. "It doesn't matter, Mom. You don't have to say anything."

She nods quickly, sliding the tin of pills from her bathrobe pocket and pressing one on her tongue. She reaches for her water glass and takes several big gulps. Then she sets it back on the table, looks at the ceiling, and sucks in a deep breath as if convincing herself to jump from the highest dock on the edge of the lake. And then she does it. She jumps.

"Delilah, Thomas Devlin is not your father."

Splash.

I see her mouth moving as the room swirls around her, filling with water so that everything goes in slow motion, blurred and muffled. I can hear my heart beat in my ears and the waves on the lake and the crickets, all the way out in the wheat grass, humming in their same low buzz, the big old world spinning by as it ought to.

Then it's as though two giant hands wrench me from the water, throwing me to the shore. I take a sharp breath as Mom opens her mouth to speak again.

"There's more. Listen to me. You have to know the whole truth."

I don't want to listen. My body is numb. I can't feel my skin. I keep telling my feet to move, my legs to unglue and lift me off the couch and carry me away, but they don't. They just sit here, waiting for my heart to explode.

Mom looks at me with big, sad, please-forgive-me eyes, and I almost want to. To let it go. To crawl into her lap and sob and tell her it doesn't matter, don't say anything else, let's just let it all go.

"It's about Stephanie," she says.

Stephanie Delilah Hannaford. I look at the picture between us on the couch and think of the name carved into the headstone and the diary and all the haunted dreams for the aunt I never knew. I wonder if we would have been close; if she and I were alike. Was she like Mom, serious and controlled? Or Rachel, spirited and a little zany? If she lived, could she have bridged the gulf in our family history? Would any of this be happening now? *What if? Maybe. What if? Maybe.*

Mom's voice trembles. "She was our baby, Delilah. Our little baby bird. We loved her so much. She was so young and beautiful, and when she got sick — really sick — her spark was gone. It just went out, and none of us knew how to turn it back on. The night of her funeral, her boyfriend, Casey..." Mom goes a little whiter, and though it kills me to see it, I don't interrupt or ask questions. I make her go through it. I make her tell me exactly what happened because deep down inside, beneath all the hurt and anger and disbelief and bile, I hang on to some small shard of hope that I'm wrong about this.

"Casey was so angry," she continues. "Angry at himself, angry at God, angry at Mom and Dad and us for not being able to see how sick she was in time to save her. He was even mad at Stephanie for leaving him before they could start their life together. He was only twenty-one — so young. We all were.

"I was sitting on the end of the dock the night we buried her, long after we watched them lower her into the ground. Trying to go back in time to fix whatever I needed to fix to prevent her death. Trying to make sense of everything. Trying not to jump in and slip away. The moon was high over the frozen lake. The light was so bright, I hated it for shining that night. Stephanie was under the ground, deep in the earth, and we'd never see her light again. How dare the moon rise? I was alone, shivering in the cold. Sobbing. Pounding my fists into the dock. Then I heard someone behind me. It was Casey. His hand squeezed my shoulder. He sat down next to me and put his head to my chest and sobbed. Both of us wept...then it happened."

Mom reaches again for the water, taking big gulps until the glass goes dry.

"What happened?" *Please, please let me be wrong.*

"We went to his car to warm up. No one was around. We...it was a desperate moment between two broken souls, Delilah. It was over almost as soon as it started, and we vowed never to speak of it again."

"Are you saying...did you...with your dead sister's *boyfriend?"*

"Delilah, I'm saying that Casey Conroy is your father."

Echoes of overheard arguments flash through my head, all the blanks filling in now.

Why don't you just talk to her about it?

Casey.

It's way too complicated.

Casey.

She's not an eight-year-old kid anymore, Claire.

Casey.

My mind is a tie-dye swirl of too many things — blurred images of Mom and some faceless guy on the dock, Aunt Stephanie filling her mouth with pills, Aunt Rachel and her tarot cards, Thomas Devlin tacked on my bulletin board at home, Patrick and Finn and Emily and funerals and fights and everything in between. It's all upside down and inside out, mismatched and chipped and forgotten like Nana's old dishes, and it's coming at me too fast to make any sense. In their rush to attack, all the words get jumbled up and stuck in the back of my throat. I can't speak.

"The day of your grandfather's funeral," Mom continues, "I confided in Aunt Rachel. You were eight. Until that moment, she believed that your father was Thomas Devlin. But my mother overheard, and —"

"That's what caused the fight?" I ask, finding my voice again. "That's why we left Red Falls that day?"

"That's part of it, Delilah, but it's complicated. There's a lot more to it."

For so long, she poured her energy into creating a home for this deceit, to tending and nurturing it. She kept it to the detriment of all else — her relationship with her mother. With Rachel. With me. And now, all I want to do is crush her heart.

"No, there really isn't, Mom. It's pretty simple. You slept with your dead sister's boyfriend on the night of her funeral and your family found out. No wonder Nana stopped speaking to you. No wonder she never tried to find me — she must've hated me when she found out. All because of *you*."

"Please, Delilah. Please try to understand. I was only a few years older than you are now. I didn't —"

"I can't believe I'm related to you. I can't believe my own mother would do something so low. You're *repulsive!*"

It stings her, but I don't care. She *is* repulsive. Everything about her disgusts me. Her stupid bathrobe and her wavy hair and her hands-free earpiece and her voice and her small hands and her hazel eyes with the brown triangle. For the woman who calls me *daughter*, there is nothing left but hate and revulsion.

"I deserve that," she says softly, looking at her hands. "I kept this from you. I know it's hard to hear the truth after so many years. I know you —"

"You don't know *anything* about me!" I shout across the living room. In three steps, I'm at the front entrance, flinging myself out into the rain as the wind sucks the door shut behind me.

Chapter twenty-six

Patrick is outside in a heartbeat, his phone still glowing from my frantic text.

"Put this on," he says, handing me a jacket and pulling a sweatshirt over his head. I don't have shoes and I can't even feel how cold I am, but I do as he asks, no strength in me to resist.

We back down the driveway and onto Maple Terrace in the Reese & Son Contracting truck, heading toward the desolate south side of the lake. Patrick doesn't ask any questions, but I feel his eyes on me, alternating from the road to my face and back again to the road as his hand brushes my cheek.

"We'll go to Heron Point, okay?" he asks. "We can talk there."

I don't feel like talking. I take his hand from my face but keep it pressed in mine, resting on the top of my thigh. He rubs my palm with his thumb, his other hand tight on the wheel.

The rain comes down harder, forcing Patrick to squint to find the turnoff for Heron Point. He follows a paved path into the grass at the edge of the sand and cuts the engine. Together, we face out against the all-encompassing blackness of the lake, each waiting for the other to break the silence.

Without the windshield wipers, the rain washes over the windows like waves, blurring everything until it feels like we're submerged. He shifts from beneath the steering wheel, closer to me in the front seat. His arms are around me tight, one hand warm across my shoulders, the other holding my head against his chest.

"It's okay, baby. It's okay." He rubs my back, reassuring, kissing the top of my head and smoothing the hair from my face. My heart expands and contracts, banging against my ribs like the cardinal trapped in the sunroom, looking for a way out. I don't know if it's the blood racing too fast or the late hour or the rain pounding furiously against the roof of the truck, but something inside me switches off. I don't want to tell him what happened. I don't want him to know about my cheating father and my weak mother and all of the lies. I dug up the past and sifted through the rubble and counted all the bones, and now I want to throw them all back in the hole under a hundred shovels full of earth. To *forget*. To erase it all, just like before, lying in the woods with my shoulders pressed into the dirt and the old Seven Mile Creek rushing past, sweeping it all away.

I wrap my fingers around his wrists and pull his hands from my face, pinning them down as I climb on top of him. I press my body against his like it's all that will keep us from being carried off in the storm. I feel him shift beneath me, his breath going shallow as I release his wrists. His hands find their way up my back, resting on my neck and pulling my face to his.

He takes a breath and opens his mouth as if to speak, but I don't let him. I kiss him and I want only to get close to him, *closer*, as close as possible, pulling his sweatshirt over his head so I can feel the heat of his chest through my clothes. The wind howls against the truck, pounding us with rain louder than his quickening breath in my ear, but in here, we're sharing the same air, and that's enough. It has to be. That's all there is.

I slip out of my jacket and T-shirt. His hands move over the skin on my back and I reach down to the waist of his shorts, fingers brushing lightly against his hip bone.

"Delilah," he says, hot and breathless on my neck. "Del, wait."

I ignore him. I kiss away his words. He stops protesting for a moment, but something holds him back.

"What is it?" I ask, barely breathing. "What's wrong?"

"We can't." His hand is flat on my chest now, holding my heart together, keeping everything from exploding out. His fingertips reach my collarbone and push me gently, a whisper-thin force that stands in the way of the inevitable end of things between us. The grand finale. The fireworks, exploding in a bright weeping willow star across the sky, falling down in a rain of smoke and ash.

Poof...

"This isn't what you want?" I ask.

"We can't do this, Delilah."

"Yes we can. No one is out here but us."

"It's not that. It's just —"

"I thought you *wanted* to be with me."

"Delilah," he whispers. "You're killing me, you know that?" His eyes are sad and deep and full of fire even in the dark of the storm, holding mine just inches away. "I haven't had one innocent thought since you came back to Red Falls."

"Then why are we still talking about this?" I kiss his face along the firm line of his jaw, but the mood is already shifting, my lips going cool in the absence of his.

"No. Not like this. I'll probably kill myself for this tomorrow," he says, his eyes closed, "but I can't let you do this when you're all freaked out."

"Patrick, I'm not freaked out."

"You don't remember that text you just sent? The look on your face when I came outside? Now? Come on."

"I'll be *fine*."

"You'll regret it. And so will I. Something happened at the house tonight, and maybe you can't tell me about it right now, but I'm not going to let you self-destruct."

"So now you're a fucking shrink? *Please*. Maybe you should stick to fixing houses and guitar strings."

"Oh, Delilah," he whispers, honey eyes and stupid, stupid dimples fighting against a frown. "Don't. Please, don't."

I see the hurt filling him like water in a broken glass, but I can't stop. "Forget it. All of it."

"Del —"

I grab my shirt and pull it back on over my head, untangling my arms and legs and throwing myself out of the truck.

"Wait!" Patrick comes after me, shirtless, following me to the shore. The rain flies at us sideways in a million cold little needles, but I'm going numb.

He shouts over the noise of the wind. "I'm sorry, okay? I'm *sorry*! Get back in the truck so we can talk!"

"I don't want to talk! Talking is what keeps messing me up!"

He tries to grab my hands, but I snatch them away. Seeing him shivering and dripping with rain and rage and fear and something else I can't name because it hurts too much to imagine — I can't breathe. I almost don't want to.

"I thought you wanted to be with me, Patrick."

"I do," he says. "More than anything."

I shout at him on the shore. "How can I believe you? You

can't even tell your father about the career you want most in this whole world. Your life is a lie. So go hide behind your bullshit music and just pretend I never came back here this summer."

It hurts him. I know, because it hurts me to say it, words slapped against faces like an open palm, raw on sensitive skin.

"Oh, so you're untouchable, huh, Delilah? You and your fucked-up relationship with your mother and everyone else in your life? Great. Does getting pissed at me make it better? Does it fix *anything*?"

"You! Can't! Fix! Me!" I'm screaming now, howling over the lake and the rain and the wind. "You can't just be my best friend all summer and make me feel all these amazing things and then turn around like none of it means anything! You're making me crazy!"

"Delilah Hannaford, *you* are making *me* crazy! Don't you get it?"

"What's to get? You're just —"

"I'm in love with you!"

Patrick stands there in the rain, illuminated by intermittent flashes of lightning. For a second, I forget everything. I forget the rain and all the words we've hurled and I think about him onstage, colored lights flashing around him, smiling and laughing like everything in the world is just *our* thing, his and mine.

But when the lightning stops, I can only see the sadness in

his face, wet hair hanging on him like it was flung there, rain running into his eyes and mouth.

I turn my back and run away on bare feet, cutting through the storm and following the shore to the docks and bleachers at the bottom of what I hope is Nana's hill.

Patrick doesn't come after me, but when I finally get back to the house, he's waiting near the porch in the shadow of the maple trees. The rain and the long jog home tamped out my anger, leaving only a deep gash in my heart and one on my shin from crashing into the docks in the dark. He walks toward me when he sees me trudging up the hill, his hands suddenly on my arms. I want to collapse into him. I want to tell him how I fell in love with him under the bleachers the moment he turned his hat around and smiled and his honey eyes lit up brighter than the sun, even though it took me this long to let myself believe it.

But I can't. I don't.

"Are you all right?" he asks, hands tightening on me as he looks down at my shin.

"It's just a cut."

"Good. Go inside." His hands unclamp from my arms.

"Patrick, wait." I lunge for him, grasping at nothing in the place where he used to be as he turns back toward his house. I run to catch up, trying unsuccessfully to lace my fingers in his. He stops, but he won't look at me, not even when I put my hands on his face.

"Patrick... I'm so sorry."

"Don't, okay? Just don't." He finally looks at me when he says it, his eyes black and icy as he pulls my hands from his face. I watch him leave. I watch him walk away. And I wait forever for him to turn around, to come back, to forgive me, to kiss me again in the rain like nothing else matters.

But he doesn't. He fades into the shadows and never looks back, leaving me exposed by the soft yellow light of the porch, rain falling all around me.

Chapter twenty-seven

"Delilah!" Mom is in the kitchen in that awful bathrobe, rocking on her feet like she's trying to decide whether to run over and hug me or launch into another lecture about my poor decisions.

It's late, I don't know what time, and seeing Mom with her twisted-up face and her arms folded and the coffeepot sputtering reminds me of that night in early June, a thousand years ago after Finn dropped me off and I crawled through my bedroom window to find out about Nana's death and our unplanned trip back to Red Falls.

"Are you okay?" Mom crosses the room in two giant steps. When she puts her arms around me, I move to shake free, but she only holds me tighter. I almost give in to the smell of her perfume and the softness of the robe against my cheek. My chest aches, my head is throbbing, my shin is bleeding, my body is shivering, and I just want her to promise me. To hold on to me and mean it and make it all disappear.

But I can't pretend anymore, and neither can she. I can't even look at her face when I push her arms away.

Upstairs, I shed my wet clothes and try to lose myself in a searing shower, inhaling big gulps of steam with my eyes closed, hot water pruning my skin. All I can see is Patrick's face, pleading at the beach, the chill between us at the end. The weight of my own heavy heart drags me down; I want to carve it out and leave it in the basement in one of the old canning jars, shelved right between the colored Christmas tree lights and the Ouija board. To go on without a care, without fear and doubt and regret. For everything in my life to be like that trip to Connecticut when just watching a hermit crab scurry through the sand was enough to amaze and elate me for an entire year.

Back in the bedroom, I look through the window for a sign from Patrick, a light, a movement from his bedroom to give me even the tiniest sliver of hope. But all along the stretch of space between my room and his, there is nothing, nothing but blackness, nothing but emptiness seeping into the night like blood.

I'm pacing, pacing the small box of this bedroom as words and pictures whir and crash together in my head. My mother telling me about my real father. Aunt Rachel, still out with Megan and unaware of the storm exploding at the lake house. The town of Red Falls and every single person who knows more about my family history than I do. And me, charging out. Stomping away. Spitting venom at the one person in all of Vermont who least deserves it.

I call Patrick's cell. He doesn't answer. The light in his room doesn't click on. I call again. Again and again and again and oh my *God* I'm going out of my mind as I walk the planks of the room from one end to the other, wishing. Wondering. Hoping. *What if? Maybe. What if? Maybe.*

The mason jar of Nana's mismatched buttons shines from the top of the dresser, undaunted as my hand lunges forward. Fingers curl around it, the veins beneath my skin pulled into small blue ropes as I heft the glass above my shoulder. The buttons *click clack, click clack* inside, huddling together as I arch back and throw it, as hard as I can, all of them at once sling-shotted and shattered against the wall, broken glass and buttons like a billion brilliant rain-stones *plink-plink-plinkering* to the floor.

"Delilah?!" Mom's voice arrives first, her body a split-second later in the doorway, mouth and eyes wide over everything shiny and broken and me in my bare feet, watching the light reflect in the glass.

"Are you hurt?" She tiptoes her way around it to reach me. She whispers. Her hands hover over me like the seagulls over the lake, gliding and floating and skirting.

"What do you think," I say. It's not a question.

"Delilah, we have to talk about —"

"No, we don't."

The seagull dives; Mom's hand squeezes my arm, too tight.

"Don't touch me! Don't you ever fucking touch me again!" I knock against her shoulder and push through the doorway, cutting my toe on a piece of glass. I'm on the stairs now, and hell yes, I'm leaving. No money, no food, no bags, wet hair, bloody foot, bloody shin, but I'm walking out that door and into the street and up, up, up as far north as I can go before I die.

And *bienvenue au fucking Canada*, I'm not coming back.

She follows me, each of us taking two stairs at a time to keep up with the accusations. *I* don't understand what it's like to lose a sister. *She's* a monster for keeping me from my real father. *I* should show some maturity and compassion. *She* should go to hell.

When Mom and I reach the kitchen, Rachel is standing in the doorway, purse clutched in her hand, mouth just hanging open over her *Well-Behaved Women Seldom Make History* sweatshirt like she's some kind of statue from the Susan B. Anthony wax museum.

"You wanna smash things, Delilah? Okay. Let's smash things." Mom ignores her sister, flinging open the glass-front kitchen cupboards to expose the rows of mismatched dishes not yet tagged for the final sale, all the plates and saucers and table decorations Nana collected from gift exchanges and

241

grocery store giveaways and other people's kitchens. I grab a coffee mug with a picture of a sleepy-faced puppy that says "Mornings are Hard!" and slam it on the floor. Mom mirrors me with two unrelated dinner plates, scattering orange and white porcelain flowers across the tile.

"What the hell is going on?" Rachel yells, finally finding her voice.

I keep smashing, breaking two more ugly coffee mugs with stupid-cute animal sayings as Mom, who is clearly out of Xanax, recaps the evening's events for her sister at warp speed.

Mom and Aunt Rachel are arguing again, but I can't hear their words. I'm still dropping dishes, thinking in slow motion about the GPS woman in Mom's car. I imagine her beckoning me from outside the kitchen window, illuminated like some robot-angel, calling me forth to the Lexus where she will ferry me off to that planet of monotonous peace, that special, otherworldly place where all the residents are relaxed and confident and completely numb.

Your life will. Get better in. Six. Point four. Million. Miles.

Voices escalate as Rachel tries to sweep up some of the dish shards, but I'm still not listening. I grab the thing on the kitchen counter nearest my outstretched hand. The Hannaford sisters see me and read my mind and their eyes get round in their heads as I look at them with my arm held high over everything, daring them to say a *single* word.

"Delilah, *no*! Not the blue —"

Rachel and Mom reach for me, all four arms like tentacles springing forth and then recoiling as I slam the stupid blue cow creamer hard into the sink.

"*Delft.*" Rachel's voice shrinks away. "Goddamn it, that ugly cow was the only thing worth any real money in this entire house."

I hover over the sink and peer down at the pieces of her, ass end up in the drain, beheaded and de-legged. She's broken. I'm broken. The fight in both of us is spent.

"Four thousand dollars," Mom says, waving her hand over the basin, the edges in her voice smoothing out. "Right down the drain."

That's it.

All the madness leaks out of the room like air from a balloon, making way for the insane laughter that follows. Rachel first, then Mom, and soon the three of us are cracking up like it's double-dose day at the crazy house.

"That cow was the most ridiculous..."

"Of all the stupid trinkets..."

"*Moooo!*"

When I can no longer discern the laughing from the crying, after all of the running and screaming and dish-dodging, after all of the hating, my legs give out. I slide to the floor, leaning against the cupboard under the sink.

Rachel and Mom slide down on either side of me.

243

We sit there listening to one another's heartbeats and jagged breaths for a long time, waiting for someone to tell us what to do, to show us how to make everything right. No one volunteers.

Eventually, we move to the living room, away from all the broken things. There isn't a lot of talking. I fade in and out like an old radio, vaguely aware of Rachel cleaning my toe and shin with anti-bacterial stuff that smells like peppermint but doesn't sting. Mom unfolds the blanket from the back of the couch and covers me with it.

It feels like another dream.

"Do you remember that time Dad went shopping for a used car after that old Chevy died?" Aunt Rachel whispers to Mom.

"He came home with an ice cream truck," she says, on the edge of laughter.

"The music trickled in the front door..." Rachel says.

"And we ran out to see..." *Mom.*

"It was Dad..." *Rachel.*

"Free ice cream for everyone!" *Mom.*

"The look on her face..."

"...slept on the couch for a week!"

"And when they finally had to take his leg..."

"'*That settles that!*' Mom said."

"Ah, that music!"

"Deedle la dee da dee da dee da dee..."

"Are we going to be okay, Rach?" Mom asks at the end of it. If Rachel responds, I don't hear. Sleep finally invades my body, carrying me up off the couch, out of the living room, out of Red Falls, and out of the world. Mom and Rachel blur and disappear. Outside, a light breeze jostles the rainwater from the maples and my entire mind goes as endless and black as the midnight sky.

Chapter twenty-eight

I'm the first one awake. Through the kitchen, the sun is shining white-hot against the windowpanes and the lake beyond is as blue and promising as ever, all evidence of last night's storm forgotten.

My head aches. My throat is raw and tight.

The new light of day sharpens the pain by degrees: the harsh contrast of sunshine and hope against the angry things that came out since I last saw the morning sky.

It wasn't that many hours ago.

Most of the dish shards have been swept into a pile in the corner, but the Delft cow is still in pieces, ass end up in the sink. I dig through the kitchen drawers for some Super Glue to make her whole again, setting her to heal on the windowsill behind the red-and-gold roosters marching across the curtains.

When Mom and Rachel join me downstairs, we pass one another in the kitchen, everything around us slow and heavy as though we're walking underwater. *Did you eat?* Mom wants to know. *Are there any clean mugs?* Rachel. She opens the window behind Moo and lights a sage stick. Mom comments on the sunshine and the lake, and I nod and shrug and none of us means any of it so I decide to hide out in the basement with a box of granola bars and some bottled waters, still dressed in the pajamas I put on last night before all the smashing. Jack is coming over to work on the sunroom and Patrick won't be with him and nothing else matters.

I don't know how long I sort through the final musty shelves of holiday decorations and bicycle parts and half-melted candles downstairs, but no one disturbs me, and when I finally tire of the damp cement walls, the sun has been snuffed out and the house is quiet. From the kitchen, the remnants of last night's breakdown are gone, all of the broken things swept out the door.

When the clock on the oven says nine thirty, I know that I'm officially breaking my promise to Patrick — I'm not going to his show tonight. As last call at Luna's approaches, I'm drawn to the front window to watch for him with nothing but hope and sadness and longing stuck on me from every direction.

I finally see the shape of him on the sidewalk, getting

closer. I kneel on the living room floor with my elbows on the windowsill and my chin in my hands and watch him nearing the house, the guitar case slung over his shoulder as black and heavy as I feel.

Look up. Look up. Look up. Look up and see me and stop and lay your guitar in the grass and run up the path to my house and throw open the door and find me here, just find me, find me here crying over you, needing and wanting you more than anything in my life. Look up, Patrick Reese. Look up look up look up…

But he doesn't look. He shifts his case to the other side and I can't see his face as he comes and goes like I'm not even here — just another invisible ghost in the old Hannaford lake house.

Up in the sewing room, the wood floor shines, cleared of glass and buttons, and the air is lemony and crisp. The day bed is made with fresh sheets, and on the end, folded in a neat rectangle, is the beige sweater I borrowed from Nana's bedroom the night I found her pills. It must have slipped behind the bed. I forgot I had it, and I know before I see the name on the inside label — scrawled between two hearts — what it's going to say.

Handmade by Alice.

I think of the woman with the dyed red hair at the estate sale, CEO of Creature Creations. *Sorry, Alice. Ollie stays with me.*

I pull the dog sweater over my head and scroll through my phone for Emily's cell number. She picks up on the first ring.

"All right, Del. Patrick was a mess tonight. What the hell is going on with you guys?"

Chapter twenty-nine

It's been four days since the fight. Em's been over here every
night since my tragic phone call, listening to the whole saga,
holding me when I cry, bringing me chocolate hazelnut lattes
from Luna's. She doesn't say whether she's talked to Patrick
about me, and I don't ask.

I haven't seen him since that horrible night, Jack telling
me only that he asked for some time off. I try to block it out of
my mind, helping Rachel lug the boxes of remaining collect-
ibles out front for the final sale, setting up tables with the last
porcelain animal statues. Glassware featuring each of the fifty
states. Ski boots. Needlepoint kits. The day passes slowly as
my gaze drifts always to the blue-and-white Victorian, waiting

for him to march out the front door and over here, right past the encyclopedias the old people didn't buy and the bowling pin salt-and-pepper shakers priced at one dollar, right to *me*.

"Hon, why don't you just talk to him?" Rachel says, probably seeing the whole thing unravel in the cards over her black-and-silver cloth.

"We're not speaking," I say.

She frowns but doesn't push for details. "Maybe you should go over there. I'm sure when he sees you again, he'll realize —"

"I'm *fine*, Rach."

"You haven't touched the flourless chocolate torte I made. And your shirt is on backward. And inside out. And what's going on with that *hair*?" Rachel makes a swirling motion above her head as I tug at the shirt tag beneath my chin.

"I'm just tired, okay?"

"Listen, Delilah. Your mother and I are burying your grandmother in less than two weeks. We let things go unsaid for eight years, and now it's too late. Life is short. You don't always get another chance to make it right. So enough of this *tired* crap, okay? Shake out your hair. Fix your shirt. March your ass over there and tell him how you feel."

"Did you draw the Lovers card again today?" I ask. "I told you, I'm just —"

"Enough!" She points next door to Patrick's house. "This has nothing to do with tarot cards. Now *go*."

The thought of facing Patrick after all these empty days sends a sharp jolt through my insides, but Rachel is right. I don't even know if Patrick *wants* to talk. But that night on the beach, when we got out of the car in the middle of everything, rising above the shouts in the storm, there was something else. Something in his eyes. Something he said.

"Don't you get it? I'm in love with you!"

Patrick's front door is open, the summer breeze carrying honeysuckle-scented air through the screen door. I hear the sweet warmth of his voice as I wrap my hand around the door handle, pull, and step inside.

"Em," Patrick says from the living room. He doesn't see me. Doesn't know I'm watching. "You're amazing. I don't know what I'd do without you."

"Same here," Emily says, standing on her toes. She reaches around his neck, pressing herself to him and choking all of the air from my lungs. He rubs her back and smiles and then she says it, those awful little words that were supposed to come only from me. "I love you, Patrick."

I take a clunky step backward, startling them both. Patrick lets go of Emily and finally notices me, his pained, frantic eyes holding mine. It's as if we're both being electrocuted by the same current and neither of us can let go or knock the other out of harm's way.

"Delilah, wait!" His hand reaches out.

"I can't..." I stumble backward. "I thought... I..."

"Whoa, Delilah. It's not what you think," Emily says,

waving her hands to erase the image of their embrace from my mind. "It's *soooo* not what you think."

I look at Patrick. "At least you're ditching the work next door for something good."

"I *told* you," Emily says, but Patrick stops her, grabbing her hand in an affectionate squeeze.

"Don't," he says to Emily. "You don't have to explain *anything* to her."

"But this is insane," she says. "I don't even —"

"It doesn't matter." Patrick stops her again.

The three of us stand near the door, me staring at Patrick, trying to keep myself from collapsing, Patrick and Emily staring at each other and then back at me.

Finally, Emily shakes her hand free and Patrick breaks the silence.

"Did you need something, Delilah?" he asks. "Or are you just trying to make everyone in Red Falls as miserable as you are?"

My stomach tightens, but I ignore the sting. "I wish I never found you again. I liked you better when we were kids!"

"Finally!" he shouts. "We agree on something!"

"Oh, you know *what*?"

"Why are you still here, Delilah?"

"Stop it!" Emily yells. "Both of you! Just stop!"

"FINE!" Patrick and I scream at her, and at each other, and at the seagulls all the way down on the lake, floating blissfully ignorant over the blue abyss.

Emily pushes past me through the doorway, outside, down the steps, sneakers throwing tiny stones at the house as she bolts toward Maple Terrace. I stumble onto the porch and Patrick slams the screen door and I run back to Nana's, faster and faster as I try to outpace my own heart. There aren't that many steps between the two houses, but I take them in double time, triple, quadruple, speeding toward Rachel and her army of ten-cent trinkets, bashing my hip into the table and taking out a whole section of fake plastic fruit and ice-skating frog figurines, Megan's words from so long ago boiling up like hot tar to fill the black holes inside.

We all long for what could have been.

Chapter thirty

On the morning of Nana's memorial service, I'm awake at four o'clock, thirsty and restless and unable to fall back asleep. It's been two weeks since I learned about my real father and the things that have wedged my family for generations. Almost as long since I've seen Emily or spoken to Patrick — when he returned to work on the house with Jack, it was with renewed efficiency, no longer needing my assistance with the shutters or the gutters or the painting of the shed. No longer seeking my conversation. No longer searching for my eyes across the kitchen table during breakfast. To him, I simply don't exist.

At five, I pull on the dog sweater and head out the front door to watch the sun fight against the fog. Cool mist swirls around my feet, swallowing me in a giant cauldron, a pinch of insignificance in a complicated magical recipe whose ultimate purpose is yet to be revealed.

Next door in front of Patrick's house, the mist breaks in the street, billowing out before a dark, hulking mass. I take a few steps back from the road as the figure moves closer, its breath white on the air just ten feet from my unblinking eyes.

It's a moose, tall and chocolate-brown, standing in front of my grandmother's house. Her head bobs gently and I smell her through the stew of the fog, her scent mingled with the earth and the tang of an earlier rain. I don't move.

My heart bangs beneath my shirt as two calves appear through the fog behind her. Time holds us all as she sniffs at the air, judging whether I'm friend or foe, whether she should challenge me or let us all pass in peace. After a series of long sighs and grunts, she raises her head and moves aside, waiting for her charges to hobble up next to her. Eight short legs move quickly, mother nudging gently with her nose. Still, I don't breathe. When the babies are finally in front of her, she moves on, vanishing in the haze.

My mother and aunt are awake when I go back inside, none of us able to sleep on the morning of Elizabeth Hannaford's burial. We eat breakfast together with little conversation, forks and knives clinking against three mismatched plates. When we do talk, we keep it safe — *the bacon isn't bad, considering*

it's soy. I hope the weather holds out. Who wants more coffee?
None of us speaks of the real things filling our hearts like deep,
cold water — the funeral. Who's going to carry the urn. The
weeks of tension and our explosive argument. Our impending
and final departure from this house. This place. This story.

An hour before we're scheduled to leave for the funeral,
Mom finds me in my room, sitting at the edge of the bed and
staring out at the lake. The door is open, but she lingers in
the hall, waiting for permission to enter as if she no longer
has the right to ask. I give it to her.

"I'm burying my mother today." She sits next to me and
puts it out there, just like that. I think about the black box
etched in gold flowers on my grandmother's dresser, wondering how it will look in my mother's hands as she shakes out
the ashes of my grandmother over Red Falls Lake.

"Can we talk?" Mom asks, putting her arms around me.

I shrug. Words won't come to my lips. In the rawness of
her open affection, I've forgotten how to make them.

"Okay," Mom says, brushing the hair out of my eyes. "I'll
start."

There's a stray button on the floor. They must have missed
it when they cleaned up the glass from the jar.

*Did she buy the button on its own, or was it an extra from
a new blouse?*

"There were so many times I wanted to tell you about your
father," she says.

257

I wonder what happens to all those extra buttons that come with new clothes?

"But as you got older, I thought if you knew the truth, you'd look at me the way my mother did when she found out. I couldn't bear that, Delilah. I never wanted to see that kind of hatred in your eyes."

Maybe we should give them to Alice for her creature creations.

"Please say something, Del. Even if it's something angry."

I wonder how many loose buttons there are in this world, just rolling around in a jar without a mate or a blouse to go on. No destiny. No purpose. Just sitting there, unnoticed. Forgotten.

"Delilah, *please?*"

I look at my mother, deep lines in her forehead, no makeup to fill in the wrinkles around her eyes. I wasn't prepared for it, and the immensity of my sadness wrings the anger out of me me until all of the harsh words escape like water squeezed from a sponge.

"I'm not mad that you were with Casey," I say. "I'm mad that you lied to me. And that you kept on lying to me every time I asked you about Thomas Devlin. You never wanted to talk about my real father."

She nods, pulling at the collar of her robe. "It killed me to pretend like that, but there was always some reason not to tell you."

"Mom, I hate…" *I hate you for being weak and needy and*

stupid. I hate you for making a mistake. I hate you for not being perfect. It's what I want to say, but the thoughts evaporate almost as quickly as they appear. How can I fault her for trying to bury a truth that when exposed to air and sunlight could only hurt the ones she loves? For doing with the story of my father exactly what I've done with my own stories for so long? All the stories we've told each other were broken or incomplete, truths stretched thin and riddled with holes where the light shone through.

"I didn't plan that night with Casey. You know that much, right?"

"I know," I say. "I made a lot of mistakes, too. Especially with guys. I get that part of it." I stare at the button on the floor again, bright white against the dark of the wood, wishing I could press it and open a hidden passageway into Red Falls Lake where I could breathe underwater and watch the sun blaze beneath the surface.

"Mistakes? Delilah Elizabeth Hannaford, the mistake I made was not telling you the truth. Casey was not a mistake. From the moment I learned I was pregnant, I've never regretted that night — not once — because at the end of it all, I got you."

Mom kisses the top of my head and squeezes me closer, the rise and fall of her chest uneven as her arms tighten around me.

"But why did you take me away from here?" I ask. "Why did we stop coming? Why did we stop talking about them?

Okay, Nana was upset. But did she really cut us off because of that one time between you and Stephanie's boyfriend?"

My mother takes a deep breath and looks out the window, pulling a tissue from her bathrobe pocket.

"Your grandmother was a difficult woman. None of us was ever very close with her, but that was especially true with Steph. They never saw eye to eye on anything, and when Rachel and I got older and moved away, Steph was left here to deal with Mom on her own.

"After Stephanie died, Mom felt a lot of guilt about their relationship, and she resented me and Rachel for not being able to save her. 'You were her sisters,' she always said. 'You would've noticed something was wrong, but you were too busy to bother with Red Falls.'

"Eventually we got past that part of it, but, Delilah, you have to realize what suicide — or any death with questionable circumstances — does to the people left behind. Not only do we grieve the one we lost, but there's this whole new layer of guilt and accusation and fear. None of us could talk about her, because we all felt responsible for what happened. Why didn't we know she wasn't taking her medication properly? Where did she get sleeping pills? Why didn't anyone notice? Did she take her own life, or was it truly an accident — the mistake of a depressed girl who just wanted to fall asleep that night? Even trying to talk to people outside the family, like Megan or any of her other friends, was impossible. Everyone wanted it to be someone else's fault. We all needed someone to blame. Someone to scream at. Especially Casey. He didn't leave town because of what happened between us. He left because he couldn't face life here without her, the constant questions, never knowing if he or any of us could have made a difference before it was too late. He told us he would go, even before that night on the docks, and he did it."

I shift on the bed, wrapping my arms around myself as an edge creeps back into Mom's voice. She shakes her head and continues, the creases between her eyes deep and long.

"You know, when a person is murdered, you can miss that person and put all of your anger into hating the killer, even if you don't know who the killer is. You also have the choice of forgiveness. But when someone takes her own life, she *is* the killer. So we missed our sister, and at the same time, when we thought about the possibility that her death was her own doing, we *hated* her for leaving us. God, it's been almost twenty years, and some days I still pick up the phone, hoping she'll be on the other end, wishing I could forgive her. I just can't believe she really…it never goes away, Delilah. That feeling. It's always with me."

Mom presses the tissue to her eyes and I don't say anything for a long time.

"I don't know how much of this you remember," Mom continues, "but sometimes on our summer visits, your grandmother would refuse to leave her room, sometimes for days on end. Or she'd go stay with a girlfriend across town until she felt like dealing with us again. She was not well, Delilah. Clinically. Like Stephanie."

"I know," I say. "I found the medications in her dresser drawer that night I was in her room."

"Well, she'd been on them for decades — even before we lost Steph."

"I guess that's why I don't have that many memories of her," I say. "Seems like she didn't want to be around much."

"She loved you, Delilah. But she didn't show it like Papa did. She couldn't."

Mom's right; my grandfather adored me. Every time he'd sit me on his lap and race me around in his wheelchair, or read the comics to me, or laugh at my silly endless knock-knock jokes, I knew that I was the light of his life. I haven't thought about him this summer as much as I've thought about Nana and Stephanie and all of the secrets, but when I do, I miss him all over again, like I just got the news this morning. It's as if he'd been part of our lives all along, and now the doctors called to tell us there wasn't anything they could do.

"After my father died," Mom says, "I was overcome with grief and shame. I had to talk to someone. I had to confess the secret I'd been carrying since that night with Casey. So I told Rachel. I knew she'd be upset about what happened, and hurt that I'd never told her. I knew it would change things between us. But I also knew she wouldn't turn her back on me . . . or on *you.*

"My mother overheard the entire conversation. She snapped. She said horrible, hateful things to me and even to Rachel, whose only crime was to hear my confession."

"What things?" I ask.

Mom closes her mouth to hold back the words like a dam. "Remember that she wasn't herself, Delilah."

"But I —"

"It's not important anymore. She's dead."

"It's important to me, Mom. I need to know. Please stop trying to protect me from my own history."

Mom takes my hand and closes her eyes, nodding slowly. "After my mother found out that Casey was your father, she accused me of robbing you from Stephanie. She said that Casey and Steph would've been married one day, and that you should have been theirs. She screamed at Rachel and me on the day we were supposed to bury my father. Shouted it through the whole house. That when God took Stephanie, he took the wrong child. That he should have taken one of us. That we weren't good enough to save Steph, and for that we didn't deserve to live."

Mom's face takes on an intensity that I don't recognize; a pain I've never before seen in her eyes despite the long and troubled story of us. It makes me want to take her away from all of it, to become the mother just this once, to rock her until it's okay again. All the times I hated Claire Hannaford Speaking, smile-as-you-dial, the constant buzzing of mobile communications devices, I'd give anything now for a call from

263

her assistant. To see my mother clear her throat and shake it off and answer that phone, large and in charge.

"God, Mom, I'm so sorry." I rest my head on her shoulder and squeeze her hand, all of the comforting, right words lost.

"There's more," Mom says, steadying herself with a deep breath. "Delilah, Rachel and I stood in the living room of this house, in this home where we'd spent our entire young lives together, and we heard my mother make a promise to God that if after all of her praying and sacrificing he still didn't take us, she would spend the rest of her life begging him to take you instead, just... just so I could know the pain of burying a daughter. After all the fights in our past, the days she'd go without speaking, the cruel words for which her illness was always a ready excuse — that promise was *it*. That's why we left. It didn't matter if it was the depression talking or the shock of hearing about Casey and me or the loss of her husband or anger and guilt about Stephanie or the medications... her words were enough. Rachel and I couldn't bear to be near her after that. By the time some of our anger had subsided, months turned into years, life went on, and we just never came back. And now, she's gone."

I replay my grandmother's words in my mind only once, trying instead to think about the orange pill bottles. Trying to remind myself that through the burden of her depression, Nana had also suffered the deaths of her young daughter and husband and had just learned that I was the child of her dead daughter's boyfriend who'd since vanished from their lives. Deep down, she probably blamed herself for Stephanie's illness and her eventual death. And I believe she loved me once. Maybe she always did. It doesn't lessen the scorch of her jagged, vengeful vow, but it helps me understand things just a little more.

When I'm all out of questions, Mom picks up the pink jewel box sitting in the windowsill — the one I bought from the first estate sale.

"What's this?" she asks. "Was it hers?"

"I think so. Something told me to keep it when I saw it with the other sale stuff. I don't know where —"

But I *do* know where. It's here now, the memory materializing before me like the moose in the morning fog.

"It's my box of tears," Nana said. "Whenever I'm feeling sad, I open it up and cry, cry, cry till I can't anymore."

"Can I cry in the box, too?"

"Of course. Just come in here and get the box, hold it in your hand, and think about why you're sad. It holds all of our sadness, so we don't have to do it alone."

"Won't it overflow?" I asked. "From all of the tears?"

"No, Delilah. This is a magic box. There's room for lots and lots."

"Are you sad right now?"

"Yes. But I'm happy, too. I'm happy that you're here. You and your mom and Aunt Rachel..."

"I don't know," I say again, but I *do* know, and it's a real memory, one that's mine and my grandmother's alone. "It just reminds me of her — the good things about her."

"It's beautiful." Mom runs her finger over the velvet inside, then closes the lid. She looks at me for a moment as she returns the box to the sill, still trying to get comfortable with the silence that sometimes falls between us.

"I love you, Honeybee," she says. She smiles and squeezes my shoulder, rising from the bed and walking out the door, the tail of her Chanel robe billowing out behind her like fog through the trees.

Chapter thirty-one

I stand on the high bank of Point Grace with Mom and Aunt
Rachel, shoulder to shoulder, our backs to the water at the
deepest end of Red Falls Lake. The three of us face a sea of
faces sailing in the black ships of their mourning clothes, all
here to remember Elizabeth Rose Hannaford. Among them,
Jack is here, and Luna and Megan, and people I remember
from the estate sales, like Alice with her dog hair purse. The
coffee cake people, too — all of them here to share the burden of this loss and seek comfort together.

Patrick, though, is not with his father. The weight of his
absence presses noiselessly on my heart with the sadness of
losing my grandparents and the aunt I never knew, gone

to death and depression, to silence and old wounds. With each passing day, hope that Patrick and I will ever again meet under the bleachers fades. But like the memories of my grandmother, nothing is ever all bad. In the aftermath of our end, I'm trying to think about the good things — his familiar smile that first day after our long summers apart. Eating maple drizzlers at the Sugarbush Festival. The fireworks show under the willow and the songs he sang and the kissing...still, it's all too close to become a memory, so I hold on, not ready to let it slip away.

Through the smoke of the sage bowls Rachel lit beneath the table holding the rose-etched urn, my mother reads an old poem about all of the unsaid things that pass between the living and the dead. Lost in the cadence of her voice, I don't follow the verse as much as the imagery, thinking about the intersections of our lives in Red Falls — lives that only three months ago had been separate. After all the years of hurt and silence, however late in the season of our relationships, my grandmother brought us back together.

"It was my mother's wish that part of her be scattered over Red Falls Lake," Mom says, dabbing her eyes with a tissue. "She will also be buried in Forest Lawn Cemetery next to our father, Benjamin, and our sister, Stephanie." She and Rachel remove the urn from its pedestal and carry it together to the edge of the bank. Rachel holds the lid while Mom shakes some of the remains into the air over the water.

Remains. As the gray dust swirls and floats down to the lake like falling stars, I look at my family and the people of Red Falls, all of us crying and smiling and remembering and thinking about the same person, and I realize that remains is the wrong word. The ashes of a body are just that — ashes. The dust of our bones. What *remains* are the people she left behind. The wake of history and love, however confusing and imperfect, she left for her family. When I think of Elizabeth Rose Hannaford, I won't remember the ashes over Red Falls Lake, or the pill bottles, or the cruel words she spat at my mother eight years ago. I'll remember her life — the good things. The happy stories from the people in Red Falls who knew her later, when she was finally able to crawl partway out from under the dark cloud of her depression and enjoy her days here.

Elizabeth Rose Hannaford, the mother. The grandmother. The trunk of the family tree from which we all branch and flower.

As we begin our quiet march down the hill to the cars that will ferry us to the cemetery, I look behind me at the old weeping willow — our fireworks willow. Beside its tangled leaves, Patrick is there, his suit dark, his hands folded peacefully in front of him as we file past. I look for him again when we reach the cars, but he's gone.

The cemetery service is shorter and smaller, only her closest friends and us, only those who know the meaning of the inscription on the headstone: Elizabeth Rose "Ollie" Hannaford. Patrick is again in the background. He doesn't approach.

After the final words when Mom closes her book of poetry and the remaining mourners leave white roses on top of the urn, I ask for a few minutes alone with my grandmother and Ollie.

I reach into my pocket and pull out the pink box of tears, following Nana's instructions. I open the lid, run my finger along the velvet, and give over all of my sadness, tucking the box into the pile of flowers.

"So you don't have to do it alone," I whisper, still hoping for the sign I sought in her bedroom that night, reading her books and trying on her costume jewelry. I wait, eyes closed, eyes open, but nothing happens. The rain doesn't fall from the gray sky. The trees don't shake. Neither does the wind blow nor the ground split open to wake the dead from their eternal slumber.

But she heard me. I know she did.

"Delilah?"

As I turn from my grandmother's grave, I see the girl approaching. Shame burns my face.

"Emily! I — I'm . . . I didn't . . . thank you for coming."

Em shakes her head and throws her arms around me, pulling me close against her dark green dress. "I am so, so sorry about your grandmother, Delilah. And for everything your family went through. I didn't know Liz well, but she was close with Luna. She came in for coffee sometimes, and I'd give her the day-old pastries to take home for Ollie. He liked the cranberry-orange scones best."

I smile, picturing a big sloppy Saint Bernard eating scones with his pinky up.

"Thanks, Em. I'm glad you're here. I wanted to talk to you after everything that —"

"No. You listen to me first. I know this isn't the best place for it, but I have something to say." Emily pulls away, keeping her hands firm on my arms. There's a fire behind her bright blue eyes and I know that whatever comes from her mouth next, she means it. I look at her and wait for the angry words I so deserve.

"You know what your problem is, Delilah Hannaford?" Em stares right inside me. "You refuse to see what's in front of your face. It's easier for you to invent reasons not to like me than to accept that someone might actually want to be your friend.

"The first time I met you, I knew there was something real about you. Way more than what was on the surface — that was obvious. I trusted you. You were nothing like the other girls that come through here all summer chasing after Patrick. He knew it, too. The three of us had so much fun together. You never got jealous or weird about my friendship with him until

271

that day in his house. Which was so crazy, because Patrick and I are practically siblings — *that's* the way I love him. I love you *both* that way. But you totally turned on me."

"Emily, I'm sorry. I just —"

"Patrick couldn't even do his show that Thursday after your fight on the lake because he was so upset. He said he had a strained vocal chord, but all of us knew the deal. I tried to talk to him after you and I spoke on the phone, but I couldn't get through to him. All week he just sat at the counter, drinking coffee nonstop, babbling about how he screwed everything up. We all knew he could fix it if he'd just shut up and talk to you. But he didn't want advice. He just... 'Delilah this, Delilah that.' He left Luna's in a daze last Saturday, so I followed him home to try once more to talk some sense into him. He asked if I knew what happened that night with your family — if I knew why you were so upset. I couldn't lie to him, Del. I told him everything. He was about to go look for you, and then you showed up and undid everything. And by the way, Miss I've Got It All Figured Out, there's —"

"Em, stop, okay? Right now, I want to talk to *you*. I'm sorry. I'm so, so sorry for the way I treated you and for freaking out like that. I didn't really believe you guys hooked up. I was just really, really messed up that day. It's not an excuse, but it's the truth, and I'll spend the rest of my summer trying to make up for it if you'll just let me be your friend again."

Em looks at me before the headstones of my family, the smell of roses and freshly dug earth strong between us.

"Actually," I continue, "I've been really, really messed up for a while now. Since before I got here. Family stuff, as you've seen. School stuff. Friend stuff. Me stuff, mostly."

Em smiles and shakes her head. "Join the club."

"I'm the *president* of that club," I say.

"I'll accept your apology if you let me be second in command."

"Done."

"Then I forgive you."

"Just like that?" I ask.

"Oh, get over yourself, Del. You're the first cool girl to come to Red Falls since...well, ever. I don't know how you do it in Pennsylvania, but Vermont chicks? We don't let stupid fights mess up the real deal."

"Right. I think my entire family was absent the day they taught *that* lesson."

"Yeah, well...my father must have been out drinking with your family that day."

I laugh. "Still no progress on the dad front, huh?"

Em shrugs. "He'll come around eventually. He just needs some time to accept the fact that his little girl...*you* know..."

"Is all grown up?" I ask. Despite feeling like I have two fathers now, the reality of the father-daughter dynamic is completely alien to me.

Em meets my eyes, her smile fading. "His little girl... likes...*girls*," she says.

273

"Likes... *what* did you just say?"

"Girls, Delilah." Emily nods slowly, watching me as if she can see all of the things in my head clicking into place as I recall our summer together. Did she ever mention guys when I talked about Finn or Patrick? Did she ever name a past boyfriend or even a crush? Then, that fight at Patrick's house, she said she was... *God*, she probably tried to tell me about a million times, but I was so wrapped up in making everyone talk about things they didn't want to remember that I didn't even know someone else actually *wanted* to talk.

"More than a friend?"

My eyes fill with tears. "Remember my friend in Montreal?" she asks. "Her name is Kate."

Emily nods and reaches for my hands. "Please don't hate me for not telling you before. I wanted to. It's just not something... I mean, it's not the easiest thing to bring up in conversation, especially with girlfriends — er, friends that are girls. I'm always worried they're going to think I'm checking them out and then it gets all weird and I'm so tired of losing friends over this and I just want to be myself and I really wanted you to meet Kate and I really wish —"

"Emily?"

"I know I should have told you sooner, I just —"

"*Em!*"

She looks at me, tears spilling onto her cheeks as her hands let go and drift back to her sides.

"Do you think the two of us can stop crying long enough

to get some lunch?" I ask, putting my arm around her. "I mean, away from all the funeral people? Sounds like we have some girl talk to catch up on, and besides, I'm *starving*."

For a second, her eyes go big and wide. Then together we laugh until the tears dry, long and loud enough to wake up all the dead people, including my grandmother, whose grave stands quietly behind us, flowers leaning over one side of the black-and-gold urn as if to wink.

Chapter thirty-two

Tonight is Patrick's final summer show.

He might not want me here, but I promised Emily I would try. As I watch him arrange power cords and adjust lights and double-check his set list, I know that if I don't fix it now, I will leave Red Falls next week and never look back, disappearing from his life for the last time.

"You okay?" Emily asks, setting down my chocolate hazelnut latte. I watch the steam curl out of it and remember that first day at the lake house when Rachel lit sage in the window. *Out with the bad, in with the good. Out with the bad, in with the good.*

I shrug. "No, but that won't stop me."

She squeezes my shoulder. "No charge for this one."

"Thanks, Em."

Outside, the rain that held off for Nana's service returns, soaking the pavement with increasing ferocity as the sun sets. The glow from Luna's windows and the promise of fresh coffee and music pulls in a rush of end-of-summer tourists seeking refuge from the damp street, and soon the crowd swells to the largest Patrick has entertained all season — even bigger than the Fourth of July week mob. It's hard to see the stage now, but I'm grateful for the extra layers of bodies between Patrick and me.

Fifteen minutes into his first set, there are so many people packed into the coffee shop that I almost expect to see Mom and Rachel, certain that every last person in Red Falls has come in from the rain to see the show. On any other night, my whole body would be warm and buzzy with such energy — people singing along and screaming and whistling after every song, Patrick making the crowd laugh with his charming intermittent chatter, the cappuccino machines hissing and whirring and steaming as Emily and Luna rush to keep up with the orders. This is the kind of endless night people tell their friends about — the last big summer hurrah before the dawn of reality rises with autumn's golden leaves.

I order another latte and slurp it down fast. It burns, but it's better than the burn that scorches my stomach whenever

I catch a sideways glance at Patrick's dimpled smile across the crowd, knowing it's no longer meant for me.

By the time Patrick winds down to his last few songs, I've had four lattes, I've burnt the roof of my mouth, my bones are jittery, and I'm not one word closer to knowing what to say. How do I apologize for wanting him so much that it scares me? How can I say I'm sorry for being who I am? For all of the mistakes and bad decisions that led me here, knowing that if not for them, I wouldn't have found him again?

I shouldn't have come here tonight. I have nothing to say, no way to explain anything, no words to make an adequate attempt. And Patrick — singing his heart out like everything in the world is all right again — has clearly moved on.

The ceiling is coming down and the walls are pressing in and the crowd...*crushing*...and the warm cinnamon air... *choking*...I need to get out of here...

I twist my way through a knot of people standing at the door, dodging hot coffee and elbows and it's just four more steps to the door, two more, one, my hand is on the glass, ready to push, ready to breathe in the cool outside air. A sliver of it seeps through the opening as I move forward, one foot almost over the threshold...if I could just...

"The last one's called 'Sigh.' It's for you." Patrick's voice pierces the air like an arrow shot across the crowd, and I know, even before I look back to the stage, that he means me. I suck in one last breath of cold air, let the door click shut, and turn around to face him. He closes his eyes and leans into the mic and the entire coffee shop falls silent. Even the cappuccino machines seem to suspend their constant hissing just to hear this song. The last one. For me.

Talkin' 'round you
Kills a little more each time
A murderous seduction would kindly suffice

The poet she sighs
As the night floods her eyes
And a sonnet succumbs to a bad, bad rhyme
No-o-oh

You won't let it go
So you try and fake it
'Cause nobody knows who you are

I hang around and take it…

'Cause like an outlaw desperado
I would fight all the world to run with you
Like the rose to willows weeping
I would shatter the skies to be with you
I would leave it behind
To roll with you

I'd throw it all away and ride

I'd throw it all away and ride
Come away and rally love it's the good tide
The river rolls in leaps and bounds to the far side

Let it go

'Cause like an outlaw desperado
I would fight all the world to run with you
Like the rose to willows weeping
I would shatter the skies to be with you
I would leave it behind
To roll with you
I'd throw it all away and slide down with you

The last line is softer than the rest, with no guitar, just Patrick's voice fading into a whisper. There isn't enough room in the halls of my whole life to feel this much. I can't... I can't stay here.

The front door seems so far away now and my legs are too heavy to push through the crowd, the crushing, suffocating crowd, so I turn around and make my way along the wall to the side door marked EMERGENCY – ALARM WILL SOUND, and it *does*, howling up against the rain like it's the end of the world. I don't know how long it screams before Luna shuts it down — I'm already in the middle of the street by then, the lights of the coffee shop wilting in the rain behind me like tiny neon flowers. I'm shaking from the caffeine and the song and everyone watching me, tears mixing with rain and covering my face, and I don't care what happens after this. I just want everything to stop. I just want to see the headlights on Finn's old silver 4Runner flash three times under the streetlight so I can get in and go to that spot in the woods and not talk and forget everything in my entire life again, because all the stuff worth remembering hurts too much.

"Delilah, wait!" Patrick runs up the street after me. "Please," he says, one hand stretched in front of him like he has this one chance to catch me, this one chance to reach out and hold on before I slip away into Red Falls Lake forever.

I stop, but because I want to or because I'm too weak to keep going, I don't know. I let him catch his breath, and we stand in the middle of Main Street for a long time until I finally blurt it out, breaking the rhythm of the rain against the pavement at our feet.

"I don't even know who I am anymore, Patrick. I'm not faking it. I'm lost." It's the truth. I never thought it would be so hard to say it, but it is. After all I've shared with him, this one thing, this one admission giving voice to the private things that scrape against the walls of my heart, feels shamefully intimate.

"You're Delilah Hannaford," he says, shaking his head.

"The girl who complains about manual labor and gets scared on the Ferris wheel and calls Crasner's the Foo nasty." His smile is sad and fierce at the same time.

"No. You don't get it. All of those things — that's who I am with *you*, hanging out and painting fences and sneaking into your room like Red Falls will never end. But it *is* ending, and I'll just go back to —"

"No, you won't, Del. I won't let that happen. I'm sorry. I didn't mean to get so crazy about everything. I just —"

I shake my head. "You don't have to —"

"I want to. I want to say this. Sometimes I just get these really intense feelings about stuff and I don't know what to do with them so I end up saying all the wrong things, but not now. Not tonight. That night at Heron Point — it hurt so bad to push you away like that. I hated seeing your face — how it crumpled up when I stopped kissing you. You have to believe me that it just about killed me. And that day at my house with Em — she'd just finished telling me about what happened with your mom and finding out about your father. I made her tell me because I needed to know what was going on with you, and..."

He's talking a mile a minute, coming closer with every word. I turn my face to the sky and close my eyes, trying to focus on the feel of the rain on my skin. He's whispering my name again and again. It's a question at first, and then not. I'm shivering and I feel him come closer, his hands moving to the top of my shirt, wrapping it around his fingers. I open my eyes and in less than a heartbeat, he wrenches me close to him, only a sigh keeping us apart. His face turns soft and serious, so near that I can count the drops of water falling from his eyelashes.

"Don't," I whisper.

His head is shaking. My mouth opens to protest again, but he knows I don't mean it. His fingers trace my lips, the silver heart on my collarbone. His eyes follow, hands twisting into my hair, both of our hearts pounding. My eyes have nothing to do but close again, and then it's there: his mouth anxious on mine, breath hot against my lips.

"Delilah Hannaford," he says, stopping only long enough to tell me. "I'm not letting you disappear again. I meant what I said that night at the lake."

"I believe you," I whisper in his ear, breathless and weak and all out of lies. "I believe you."

The ground shakes and spins and falls away again as I collapse into him and let go, rain washing the broken pieces of me all the way down the hill, straight into Red Falls Lake.

Chapter thirty-three

On the morning before we leave Red Falls, I awake to an unusual silence. No drills and hammers and saws chewing through the wood. No estate-sale customers haggling for cheaper knickknacks. No appraisers or lawyers to usher us closer to our final good-byes.

It's the first time since our arrival that I hear so many birds outside my window, singing and chirping and wishing one another well, all the way from here to the lake.

I get out of bed slowly and stretch, enjoying the solitude as I begin to pull my clothes from the dresser and pack up my suitcase. I save Holden Caulfield for tomorrow, but I put the dog sweater in there and Patrick's green guitar pick and the rock he carved with our initials and my new friend, Moo, smiling in her way. I brought her up from the windowsill in Nana's kitchen to remind me of everything that happened this summer; how easily some things can be broken for good and for bad, and how some things, no matter how shattered, can still go back together. Like Moo, my family may never be as strong as it once was. There are chips and cracks and scars. But some of them can be repaired, piece by piece, rebuilt into something even more cherished and loved and unique. That's what I'm working for now. That's what I'm holding on to.

I don't know what's waiting for me back in Key. I cringe to think about the last time I was there, all the momentous screwups, my photo-worthy *Finndescretions*, the friends I left behind without explanation. We may not have much in common these days, but they're still my classmates. We'll still see each other in the halls of Kennedy High as we all prepare to cross the graduation stage together next spring. Our lives may be different this year, but they were once my friends, just like the people of Red Falls were once Mom's and Rachel's. And maybe, like the people of Red Falls who came back together after my grandmother's passing, there's still a way, a new way, a different way, that we can be friends again.

But if not, if they don't like the changes I've made in my life, I have to accept that. I have to be okay. Emily, Megan, Jack, Luna, Patrick . . . they helped me learn what true friendship is. It's never perfect, but it *is* important. And now that

I've had the real thing, I'm not going to settle for anything less.

As for my non-boyfriend, Finn, there is no place in my life for him anymore. When I think of him now, of our spot in the woods, all my thoughts run into Seven Mile Creek and wash away. I don't miss him. Finn and I never knew each other. Knowing each other wasn't our thing. He just made it easy for me to drown it all out. He helped me run away from myself without really going anywhere.

I don't regret my time with him. Without the dark contrast of Finn, I might never have seen the light of Patrick. In that way, I'll always be grateful that he was part of my life.

But I'm not running away anymore.

I slide my phone from my pocket and scroll to his last text — the one he sent just before meeting me on the street corner that last night in Key.

pick u up at midnite? usual spot?

The words send a familiar rush through my chest, but this time, it's the rush of something leaving. I feel the tide of it rise up inside as I delete his number from my contacts, pushing out against me until it reaches my fingertips and floats out into nothingness. Whatever happens when we return from Red Falls, that girl — the one waiting under the street lamp at midnight to sneak off to the woods and *forget* — she's gone.

"You all packed up?" Mom asks, joining me in my summer bedroom.

"Mostly." I shrug, watching a seagull dive across the lawn in front of the window. Mom tucks a section of hair behind my ear, and I find myself doing that old rock and a hard place thing with her again — the dance we've so perfected this year. Things *are* better, and I hope in time, forgiveness will come on all sides. But isn't that enough? Will it ever be enough?

"Delilah, I know you're still processing everything that happened," she says. "It's a lot to think about. I'm not expecting you to just get over it. You need time — as long as it takes." She rests her hand on my knee.

"It hasn't even hit me yet," I say. "Not really. Sometimes I try to think about it, and it's so unreal that my brain tells me it's only a movie. A story. Not my life."

"I understand. But I want things... I want everything to be out in the open now. No more secrets." Mom nods, talking faster but softly. "If you have any questions about your father or me or our family, ask. I mean that. I might not have the answers, but I promise I'll be straightforward with you."

I take a deep breath. "Mom, does Casey Conroy know about me?"

"I haven't been in touch with Casey since that night," she says. "And I doubt my mother would've tracked him down after she found out. I don't think he knows about you, Delilah. I guess I always knew that you'd learn the truth about your father, whether I told you or not. As hard as that was for me to accept, I also wanted it to be your decision to tell him or not. If you decide that you want to look for him, we can contact —"

I shake my head. "I don't want to think about it yet. It's still too soon." My chest tightens, but I fight it. I don't want to go back to the dark places — the sadness I wallowed in for days following Mom's confession.

"I'm not asking you to make any decisions about your father right now," Mom says. "Whatever you want to do — if anything — I'll support. I just want you to —"

"Mom, what was Stephanie like?" I ask. "I mean, before she got sick." Things are different now. I feel like she'll tell me.

Mom smiles. "You look like her, you know. Same mischievous grin. Same eyes. We all get it from Nana, but you look especially like your aunt, even when you were little. Megan and I used to say that a piece of her lived on in you. Sometimes when I see you a certain way, like in a mirror or through the window, I see her. Especially here in the lake house."

"Were you close? Was she funny? Was she smart?"

Mom nods, her face illuminated by the memories. "She was beautiful, Delilah. Alive. Impulsive. A little reckless, kind of like you. I always admired that about her. And about you — truly. It just conflicts with my mothering instincts."

I smile. "Yeah, I kind of get that now."

"Yes. Well, Stephie was really special, Del. Everyone fell

in love with her — you couldn't help it. It almost killed my father when she started unraveling, and by then, Rachel and I were already away at college, starting new lives in new places. We didn't see it happening right away. But before, Stephie was the light in our lives — like a bright, bright star. People always say things like that when someone dies, don't they?"

"I guess." I never knew anyone who died like that — not someone close to me. Just Papa, and I don't remember what they said about him at the funeral because the fight erupted, overshadowing all else.

"They do. But with Steph, it was true."

"I wish I knew her."

"Me, too, Delilah. You know, she almost died once before, when she was about five. She fell into the lake. I was supposed to be watching her, but Rachel and I were arguing on the dock. All of a sudden, Stephanie was just gone. The silence was deafening. I was only nine or ten myself, but I will never, ever forget the fear in my heart when I realized what happened."

"What did you do?"

"I jumped off the dock and grabbed her, but she wasn't breathing. We ran to the house. Jack was there. He took her from my arms and laid her in the grass and started CPR. It was like the whole world stopped, waiting for her to cough. Then she did. It was over. Jack never mentioned it again — not even to my mother. Stephie didn't talk about it, either. It was like she knew how serious it was. How lucky...after that, Rachel and I promised each other we'd never let anything happen to her."

Mom's eyes go far away as she finds her way back through the tangles of her past.

"When she died," she continues, "I took some comfort in the fact that after the accident at the lake, we brought her back. She was supposed to die *that* day, but we got to sneak in another fourteen years with her. I know we don't talk about her, but my God, Delilah. I miss my sister every day. Every *single* day."

Mom takes a deep breath and pulls me close to her, folding herself around me. As her tears soak into my hair, the truth of it hits me like a flash storm over Red Falls Lake. Above every role in her life — Claire Hannaford Speaking, Rachel's and Stephanie's sister, Casey's grief-induced fling, Nana's and Papa's daughter, *my* mother — she's a human being, just like me. Frail and faulty and flawed, capable of making the most heinous mistakes and inflicting the most severe pain.

But equally capable of the greatest love.

I wrap my arms around her and hold very still, grateful somehow for the twisted, rock- and root-strewn paths that brought us here.

"You're probably wondering about this Mr. Devlin character," she says. It's strange to hear her call him that — a character — as though he exists only in the pages of a novel and never as the man I've come to know, however mistakenly, as my father. It shocks me now to realize that in the weeks since I learned the truth, I *wasn't* wondering about him — not in the way Mom's playful tone implies. It was as though my heart made room for two truths that night — one real, the other safe and familiar and desirable — and even as Mom spoke the words that Thomas wasn't my father, even as I screamed at her and ran out of the house, part of me went on believing that he *was*. Believing that wherever he was, all of the joys in my life he'd witnessed and shared — all of the disappointments he'd somehow seen. Believing that through them all, he'd reached out and rubbed my back and told me I'd be okay, even if I couldn't hear his words or feel his protective hands on my shoulders. So many years ago, when my mother first gave me the article about his death and told me about their brief encounter in Philadelphia, I believed her then, too. I believed her then, *first*. Thomas has been with me a long time, and like the memory of anyone we love, a few nights without him isn't going to erase him from my life. Nothing is.

"I met him at the bar in Philadelphia — just like I told you," she says. "He asked me why I peeled the labels from the beer bottles before I drank them."

"You still do that," I say, remembering the last time I saw her drink one at DKI's company picnic.

"I know. I don't like how they feel. Anyway, he noticed, and we started chatting. We talked all night long, hanging out until the bar closed. In all this time, until you found

291

those pictures in the closet, he was the only person I ever really talked to about my sister's death. It was only a couple of weeks after her funeral. It was so much easier with him — a total stranger — than it was with my own family.

"There was a moment — a flash, really — where it could have gone another way, but we let it go. He had an early morning flight back to London and on to Afghanistan...if I had known his fate that night, I might have tried to...I don't know, Del. I guess we never know what life is going to hand us. We kissed and walked away. I didn't tell Rachel about him at first, even when I learned about what happened in Afghanistan. I still felt so guilty about Casey and so messed up about Stephanie.

"I saved the newspaper article about his death," she says, tracing the lines of one hand with the other. "I wanted to remember him. Not long after I learned I was pregnant, I found the clipping on my desk, and it happened from there. All I had to do was stretch the truth just a little, and no one would have to be hurt by what happened between Casey and me. Especially not my child. It's funny — I let Thomas walk away that night because I knew it wouldn't turn into anything. I never expected that he'd become such a part of our history."

He may not be my biological father, but Thomas Devlin was a real person, a man who lived and died for what he loved. A man who shared a few moments with my mother and who maybe, in some small way, is still connected to me on that same giant cosmic rubber band that keeps stretching and twisting and snapping us all back together when we least expect it. In that way, I'll always consider him a part of me, and me of him, even more than Casey. And maybe somehow Thomas knows about me, too. Maybe he really *is* watching over me, smiling, telling us that we're going to be okay. The daughter that was almost his. The woman with the hazel eyes.

I study the creases and curves of my mother's face as she looks at me, her story over for now. I know it's illogical, but before this summer, it always seemed that my mother sprang forth into this life fully grown, fully clothed, fully armed with her arsenal of logic and reason, unscathed by life's garden-variety heartaches. All the time I was busy resenting her, I never considered that she was ever young or starry-eyed. That before I came into her life, my mother had an entire age of happiness and sadness and elation and fear and wonder. Layers on layers on layers, all part of the history of us.

"So..." Mom stretches, putting her arm around my shoulders. "How's *Patrick?*"

"What?" My heart speeds up. "I don't know. What do you mean? Why are you asking me about Patrick? What did he say?"

Mom smiles and waits for my neurosis to pass. "Rachel tells me I don't have to worry. That everything will work out amazing with you two, so say the cards. What do you think?"

My face burns under her gaze, but I smile. I can't help it. "I don't know what you're talking about."

"Of *course* you don't. Come on, Delilah. I'm not blind. I've seen the way you two look at each other." She cups my chin in her hand.

"You have?"

"Yes. Just promise me one thing."

"What's that?" I ask.

"If you want to see him, no matter where he lives or where you live or what time it is, use the front door, okay? No more windows."

I laugh. "Deal."

"All right. Finish packing and come downstairs," she says, patting my knee. "Patrick and Jack will be here soon. Rachel and I have some news for everyone."

News?

News can only mean one thing.

They sold the house.

From the bottom dresser drawer, empty now of all my summer things, I remove the diary of Stephanie Hannaford. Seeing Casey's name again as I flip through the pages, I know that if I reread it, it will be as a brand-new story, every sentence illuminated by the light of Mom's confession. If I read it carefully, Stephanie's memories might tell me more about my biological father; about the kind of person he was before her death. The kind of person he would have remained if his life had turned out like it was supposed to.

I think of Stephanie's grave again and my heart hurts to

have missed the chance to know her in this lifetime. But, if Stephanie had lived, Casey and Mom wouldn't have had their moment, and I wouldn't have been conceived. In that way, we weren't *supposed* to know each other in this lifetime.

If I was meant to find the diary, then the universe has fulfilled that promise. I found it. I read it. And now it must go back to the house, kept safe with the history of all who've lived here until the universe decides that someone else should discover it. I close the latch and run my hands over the faded gold rose on the cover one last time before placing the diary back beneath the floor in the closet. Over the hole, I snap into place the board I knocked loose that first week, inserting four nails and hammering it back down, swift and certain.

I lay my hand flat against the wood for a moment, the last I'll have in this room before it's time to say farewell to the house on Maple Terrace forever.

"Good-bye, Aunt Stephanie," I whisper. A breeze blows through the open window, billowing the curtains out over the bed, and when I look up at the sunlight, I see the red cardinal, perched on the ledge outside the window. He watches me for a moment, and then, without fanfare, turns and glides away.

Chapter thirty-four

Downstairs, as I look around at the half-packed boxes of Mom's computer accessories and dry cleaning bags of pant-suits and the remaining spoons and forks we saved for our last few meals, I feel an emptiness in me. Tomorrow is the last time I'll see this house. The last time I'll watch the roosters dance over the kitchen sink or the ants scurry from under the stove. The last time I'll make any memories in my grand-parents' home.

Jack and Patrick are here, and Mom and Rachel assemble us all outside for their big announcement. From the front lawn, I look up at the house — *really* look at it — for the first time since our arrival in June. I know the third step on the porch still creaks. The shutters, under the weight of their new paint and some possibly missing hardware which may or may not be my fault, aren't one hundred percent level. And there's no guarantee that the gutters will stay clean or the paint won't peel again or the newly remodeled sunroom will keep the cardinals out.

But those shutters were painted and hung with love. The flower beds have been replanted. The trees and honeysuckle vines were trimmed and the carpets steam-cleaned and the windows reflect the sky and the entire house radiates like a gold beacon in the warm yellow of the sun, high on the hill above Red Falls Lake. Like the women that have called it home for hundreds of years, the house on Maple Terrace is beautiful. Within its creaks and cracks and flaws, it holds the memories, hopes, and dreams of all of us. Today, our summer of work has come together — the shutters and the gutters and the painting and the flowers — and I *know*. I know that it was worth it.

We arrived in Vermont expecting to fix up the old lake house. But in the end, it was the house that fixed *us*. I knew in my head that we'd never see it again — the place that reunited the Hannaford women. But my heart had different ideas. Crazy ones, faraway ones, like maybe, somehow, we could spend one more summer here. One more Fourth of July at the Sugarbush Festival. One more week washing windows and taking down shutters. One more season sipping lattes with Em and listening to Patrick sing at Luna's.

"You guys, look at this place!" Rachel says, her pale pink *Save 2nd Base — Get a Mammogram* T-shirt clinging to her body in the heat. "Look at what we accomplished this summer!" She puts her arm around Jack.

"She's a true beauty," Jack says. "I've worked on lots of remodels, but this one, *man*. I'm really gonna miss 'er."

I take a deep breath, honeysuckle overflowing in the late summer air.

"Well," Mom says, "after three months of hard work and a lot of tears, Rachel and I have some really excellent news for everyone."

Patrick squeezes my hand as I steady myself for the news I've waited for all summer. The news I couldn't hear soon enough when we first arrived. The news I'd give anything to put on pause now, just for a few more days.

Mom speedwalks across the grass to the front end of the driveway. There's a sign staked into the lawn on iron post, wrapped in a white canvas tarp. It seems strange that she'd post a FOR SALE sign if they've already accepted a private offer, but it's probably just another one of those weird historic town ordinances. I shield my eyes from the sun as Mom tugs off the canvas to reveal a simple wooden sign swinging gently on its post.

FUTURE SITE OF:
Three Sisters Bed & Breakfast
A Hannaford Family Guest Home

"We wanted to tell you guys first," Rachel says. "We'll start accepting reservations next summer. The news will be announced officially in tomorrow's *Bee*."

Who needs the *Red Falls' Bee*? Once the neighbors see the sign, we're inundated with visitors and phone calls, everyone wanting a tour, wanting to know more, wanting to bring coffee cake. Hours later, when it's just us and Emily and Patrick and Jack sitting around the kitchen table for our final meal together, it's the first chance I have to ask my questions. To balance my excitement at the romantic idea of it all with the unlikely reality of Mom giving up corporate life.

"I'm great at my job, Del," Mom says. "For years, it's been my priority."

"Right," I say. "I don't think they'll let you go."

"A born project manager like you?" Jack asks. "*I* wouldn't let you go. If half the sites we worked on were run like this remodel, I'd come home with a few less headaches. Just the ones the kid here gives me."

Patrick throws a cherry tomato at his father, but Mom presses on. "I've been buried in project spreadsheets and other people's marketing plans for too long. I love my work, but it's stressful. I'm dependent on the cell phone, dependent on the computer, dependent on . . . well, other things I no longer want in my life. It took me the whole summer to figure it out, but now I'm one hundred percent sure. I'm ready for a change."

"But Mom, running a B and B is a *huge* change. It's like a hotel, right? *And* a restaurant. *And* a museum. *And* you have to work with people — in person, not on e-mail." Emily, who rushed over as soon as she heard the neighbors gossiping at Luna's about the news, kicks me under the table.

"It's still a business," Mom says. "And that I *can* do. With my management and marketing skills, and Rachel's creative energy and way with people and food, we can make this work. I've looked at the numbers, Del. The tourist industry up here is on the cusp right now. Rachel and I have already met with the bank and the Chamber of Commerce. We've got some money saved, and your grandmother was smart with hers. With the assets from her estate, we can afford the risk."

I swallow a bite of sautéed zucchini and look at her with raised eyebrows. "Mom, you don't do risk, remember?"

"Well, this one's a very *calculated* risk. I've done financial projections across several market scenarios, accounting for climate changes and fluctuating maple production levels, both of which directly impact the tourist industry in Vermont. I also looked at…hey, don't laugh! It's still a risk! Anything can happen. It'll be an adventure."

"So…we're moving to Vermont?" I ask.

"Not right away," Mom says. "Not necessarily at all. It'll take time to get all the right permits to get it zoned and up to code. We'll need to do some upgrades, which I'm leaving in Jack's capable hands, and I need to plan my transition from DKI. Rachel needs to work out her catering schedule for the

Toronto Film Festival and Sundance before she can commit to dates here. And you need to finish out your senior year at Kennedy and decide what comes next. One day at a time, right?"

I consider her plan, not surprised that she's accounted for everything.

"Besides," Mom says, "Rachel did our cards, and according to the Eight of Wands, it's time for some fresh opportunities. Oh — I also got the Ten of Pentacles in my 'best outcome' spot. Abundance, family traditions, strong family ties — I thought that was telling."

"Absolutely," Rachel says, pouring us all another round of hibiscus tea. "I also thought it was cool that the Empress appeared in both of our spreads this morning. That means it's a good time for female creativity, and work ventures will likely lead to material comforts."

"Whoa. I want my cards read!" Patrick says.

"Seriously," Em says. "You should do lakeside readings for the guests. Um, starting with us."

"That's not a bad idea," Rachel says, reaching for Mom's notebook on the counter behind her.

Everyone around me is laughing, chatting, passing food, telling stories, eating, forks scraping on mismatched plates, chipped cups clinking together, no more invisible guests for invisible dinners at the big empty table.

"Okay," I say over the happy sounds filling the room. "You win, guys. Three Sisters B and B. I'm in." I spoon another pile of mango chutney over Rachel's organic grilled seitan. "I just hope next season's guests aren't holding out for actual *bacon* with their breakfast."

Mom laughs. "We said one day at a time, Del. We'll cross the bacon bridge when we get there."

After dinner, Mom packs up the rest of her mobile office while Rachel walks Emily back to Luna's. Everyone promised to come over tomorrow morning to see us off, but tonight is the last I'll have alone with Patrick before my summer in Red Falls draws to a close.

Side by side, we walk along the lake shore, watching the turtles and sailboats like we did the first time we saw each other under the bleachers that day. Neither of us wants to acknowledge the good-bye sitting there on the horizon, to ask the questions about when we'll see each other again. They're not on our lips, but I know they're in our minds, both of us silently counting and recounting the hours and the miles between New York and Pennsylvania.

"I told my father about college," Patrick says. "He knows I'm going."

"How did he take it?"

"He didn't freak out as much as I expected. He was more upset that I didn't tell him how I really felt a long time ago. He said that he never meant to push his own dreams on me, and that if I don't want to work for Reese and Son, he can hire another partner. He actually seemed kind of proud about the college thing. But I know he's not crazy about the music major. I don't think he'll ever be comfortable with the artist gene in our family."

"Did he try to talk you into a new major?"

"Architecture. But only for about thirty seconds. Then he said that as long as I don't expect him to take the subway or a taxi, or wear a suit, he might possibly perhaps *maybe* come to one or two of my shows in the city. That is, assuming I find any work." Patrick laughs.

I hate thinking about him not being right next door after tomorrow, but picturing him onstage again, even if it's all the way in New York City, makes me smile.

"I'm really proud of you," I say. "For telling your father the truth and for following your heart. Just promise me something, okay?"

He puts his hand over his heart. "Anything."

"Don't sing that song for anyone else, Patrick. I mean, unless you get a record deal or something. Then I'll make an exception."

Patrick wraps my pinky in his. "If I get a record deal, I'll fly you down to the studio so I can sing it for you there. Promise."

I smile, pulling him closer.

"So aside from visiting me like every single weekend in New York, what are your plans after Red Falls?" he asks.

"Plans. Let's see. Big plans. Well, there's another exciting year left at Kennedy High."

"Senior year," Patrick says. "The home stretch."

"I guess. I'm also thinking of getting a job at a coffee place or something," I say. "Just a few hours a week. Get some job experience before college."

"That sounds cool, but if you're going to work in a café, you have to promise *me* something."

"What's that?"

"Don't let anyone else sing to you."

"Oh, no problem." I hold up my pinky again. "I'm only doing it for the free chocolate hazelnut lattes."

Patrick squeezes my hand. "Delilah?" he asks. "What about . . . are you going to look for your father?"

My father. I turn to watch a small blue sailboat making its way across the lake, wondering if I'll ever have the answer to that question. That first night I found out? *Yes.* I wanted to look for him. I was mad, and I needed someone to scream at. If I had the money, I probably would've bought a ticket to L.A. just so I could track him down and stand in front of him and tell him *all* about it.

Now, I don't know. I don't know what I'd really say or do or feel, and I don't *want* to. I'm not ready to know him. I'm not ready for him to know *me.*

More than that, there's still Thomas Devlin. And I'm not ready to say good-bye to him.

I pick up a rock from the path and throw it sideways at the lake, watching it skim the water twice before it disappears. "Honestly, I have no idea what to do about Casey Conroy,"

I say. "I'm not ready to think about it yet. I'm keeping Thomas for a little while. Maybe a long while."

Patrick smiles.

"I was just thinking about this story he did on elephant poaching in Africa," I say. "He basically lived with them on these wildlife preserves where different animal rights groups were working to rescue and treat the elephants wounded by poachers.

"In the article, he talked about family dynamics in elephant herds. The matriarch builds up a kind of social memory, so the older she is, the more she remembers about the family and the rest of the herd, about which outside elephants are friendly, about where all the best food is, stuff like that. But these older elephants are usually bigger, with bigger tusks, and that's what poachers go for. When the matriarchs die, all of those memories go with them, and the rest of the herd is kind of lost."

We stop to watch a family of turtles scuttling up a rock near the shore. Patrick puts his arm around me.

"At first, the story kind of reminded me of my grandmother and how everything got so screwed up and lost when we left Red Falls that year. But then I realized something."

"What's that?" Patrick asks.

"We're not exactly like the elephants. We have the ability to pass our memories on. We just have to tell them to someone."

"All right," Patrick says. "Here's one for you. My earliest

memory of Red Falls Lake happened right over there." He points along the shore past the turtles. "I must have been about four. I was playing in the sand when I noticed these tiny silver fish swimming in a shallow pool next to the lake. They looked so sparkly, like little flashes of light in the water. I remember how much I wanted to see them up close, to see if they would still sparkle in my hand.

"I tried to grab them, but they were too fast. They kept speeding away whenever I got close. A woman was watching me from the beach, and when she figured out what I was doing, she came over with a red bucket, crouched down next to me, and scooped up the water and the fish so I could get a better look."

I lean into him, closing my eyes to envision the story of Little Ricky and his shiny silver fish. The more he talks, the sharper the picture becomes, until finally...

"Patrick, wait! I totally remember that day! I was there!"

Patrick smiles. "You know, I tried to write a song about it once — about that moment — but the words kept slipping away, just like the fish. I guess it was only meant for us."

"Look at the fire fish," I whisper. "That's what she called them. That's what she said to me." It's all there for me now, the old lake stories sailing clear and bright into my mind like they were there all along, waiting for the sun to shine sideways and reveal them swirling and bobbing below the surface like the little silver fish. My grandmother waved me over to peek inside the red pail with Ricky, holding our hands on the shore as she smiled in wonder at the way the fish sparkled like diamonds in the water.

"See," Patrick whispers. "You didn't forget anything." He pulls me into a kiss, and as his arms close around me, I know that of all my Red Falls memories, this will be my favorite. After we leave tomorrow, no matter what awaits me in Key as Mom and I put the pieces of our lives back together, no matter what I decide to do about my real father, no matter what happens at school, no matter how long it takes to open Three Sisters, I will always come back here. I will close my eyes and smell the summer honeysuckle and feel the setting sun on my face and Patrick's lips against mine and I will come right back exactly here, back to the turtles and the fish and my grandmother holding our hands, back to this kiss on the best and last night of my *second* first summer in Red Falls, Vermont.

"Delilah, I know we haven't worked out visitation rights for Holden Caulfield yet, but I've decided that *you* should be the official keeper of the family portrait." Patrick passes me a square of paper from his pocket and I unfold the caricature of us he commissioned at the Sugarbush Festival, studying it until I've learned the curve of our smiles and my tears blur the exaggerated lines of Holden Caulfield's big, beige antlers.

"I miss you already," I say, resting my head against his chest. "Thank you for this. And for Holden. And the fish story. And the song. And about a million other —"

"Delilah," he says, lifting my chin, "you're missing it." He stretches his hand toward the blazing orange and purple sky before us. As we watch the last sliver of sun dip behind the water, he whispers against my lips those words from the lake that night and I memorize them and the smell of his skin and the honey light in his eyes and the fish sparkling in the water and I know that *this* time, whatever the universe is saying, I'm listening.

And this time, I'm not going to forget *any* of it.

ACKNOWLEDGMENTS

The inspiration for *Fixing Delilah* belongs in part to the women of my family: my late great-grandmother, Florence, and my late grandmothers, Marjorie and Elizabeth, who filled my childhood with memories of the big yellow house on the hill, "Betty's Boutique," and a thousand hidden treasures among the old things; my mother, Sharon, who stayed home with us for as long as she could; my aunts, Linda (my sage, tarot-reading OMLFG), Shelly, Connie, Amie, and our beloved angels, Marcy and Sharon, who brought food and laughter; and my beautiful cousins, Joycene, Katie, Kellie, Allie, Haley, and babies Julianna and Kenna, who carry on the stories. I am also indebted to Brandi Carlile, whose music was the muse that brought the Hannaford women to life. "The Story" says it best.

Though writing is often a lonely endeavor, a great community of people supported Delilah on her journey from these early inspirations to her final place on the bookshelf.

My editor knew Delilah's heart from the first draft, and while her quest to make me cry was unsuccessful, her vision for the Hannafords was not. Thank you, Jennifer Hunt, for your wisdom, your trust, and your sense of humor. Because of you and the Little, Brown Books for Young Readers family, including Saho Fujii, Pamela Garfinkel, Amanda Hong, Alvina Ling, Zoe Luderitz, Ames O'Neill, Andrew Smith, Victoria Stapleton, Kate Sullivan, and many others, Delilah is out in the world of books at her absolute best.

"Sarah, if anyone can do this, it's you," Ted Malawer said (as many times as I needed to hear it [and maybe a few more]). Ted, your encouragement, guidance, friendship, and mutual appreciation for dessert have set the gold standard to which all literary agents should aspire.

Librarians, booksellers, teachers, bloggers, and readers, without your passion for young adult literature, my stories would be trees falling in a desolate forest. Thank you for hearing me, and for telling the world about the books you love.

To borrow Patrick's words on true friends, "I wouldn't trade one of them for a hundred of the other kind." Amy Hains, my WBF, Delilah's strength is yours, and Emily is infused with the goodness of your friendship. Rachel Miller, Delilah's admiration for your namesake character is matched only by my admiration for you, and that's not an uncompliment. Thank you both for reading my work, crying at all the right parts, and always believing in me.

My family, my family-in-law, and my lifelong Dunkirk crew are the ones who keep showing up, buying books, and squealing in my general direction at public venues. You crazy people really know how to make a girl feel like a star.

From Delilah's first words in Fairplay, Colorado, to her last in Buffalo, New York (and that whole teeth-gnashing part in the middle), lots of readers and writers donated their time, expertise, and literary companionship to the noble purpose of keeping me sane. Thank you, Danielle Benedetti, Megan Frazer, Cheryl Renee Herbsman, Jennifer Jabaley, Sarah MacLean, Jenny Moss, Jackson Pearce, Carrie Ryan, Meredith Sale, Kurtis Scaletta, Sharon Somers, Michelle Zink, Lighthouse Writers Workshop, The 2009 Debutantes, and The Tenners.

Above all, my deepest gratitude is for Alex, my pet monster, my best friend, my husband, my heart. You are the reason it's easy for me to write about falling in love. There are pieces of this story that once belonged to you, and I love you for making them ours. Thanks for "hacer-te-ing the café" and wandering this world with me in the middle of the night. I'm totally keeping you.

For more summer romance, friendship, and fun,
check out TWENTY BOY SUMMER
by SARAH OCKLER.

According to Anna's best friend, Frankie, twenty days in
Zanzibar Bay is the perfect opportunity to have a summer
fling, and if they meet one boy every day, there's a pretty
good chance Anna will find her first summer romance. Anna
lightheartedly agrees to the game, but there's something she
hasn't told Frankie—she's already had her romance, and it
was with Frankie's older brother, Matt, just before his tragic
death one year ago.

Turn the page for a sneak peek!

AVAILABLE NOW

*I*t was just over a year ago.

Twelve months, nine days, and six hours ago, actually.

But thirteen months ago, everything was . . . *perfect*.

I closed my eyes, leaned over my candles, and prayed to the cake fairy or the God of Birthdays or whoever was in charge that Matt Perino — Frankie's brother and my best-friend-that's-a-boy — would finally kiss me. It was the same secret wish I'd made every year since Frankie and I were ten and Matt was twelve and I accidentally fell in love with him.

Frankie, Matt, and their parents — Uncle Red and Aunt Jayne, even though we're not related — celebrated my fifteenth birthday in our backyard with Mom and Dad, just like always. When all the singing and clapping and candle blowing stopped, I opened my eyes. Matt was right next to me, *beside* me, sharing the same air. Mischievous. The back of my neck went hot and prickly when I smelled his apple shampoo — the kind from the green bottle he stole from Frankie's bathroom because he liked how it made his hair look — and for one charged-up second I thought my birthday wish might finally come true, right there in front of everyone. I didn't even have time to *think* about how embarrassing that might be when Matt's hand, full of birthday cake, arched from behind his back on a not-so-slow-motion trajectory right into my face.

While cake in the face was clearly progress from the previous year's Super Bowl coach–style shook-up soda over the head, something in the wish translation was still getting lost as it blew across my candles into the sky. I made a mental note to clarify my demands next year in bullet points with irrefutable examples from Hollywood classics and screamed, shoving both hands into the mangled confection on the picnic table.

I scooped out two giant corners overloaded with frosting flowers.

Then, I charged.

I lunged.

I ran.

I chased Matt around the yard in laps until he dropped to the ground and wrestled the extra pieces from me, rubbing them into my face like a mud mask. We went at it for ten minutes, laughing and rolling around in the grass, Frankie and our parents cheering and howling and throwing more cake into the ring, candles and all. When we finally came up for air, there wasn't much cake left, and the two of us were coated head to toe in blue rainbow-chip frosting.

We stood up slowly, laughing with our mouths wide open as we halfheartedly called a truce. Dad snapped a picture — Matt's arm around my shoulders, bits of cake and colored chips and grass clinging to our clothes and hair, everything warm and pink in the glow of the setting sun, the whole summer stretched out before us. It didn't even matter that Matt was going to college in the fall. He'd be at Cornell studying American literature, just over an hour away, and he'd already started talking about my and Frankie's weekend visits.

When the novelty of the birthday cake wrestling match finally faded, Matt and I went inside to clean up. Beyond the sliding deck door, shielded in the cool dark of the house from everyone out back, we stood in front of the kitchen sink not saying anything. I stared at him in a sideways kind of way that I hoped didn't expose the secret thoughts in my head — thoughts that, despite my best efforts to contain them, went further than I'd ever let them go before.

His messy black hair and bright blue eyes cast a spell on me, muffling the chatter outside as if we'd been dunked under water. I held out a sticky hand and threatened him with another gob of frosting in an attempt to break the silence, afraid he'd hear my heart pounding under my T-shirt. *Thump-thump. Thump-thump. Thump-thump-thump-thump.*

Matt scooped some frosting from my outstretched hand and moved to close the space that separated us, changing absolutely everything that ever was or wasn't between us with a single raised eyebrow.

"Anna," he said, dragging his frosted fingers through my hair. "Don't you know what it means when a boy pulls your hair at your birthday party?"

No. Just then, I didn't know what anything meant. I couldn't remember how we'd arrived in the kitchen, why we were covered in cake, why my best-friend-that's-a-boy was looking at me so differently, or even what my name was. I bit my lower lip to prevent my mouth from saying something lame without my brain's permission, like "Oh, Matt, all my wishes have come true!" I felt the stupidity rising in my throat and bit down harder, staring at his collarbone and the small piece of blue sea glass he wore on a leather cord around his neck, rising and falling.

Rising.

Falling.

Seconds? Hours? I didn't know. He'd made the necklace the year before from a triangular piece of glass he'd found during their family vacation to Zanzibar Bay, right behind the California beach house they rented for three weeks every summer. According to Matt, red glass was the rarest, followed by purple, then dark blue. To date he'd found only one red piece, which he'd made into a bracelet for Frankie a few months earlier. She never took it off.

I loved all the colors — dark greens, baby blues, aquas, and whites. Frankie and Matt brought them back for me in mason jars every summer. They lived silently on my bookshelf, like frozen pieces of the ocean I had never seen.

"Come here," he whispered, his hand still stuck in my wild curls, blond hair winding around his fingers.

"I still can't believe you made that," I said, not for the first time. "It's so — cool."

Matt looked down at the glass, his hair falling in front of his eyes.

"Maybe I'll give it to you," he said. "If you're lucky."

I smiled, my gaze fixed on the blue triangle. I was afraid to look at him, because if I let my eyes lock on his, he might try to — and then everything would be — and I might just —

"Happy birthday," he whispered, his breath landing warm and suddenly close to my lips, making my insides flip. And just as quickly as he'd surprised me with the cake, he kissed me, one frosting-covered hand moving from my hair to the back of my neck, the other solid and warm in the small of my back, pressing us together, my chest against his ribs, my hip bones just below his, the tops of our bare summer legs hot and touching. I stopped breathing. My eyes were closed and his mouth tasted like marzipan flowers and clove cigarettes, and in ten seconds the whole of my life was wrapped up in that one kiss, that one wish, that one secret that would forever divide my life into two parts.

Up, down. Happy, sad. Shock, awe. Before, after.

In that single moment, Matt, formerly known as friend, became something else entirely.

I kissed him back. I forgot time. I forgot my feet. I forgot the people outside, waiting for us to rejoin the party. I forgot what happens when friends cross into this space. And if my lungs didn't fill and my heart didn't beat and my blood didn't pump without my intervention, I would have forgotten about them, too.

I could have stayed like that all night, standing in front of the sink, Matt's black apple hair brushing my cheeks, heart thumping, lucky and forgetful. . . .

"What's taking so long?" Frankie asked, running up the deck stairs outside. "Come on, Anna. Presents."

I pulled away from Matt just before she pressed her face against the screen to peek inside.

"Yeah, birthday girl," Matt mocked. "What's taking so long?"

"Be right out, Frank." I gave him my Don't You Dare face. "I just need to change."

"Can I come?" Matt whispered against my neck, causing a shiver. Or an earthquake.

I suddenly remembered all the baths we'd taken together as little kids, before we got old enough for it to be dangerous. The memories seemed different now. More vulnerable. Raw. My face went hot, and I had to look away.

"So?" Matt pinched my arm as Frankie headed back to the picnic table.

"So you're lucky Frankie didn't see that," I said, not sure I meant it. "And you have to go change your *own* shirt. In your *own* room. I mean, over —"

"Mmm-hmm." Matt grabbed my hand and pulled me in tight for another kiss, his other hand on my cheek, quick and intense. He pressed his body against mine in the same configuration of hip bones, stomachs, and ribs as the first time. I pressed back, wanting to wrap myself around him, anchor myself to him. It was all that kept me from floating away like a tiny, iridescent bubble.

"Do you think she saw us?" I asked when we finally stopped.

"Nah." He laughed, still holding my hand. "Don't worry. It's our secret."

Alone in my bedroom, I shoved my frosting shirt into a plastic bag to deal with later. I rinsed my face and hair with cool water, but my legs wouldn't stop shaking and I couldn't catch my breath. The brain that was conspicuously absent for the kitchen sink rendezvous was suddenly hyperaware, modeling scenarios and impossible questions that were about twelve-and-a-half minutes too late:

What now?

Will this kill our friendship?

What about our parents?

Does he like me, or was he just messing around?

Will it happen again?

How do we tell Frankie?

Why did he say it's our secret?

Made-up answers raced through my mind, and I had to close my eyes and count to fifty to calm down. Fifteen minutes after everything changed was too soon to start obsessing about the what-ifs of the future.

Back outside, warm and giddy in front of Dad's bonfire, I spent the rest of the night not touching Matt, not laughing too hard at his jokes, not looking at him, afraid that someone would read the thoughts written on my face. After the fire had faded to a soft glow and I'd opened all the gifts, it was time for the Perinos to head back to their house next door. I said my goodbyes and thank-yous to Frankie, Uncle Red, and Aunt Jayne and looked at my feet when it was Matt's turn.

"Thanks for the cake," I said. "And the journal." He knew how much I loved my diaries — as much as he loved his books. It was the best present ever. Well, second best.

"Happy birthday, Anna," he said, picking me up and spinning me around in a giant hug, telling me with a wink that he'd see me tomorrow, just like he'd done on a thousand other nights. "Write something for me tonight."

To everyone else he was regular Matt, the big brother part of the inseparable Anna-Frankie-Matt triangle, the boy who used to bury our Barbies in the backyard and read us adventure stories when we couldn't sleep. But to me, he'd become something else as soon as he pulled my hair at the kitchen sink. Something *other*. Something that would never be the way it was before.

You awake? Matt's text message lit up the phone on my night table later that night.

Ya.

Of course I was awake. In the hours since the party, my heart hadn't slowed its furious beat. Sleep was out of the question.

Meet me out back, k?

K. 5 min.

I pulled on a sweatshirt, brushed my teeth, and put my hair in a loose ponytail. I started to dig for my eyeliner but decided it would look a little strange (and obvious) if I showed up behind the back deck at one in the morning in full makeup. Instead, I opted for hair down with a little mango-flavored lip gloss — casual but cute.

It wasn't sneaking out, exactly. I mean, it was my own backyard, and if I saw any of the upstairs lights go on, I could duck back into the kitchen and pretend I was snagging the last piece of cake salvaged from the birthday battle.

Matt was waiting by the stairs when I tiptoed out the back door. My bare feet hadn't even touched the dewy grass when he pulled me against the side of the house.

"I can't stop thinking about you," he said, kissing me again, this time with a purpose and intensity I'd never seen from him in the long history of our friendship. I kissed him back, wrapping my arms around his neck as his mouth pressed against mine. I must have been shaking, because after a minute he stopped and asked if I was cold.

"Just — surprised," I said. "And happy. And scared." It was barely a whisper, but I hoped it communicated everything I was thinking. Scared of getting what I wished for. Scared of hurting Frankie. Scared of losing my two best friends. Scared of undoing everything the three of us had known and loved since we were kids.

"Me, too," he whispered, breathing hard. "Anna, did you ever —"

Before he could finish, a square of light fell on the grass from Mom and Dad's bathroom window upstairs.

"I have to go," I said. "Tomorrow?"

He grabbed my arm and pulled me close to him, a whisper brushing against my cheek. "Tomorrow."

Then he kissed my neck, his lips alighting on the skin below my ear like a spark from the bonfire that burned long after I crept back to my bed.

He called the next day.

"Hi."

"Hi." I was still dazed from the late-night backyard encounter and kiss-induced insomnia.

"Frankie and I are going for ice cream. Come over?"

Frankie.

"Sure," I said. "But Matt, should we — I mean, did you say any-thing to her?"

"Not — *exactly.*"

Does that mean he doesn't think it's a big deal? That we can just go for ice cream like any other day, like it didn't happen? Like it won't happen again?

"I want to, Anna," he said, reading my mind. "It's just — she's my little sister. And you're our best friend. And now you're my — I mean — we need to look out for her, you know?"

And now I'm your what?

"I know," I said.

"Don't worry, Anna. I'll tell her, okay? Just let me think about the best way to do it."

"Okay."

"Promise me? *Promise* you won't say anything?"

"Don't worry." I laughed. "It's our secret, right?"

I spent an hour getting ready, obsessing over hair and clothes and things that never used to matter so much. I couldn't calm the but-terflies in my stomach about seeing Matt again, about feeling his lips on me, about telling Frankie, about the rest of the summer, about the rest of always.

When I first got to their house, I climbed in the backseat of Matt's car and avoided eye contact with him, worried either that he'd already told Frankie, or that he hadn't. We rode the whole way not looking at each other, Frankie chattering in the front seat about their upcoming California trip, seemingly oblivious to the fact that the whole world had changed the night before. It wasn't until we got inside Custard's Last Stand and Frankie forgot her purse in the car that we finally locked eyes.

"Hey, you," Matt said gently, smiling at me. I opened my mouth to say something important, something witty and charming, but in the new dawn of our relationship, where everything suddenly mattered, I was tongue-tied.

"Hey," I said lamely.

Matt jangled his keys and kicked at the floor with his foot.

"What are you thinking about?" he asked, tracing a line across my forehead.

Before I could invent something better than "Last night at the party and behind the house and I wish you would just shut up and kiss me again," Frankie was back with her purse, pressing us to make the difficult decision between the banana split and the fudge brownie sundae.

Sparing Frankie any further agony over the ice-cream selections, Matt ordered one of each, along with a caramel sundae for me, and we shared everything, fifty-fifty-fifty, just like always.

As Frankie shoved a spoonful of brownie into her brother's mouth, laughing her soft Frankie laugh, a flash of guilt squeezed my stomach. Until the night before, there were no secrets between the three of us but the ones I kept for myself — my silent, formerly unrequited feelings for Matt. I could hardly look at him without my insides tying up. *Please,* please let's tell her.

"Listen," Matt said. We were out back under the stars again, sneaking out after everyone else had gone to sleep. "You know she needs to hear it from me. I think the best time for me to tell her is when we're in California. It's only a few weeks away, and then I'll have some time alone with her to tell her about everything. It'll give her a chance to let it sink in."

The thought of keeping something so important, so intense, so unbelievable from my best friend for even one more day almost killed me. Never before in our shared history did I hide so much as a passing crush — she knew everything. She'd been there for every tragedy, every celebration, every embarassing moment. She'd been with me when I got my neon green braces in fourth grade. With me in seventh grade when I walked out of the school bathroom past the entire lunch line with my skirt tucked into my tights. With me when Jimmy Cross and I kissed during the eighth grade assembly and got hauled off to the principal's office. Birthdays, dreams, fears, laughs, obsessions — everything. Inside her head, Frankie had the map to my entire life, and I to hers. I hated that my feelings for Matt were uncharted and unmapped like a secret buried treasure.

But he was Frankie's brother. I trusted him. And when he took my face in his hands and breathed my name across my lips, I knew that I would keep my promise forever.

Days passed quickly into weeks, Matt and I perpetuating our "just friends" charade as best we could in front of Frankie and our families. So many times during family dinners or casual visits in our adjoining backyards, I wanted to end the charade, to throw my arms around him in front of everyone and just make it known. I censored every look I gave him, every word, every touch, certain that I'd mess up and someone would find out.

But no one did.

To our parents and Frankie, we were the same best friends as always, innocent and inseparable. Whenever we could steal a few minutes alone, that's when we became the "other," the charged-up thing that kept me up at night, afraid of falling so fast, afraid of losing, afraid it wouldn't last once Frankie found out. We stole too-short kisses in the front hallway, shared knowing and devious looks across the dinner table when we weren't being watched. We snuck out every night behind the house to watch for shooting stars and whisper about life, about our favorite books, about the meaning of songs and old memories and what would happen after Frankie knew. It wasn't the topics themselves that changed — we'd talked about all of those things before. But now, there was a new intensity. An urgency to know as much as we could, to fit as much as possible into our final nights before Matt revealed the secret.

On their last day before the trip, after they'd finished packing, the three of us went back to Custard's for an ice-cream send-off. I ordered the mint chocolate-chip brownie sundae, Frankie got a dipped cone, and Matt got a strawberry shake. Matt and Frankie were buoyant, floating on the anticipation of their upcoming trip, carrying me along in the current of their excitement. I couldn't wait for them to get to Zanzibar, to their summer house, down to the beach where Matt would tell Frankie about us and she'd smile and laugh and hug him and everything would be perfect again.

"It will be fine, Anna. You'll see," he whispered to me when Frankie went up to the counter for more napkins. "I know we're dragging it out, but she's my little sister — I can't help it. We just have to look out for her."

I smiled, envisioning our final kiss before tomorrow's departure, later tonight at our usual meeting place behind the house.

We split our ice creams three ways again, saving just enough for the ride back home. In the car, Matt turned up the volume on his favorite Grateful Dead CD. Frankie and I sang the melody while he filled in the harmony, his face tight and serious as he concentrated on the words. He drove with one hand on the wheel, the other tapping the dashboard, then his thigh, then back to the dashboard — a wild imaginary drum solo. I stopped singing long enough to shove in another spoonful of my mint chocolate-chip sundae, a pothole causing me to miss, the ice cream toppling down my shirt to my lap. I was in the front seat, right next to him, and I didn't care. In just three weeks, my best friends would be back home, helping Matt get ready for college, enjoying the sunsets of summer, and looking forward to the rest of our days — the rest of our forever.

The chorus started again through the speakers and I sang louder, *"Ca-sey Jones you bett-er . . . watch your speed . . ."* Frankie laughing from the backseat, Matt smiling at me sideways, fingers secretly brushing my knee, the noon sun laid out and happy on the dusty road ahead.

Together. Happy. Whole.

The three of hearts.

The possibilities endless.

And then ... my sundae flying out of my hands into the dashboard.

Veering.

Screaming.

Slamming.

Broken glass.

A wheel spinning.

Casey Jones skipping, over and over. *"Watch your — watch your — watch your speeeeeed."*

Someone squeezing my hand, hushing, asking for my parents' names and phone number. *Helen and Carl Reiley. But don't tell them,* I think.

An ambulance. Paramedics. Stretchers.

"I've got him," someone shouts. "Get the girls out!"

"Can you hear me? Can you move your legs?"

"Jesus, you girls are lucky to be alive."

In the hospital lobby, I curled myself against Dad's chest, letting him stroke my hair and hum Beatles songs like he did when I was little to chase away the monsters. My head hurt, my knee was bandaged up, and my wrist was immobilized and wrapped in white tape. Frankie, sitting across from me with her knees pulled to her chest, had a fat lip and eight stitches sticking out like angry black spider legs through her left eyebrow. She was still — all but her fingers rubbing the red glass of her Matt-bracelet. I closed my eyes under the fluorescent lights and tried to make another birthday wish, a onetime do-over, a rebate, a trade-in on the kitchen sink kiss that started everything, offered up for just one last miracle.

I thought about Matt's clove-and-marzipan-frosting mouth and his favorite books stacked up on every flat surface of his bedroom as the doctor told us what happened. Matt wasn't a careless driver; he just had a hole between the chambers of his heart, a tiny imperfection that had lain dormant for seventeen years until that moment on the way home from Custard's when it decided to make itself known. They used a more medically appropriate term when they explained it to Red, handing him a plastic bag full of Matt's things. Watch. Wallet. The Syracuse Orangemen T-shirt he'd worn that day. But I knew what it meant. I knew as soon as Red started shouting, as soon as Aunt Jayne collapsed in Mom's arms, as soon as the hospital chaplain arrived with his downturned mouth and compassionately trained eyes.

Matt — Red and Jayne's Matt, Frankie's Matt, *my* Matt — died of a broken heart.

And everything else that ever mattered in my entire existence just . . . *stopped*. I was underwater again, seeing things in a slow-motion fuzz without sound or context, without feeling, without care. The world could have ended and I wouldn't have noticed.

In a way, it *did* end.

They must have let Red and Jayne and Frankie say goodbye to him, but I don't remember.

Mom and Dad must have called relatives and friends and funeral directors, but I don't remember.

There were probably nurses and apologies and organ donor papers and Styrofoam cups of cold coffee, but I don't remember any of it. Not in a way that makes sense.

I don't even remember how I got home. One minute I was underwater in the hard plastic hospital chair, and then I was back in my own bed with the door closed against my parents' muffled conversations downstairs and the endlessly ringing phone.

I must have fallen asleep, because I dreamed about him. In the dream, he gave me his blue glass necklace and Frankie's red bracelet.

"We need to look out for her, you know?" he said. "I have to be the one to tell her. It's the only way."

I know.

And when he smiled at me, I promised. I promised him I would protect her.

I promised him our secret would stay locked up for all eternity. And it will.